operations, and a\h. \.ng cnange \.\...
point, which I won't reveal for fear of spoiling the plot.
There was great attention to detail woven skilfully into
the writing, so I felt I learned a lot about the era by
osmosis, rather than having it thrust upon me. All in
all, a remarkable debut novel."

Debbie Young, author and book blogger

"From the start of this story I felt as if I had been
transported back in time to Regency London. Walking
in Sam's footsteps, I could hear the same cacophony of
sound, shared the same sense of disbelief at
Fauntleroy's modus operandi, and hung onto Constable
Plank's coat tails as he entered the squalid house of
correction at Coldbath Fields. I am reassured that this
is not the last we shall see of Samuel Plank. His
steadfastness is so congenial that to spend time in his
company in future books is a treat worth savouring."

Jo at Jaffareadstoo

Praise for *The Man in the Canary Waistcoat*

"Susan Grossey is an excellent storyteller. The descriptions of Regency London are vivid and create a real sense of time and place. Sam Plank, Martha and Wilson are great characters – well-drawn and totally individual in their creation. The dialogue is believable and the pace well fitted to this genre. The novel shows excellent research and writing ability – a recommended read."

Barbara Goldie, The Kindle Book Review

"Regency police constable Sam Plank, so well established in the first book, continues to develop here, with an interesting back story emerging about his boyhood, which shapes his attitude to crime as an adult. This is not so much a whodunit as a whydunit, and Grossey skilfully unfolds a complex tale of financial crime and corruption. There are fascinating details about daily life in the criminal world woven into the story, leaving the reader much more knowledgeable without feeling that he's had a history lesson."

Debbie Young, author and book blogger

Praise for *Worm in the Blossom*

"Ever since I was introduced to Constable Sam Plank and his intrepid wife Martha, I have followed his exploits with great interest. There is something so entirely dependable about Sam: to walk in his footsteps through nineteenth century London is rather like being in possession of a superior time travelling machine... The writing is, as ever, crisp and clear, no superfluous waffle, just good old-fashioned storytelling, with a tantalising beginning, an adventurous middle, and a wonderfully dramatic ending."

Jo at Jaffareadstoo

"Susan Grossey not only paints a meticulous portrait of London in this era, she also makes the reader see it on its own terms, for example recognising which style of carriage is the equivalent to a 21st century sports-car, and what possessing one would say about its owner... In short, a very satisfying and agreeable read in an addictive series that would make a terrific Sunday evening television drama series."

Debbie Young, author and book blogger

Praise for *Portraits of Pretence*

"There is no doubt that the author has created a plausible and comprehensive Regency world and with each successive novel I feel as if I am returning into the bosom of a well-loved family. Sam and Martha's thoughtful care and supervision of the ever-vulnerable Constable Wilson, and of course, Martha's marvellous ability, in moments of extreme worry, to be her husband's still small voice of calm is, as always, written with such thoughtful attention to detail."

Jo at Jaffareadstoo

"Do you want to know what a puff guts is or a square toes or how you would feel if you were jug-bitten? Well, you'll find out in this beautifully researched and written Regency crime novel. And best of all you will be in the good company of Constable Sam Plank, his wife Martha and his assistant Constable Wilson. These books have immense charm and it comes from the tenderness of the depiction of Sam's marriage and his own decency."

Victoria Blake, author

Praise for *Faith, Hope and Trickery*

"What I like about the delightful law enforcement characters in this series is their ordinariness. They are not
superheroes, they do not crack the case in a matter of a
quick fortnight, but weeks, months, pass with the crime
in hand on-going with other, everyday things, happening in the background. This inclusion of reality easily
takes the reader to trudge alongside Constable Plank as
he threads his way through the London streets of the
1820s, bringing the lawbreakers to justice."
*Helen Hollick of Discovering Diamonds book
reviews*

"The mystery at the heart of the novel is beautifully
explained and so meticulously detailed that nothing is
ever left to chance and everything flows like the wheels
of a well-oiled machine. There's an inherent
dependability about Constable Plank which shines
through in every novel and yet, I think that in Faith,
Hope and Trickery we see an altogether more
vulnerable Sam which is centred on Martha's unusual
susceptibility and on his unerring need to protect her."
Jo at Jaffareadstoo

Praise for *Heir Apparent*

"*Heir Apparent* is possibly my favourite Sam Plank book yet, with great twists and turns to the plot, and meticulous research. This author really gets the historical detail just right, but what stands out for me is the captivating character development the author has honed throughout the series, and I will own that for me the crime element is almost superfluous, as it is the characters who keep me coming back to these books."
Peggy-Dorothea Beydon, author

"There's an authenticity to the characters, particularly Sam, and his wife, Martha, which not only makes these stories such a joy to read, but which also gives such an imagined insight into life in the capital in the early 1800s so that it really does feel as though you are moving in tandem with Plank, Martha, and the intrepid Wilson as they go about their business, forever trying, and usually succeeding, to live their lives in the full glare of the criminal fraternity."
Jo at Jaffareadstoo

NOTES OF CHANGE

Susan Grossey

Susan Grossey
Publisher

With grateful thanks to Dave Ryan for arranging, and to the estate of Bob Marrion for permitting, the use of Bob's marvellous illustration of a Metropolitan Police officer on the cover of this book.

This novel is a work of fiction. The events and characters in it, while based on real historical events and characters, are the work of the author's imagination.

Book layout ©2022 BookDesignTemplates.com

Notes of Change / Susan Grossey -- 1st edition
ISBN 978-1-9160019-7-8

For my mother–
who taught me to read and then never let me stop

It is not the one who has little but the one who desires more who is truly poor.

—SENECA

Author's note

Any period of history has its own vocabulary, both standard and slang. The Regency was no different, and in order to capture the spirit of the time I have used words and phrases that may not be familiar to the modern reader. At the end of this book there is a glossary of these terms and their brief definitions.

CHAPTER ONE

Cherubs and horses

MONDAY 13TH JULY 1829

There are some men who pursue change: as soon as they master a skill or see a spectacle, they are keen to move on to the next. And there are those of us who treasure the familiar. It's not that I wish to return to the past – far from it, as anyone who has escaped the fish-stinking alleys of Wapping will agree. And I am certainly not against improving myself; I read as widely as I can, and keep my ears open and my mouth shut when I am with men who can teach me. But I do not seek novelty for its own sake – a steadfastness for which my wife Martha might be a little more grateful. Sometimes, however, the world thrusts change upon all of us, and we must make our peace with it. Next year – God willing – I shall mark my half-century. And since I was sixteen I have been a constable. I once told Martha that I wanted to be buried in my uniform, which she said was in poor taste. With Mr Peel's innovations, I may no longer have the right – or indeed the uniform.

William Wilson glanced at me as we paused to cross Oxford Street.

"Are you unwell, sir?" he asked.

"Unwell?" I repeated.

"You sighed," he explained.

"Perhaps at the prospect of being asked ridiculous questions," I said, and immediately regretted my bad temper. Ever since Wilson had told me that he had decided to join the Metropolitan Police at the first opportunity, I had been short with him – even though I had been the one encouraging him to think to his future and throw in his lot with the new force. As Martha had observed after seeing me snap at the poor lad, just because the head knows something, it does not mean that the heart has to like it.

There was a small gap between the carts heading eastwards and we stepped into the road. There was less traffic going west but we still had to wait for a neat little carriage to bowl past us, the coachman calling out a halloo of warning. The shade cast by the shuttered theatre in Blenheim Street came as a relief; although it was not yet nine o'clock, the day was warm.

"Forgive me," I said. "I am out of sorts. The heat does not agree with me – I have not been sleeping." Wilson said nothing but nodded tightly. If I let this matter lie he would be quiet for perhaps ten minutes, but there has never been anyone less capable than William Wilson of bearing a grudge or staying angry. "And how is young master George sleeping these days?" I asked.

Wilson's face broke into a smile at the thought of his baby son. "We've given up on clothes for him, in this heat," he said. "When he's asleep, he looks like one of those fat little angels you see in church."

"Cherubs," I said as we climbed the steps of the Great Marlborough Street police office.

"Less angelic when he's awake," continued Wilson. "His favourite game now is giving and taking, which he can play for hours – handing something back and forth. Me, I'm not so keen on it – everything he gives you comes with a generous coating of spit."

"Talking about one of our visitors, are you, sir?" asked Thomas Neale. Our office-keeper was making an annotation in his ledger; I'll wager that the records kept at the Old Bailey are less thorough than those in that ledger.

4 | SUSAN GROSSEY

"Constable Wilson was regaling me with the perils of fatherhood," I said.

"And how is Mrs Wilson's latest project coming along?" asked Tom. "Is she still troubled by the vomiting? I remember Mrs Neale suffering terribly."

"My mother tells me it should lessen," confided Wilson, "now that we are past the early months."

Tom nodded sagely.

"When you have quite finished with your tales of the nursery, gentlemen," I said, leaning over the counter and tapping a forefinger on the ledger, "I wonder whether there is some work to be done."

The office-keeper tutted and pulled the ledger towards him, making a show of dusting it off where I had touched it. "As you are so eager today, Constable Plank," he said, "the honour of answering our first call of the day is yours." He closed the ledger firmly before I could look at it again. "Mr Duke, clerk, has asked to have a word. The Horse Bazaar on Portman Square."

"Horses?" I said.

"Dozens and dozens of them, I should imagine," Tom replied with a smug smile. "Enormous great beasts".

♦

"You were happy enough around horses when we did that job in Covent Garden," said Wilson as we turned our step towards Regent Street, "when we worked on that watermen's stand."

"Needs must when the devil drives," I said, "but I'd rather not get too close to them. Unpredictable, they are, and no respecter of a fellow's boots." Just then, as if to prove me right, a carthorse waiting at the side of the road let loose a stream of urine that splashed onto the cobbles and steamed in the warm sun.

Wilson laughed. "Oxford Street or the squares?" he asked.

"The squares," I replied. "The coolness of the greenery will be very welcome." We crossed into Hanover Street and skirted to the south side of the square. The tidy gardens were enclosed by an elegant iron railing and a steady procession of smart carriages trotted past us, serving the fine houses that strove to outdo each other in size and ornamentation. We continued along Brook Street and emerged at the north of the much larger Grosvenor Square. Here the homes were not as grand, but somehow more pleasing – designed more for comfort than to impress. The huge central garden –

covering some eight acres, I was once told by a proud but tired gardener – was beautifully maintained, with the elm hedges carefully clipped and the grass lawns neatly trimmed. Wilson and I crossed the wide road to walk alongside the railings rather than in the dusty, glaring thoroughfare.

"If you join the new force," I said, "I hope the uniform is cooler than this one." My blue coat was smart and Martha frequently told me that it flattered me, but the heavy cloth and high collar made it uncomfortable in the summer months.

"Are you sure that you will not join?" asked Wilson.

"They'll not want a square-toes like me," I said.

"So you keep saying," said Wilson, "but a new force cannot train itself, and a seasoned constable like you would soon lick the new boys into shape. I'm sure they'd jump at the chance to have you." I stayed silent and we turned into North Audley Street. Full of tradesmen's premises, it was a lively place. Wilson stood aside to let a young woman pass; the two baskets she was carrying were already full as she surveyed the birds hanging outside the poulterer and she blushed prettily at Wilson's polite smile. I'll say this for the lad: since marrying Alice, he has not so much as winked at another woman. The traffic thickened as we forced our way across Oxford

Street and turned into the former infantry barracks that now housed the Horse Bazaar. To my relief the yard was quiet, with a single horse being inspected by three men while a dog sat in a patch of sunlight blinking lazily and reaching round to snap at fleas on its rump.

"Talking of uniforms, look at that one," said Wilson, nodding towards the groom who was holding the harness of the horse. The man was wearing a crisp outfit of white trousers, a blue spencer and a blue cap with white bands.

"Very natty," I agreed. The building at the end of the yard put me in mind of a town hall, with its unadorned clean lines and the large double doors surmounted by a generous fanlight. A young lad – a stable-boy, I guessed – walked past us and I called out to him. "We're looking for Mr Duke. The chief clerk."

"Inside, sir," said the boy. "His office is on the right."

As Wilson pushed open the door and we walked into the hallway, we could hear people walking around overhead, and there was a distant sound of conversations – rather like bees in a hive. As the lad had said, the door to our right bore a sign saying "Clerks' Office", and I knocked on it.

"Come in, come in," called a man's voice.

Had someone asked me to describe a clerks' office –
in a bank or a firm of solicitors or here in the Horse Bazaar – the scene before me was just what I would have
imagined. A row of heavy wooden chests of drawers oc-
cupied one wall while another was taken up with a range
of cubbyholes stretching from floor to ceiling, with papers and folders peeping from nearly all of them. Two
large arched windows looked out into the yard and allowed plenty of light to fall onto the huge desk which
took up most of the room. Two men sat opposite each
other at the desk, and both turned to look at us as we
entered.

"I am Constable Plank," I said, "and this is Constable
Wilson. From Great Marlborough Street. You sent
word."

The older man stood and came towards me, his hand
outstretched. "Thank you for coming, constables," he
said. "I am Frederick Duke, chief clerk, and this is my
son Francis." Glancing from father to son, I could see
the similarity: both were tall, with dark curling hair and
blue eyes, and both looked uneasy. "Francis: the banknotes."

Francis Duke reached into the long drawer on his
side of the desk and pulled out an envelope which he

NOTES OF CHANGE | 9

handed to his father, who passed it to me. I opened it: folded inside were banknotes totalling eleven pounds.

"They are forgeries, constable," said the chief clerk. "Taken by my son at the auction on Saturday, in payment for a chestnut hunter."

"You are certain they are forgeries?" I asked, removing the banknotes and looking at them.

"I have a friend who is a banker," said Duke. "He is in no doubt."

"And you wish to make a charge against the buyer?" I said. Wilson had taken out his notebook and pencil and looked expectantly at the clerk.

"That is one possibility, indeed," said Duke.

We waited but he was silent. "I can understand your concern for your son," I said, "but surely the owner of the business..."

"Mr Young," said Duke.

"Surely Mr Young would understand. Counterfeiters are very able – even to my eye these notes look credible." I picked up one of the banknotes and turned to look at it in the full light. "And you have a record of the buyer, so you know who has uttered the notes. It would be a straightforward case, I am sure, with little loss to your business, and no particular blame attached to your son."

"My father is not seeking to protect me, Constable Plank," said Francis Duke with a dry laugh. "He has already made it very clear that the eleven pounds will be coming out of my wages. But if word were to get out…. The Bazaar is a place for elegant people, and they would not like to think that they are rubbing shoulders with counterfeiters and forgers."

His father held up a hand and his son stopped speaking. "This is a delicate matter, constables. Francis, you may leave us."

The younger man closed his desk drawer and left the room. His father continued. "Francis is right, of course: we must protect the Bazaar from unsavoury rumours. But there is more to it than that – something I have tried to keep from my son." The clerk looked up at the ceiling as though searching for the right words. "Mr Young is not a man of forgiveness. If he were to find out about this he would certainly dismiss Francis – an outcome that would trouble the boy's mother greatly and me not one jot. Do you have a son, sir?"

I shook my head. "But Constable Wilson does," I said.

"Allow me to give you some advice, Constable Wilson," said Duke. "When your boy is of an age to work, do not encourage him to follow you. Either he will outshine you, which I imagine would be trying, or he will find that he has no aptitude for the work and will blame you for this, as though it is somehow your fault. Francis is an able boy in many ways, but he is not a clerk." He shook his head. "But neither of us dares to confess it to Mrs Duke, who rejoices to see us working together."

"So why not let Mr Young make the decision for you and dismiss your son?" asked Wilson.

"As I have said, Mr Young is not a man of forgiveness," answered Duke. "And neither is he a man of moderation. When crossed, he takes revenge." The clerk leaned towards us, putting a hand on the banknotes that were lying on the desk. "If I were to tell him that we had been duped, he would demand to know who had uttered the notes – and I fear what he would do. He has connections with some dangerous men, constables." His voice dropped to a whisper. "Scoundrels. Rough, coarse, violent men. If I were to set him on the man who uttered the notes, well, I could not have that on my conscience. In my view, he used the notes in all innocence." He shook his head sadly. "He is young and vain, constable, like so many fellows of his age, but he does not have the, well, the brazenness or the coolness to deliberately utter false notes."

"And so you hope that we can find the real culprit for you," I said. "The forger who created the notes. And then perhaps Mr Young's anger can be directed at the right target."

Duke nodded. "I can share with you all the information we have," he said. "When we sell an animal, we take all the details of the purchaser. Not all the horses are sold warranted sound, but it is as well to keep records in case of dispute."

"Was this horse warranted sound?" I asked.

The clerk returned to his desk and opened a ledger at a page marked with a slip of paper. He shook his head. "We find that young gentlemen are less concerned about soundness: they want an animal that is handsome, and a goer."

"And this one was?" I asked.

The clerk read the entry in the ledger and nodded. "Chestnut hunter, white blaze, three years, sixteen hands. From the fair at Boughton Green last month." He looked up at us. "Northamptonshire. Horses bred in the country are very popular with our customers."

"And who was this customer?" I asked.

"Here," said Duke, handing me the slip of paper from the ledger. "I have written it down for you."

I looked at the note. Charles Madden, number 88 Brook Street, Mayfair. "And you are certain that this is the man who bought that horse and paid with counter-feit banknotes?" I asked.

"Mr Madden has visited us on several occasions," explained the clerk. "My son recognised him when he took the payment."

"Could we speak to him about that?" I asked.

"Of course," he replied, and then called out, "Francis!" The office door opened immediately and the junior clerk came back into the room. He had doubtless had his ear pressed to the wood but tried to look unconcerned.

"Mr Duke," I said, "when you took the payment from Mr Madden, were you certain of his identity? Perhaps someone else paid on his behalf, and in the confusion and the crowd of the auction you mistook yourself?"

The young man shook his head. "We do not take money in the hall of the Bazaar. When a lot is completed, the runners note down the winning bid and the purchaser. The purchaser is given a ticket showing the purchase price and instructed to go to the cashier's office to pay. That's an office in the corner of the hall where business can be conducted more quietly."

"And you were the cashier at Saturday's auction?" I asked.

"I was, yes," he replied.

"And you recognised Mr Madden when he presented his ticket?" I asked.

"I did," confirmed the clerk. "It was his first purchase under his own name, but Mr Madden has been to the Bazaar on several occasions recently. He accompanied his parents when they bought a carriage and pair earlier this year, and then he returned with his father to look over some new harnesses."

"His stepfather," corrected the chief clerk. "Roger Forster."

"Did Mr Madden say anything about the money?" I asked. "Where it came from?"

"We do not ask such impertinent questions," said the chief clerk. "It is of no concern to us."

His son looked uneasy.

"Did you talk about it, Mr Duke?" I asked the younger man.

He nodded. "Mr Madden is about my own age," he said, "and I commented that I was envious of his being able to afford such a horse." He looked at his father. "I know we are not meant to say anything, but he was friendly and talkative…"

"And what did he say?" I asked.

"He said that he had won it. At Crockford's," replied the junior clerk. "He said I should consider it myself."

"Over my dead body," said his father. "And dead I certainly would be, if your mother ever caught wind of you going to such a place.

CHAPTER TWO

Simple but strong

TUESDAY 14TH JULY 1829 – MORNING

"What do you think, Kitty?" I asked the girl. "Violets or pinks?"

The flower-seller was about twelve years old and had worked on the busy corner of Great Marlborough Street and Regent Street for two years or perhaps more. She wore an old but carefully mended and clean dark print frock, a pair of worn-out shoes and a black bonnet that showed stark against the pallor of her skin, and the basket over her arm was full of neat little bundles of flowers tied with string. Several times a day her younger brother would arrive to refill the basket and take away the coins she had collected and deliver them to their widowed invalid father at their room in a house near Drury Lane. Kitty put her head to one side to consider my question.

"Last week you bought violets," she pointed out, "so pinks would make a nice change for Mrs Plank."

"Pinks it is," I said, digging into my pocket for the coins. "Three bunches if you please, Kitty."

Kitty was carefully picking through her flowers for me when a shout of "Constable!" from across the road caught our attention. I could see a boy waving his arms and looking for a gap between the coaches and carts. I held up a hand to halt him, calling "Wait there, lad", and handed the coins to Kitty. "I'll collect the flowers later," I said. In truth, the flowers were poor things, barely lasting a day once Martha put them in a jug, but as long as Kitty was selling flowers she was not selling herself, and that was worth a few pennies of anyone's money. I crossed the road towards the boy, who was dancing impatiently on the spot. He was one of our regular lads, who wait outside police offices and courthouses in the hope of earning a few coins by carrying notes and messages.

"Now then, Jake," I said, "what has lit a fire under you today?"

"A dead man, Constable Plank," he said breathlessly. "Out the back of St James's Street. The dustman sent me for a constable."

♦

Twenty minutes later we arrived at St James's Street.

"Down here," said Jake, beckoning me to follow him into a small side street. "It's in the dust-pit out the back of these fancy places."

"Not the cesspit?" I asked. It wouldn't be the first body pulled out of the mire by a night soil man.

"Ask him," said Jake, pointing at a man standing beside a box-cart with the name Martin & Company painted on the side. "He's who sent me. Farthing from him, farthing from you." He held out his hand.

"Your rates are steep these days, Jake," I said, feeling in my pocket and hoping that I hadn't given all my coins to Kitty.

"Mayfair rates," he said, and I laughed as I paid him – I'd have to tell Martha that one. He bit the coin I handed him – out of habit, and I took no offence – and then hared off to be of use to someone else.

"Mr Martin?" I said to the fellow who was waiting.

He shook his head. "Mr Martin's the guvnor," he said. "I'm Barnes. Dustman." He wore the familiar outfit of his profession: a heavy smock over thick trousers, with sturdy boots on his feet and a cap with a long flap hanging down his back.

"And I'm Plank," I said. "Constable."

"He's in here," said Barnes, pushing open the gate. I followed him into the yard. "It's mucky," he said over his shoulder, "but not dirty. This is Parker." Sitting on an upturned basket next to the dust-pit was another dustman. He stood as we approached and towered over both of us. "He's simple," added Barnes.

"Simple but strong," confirmed Parker with a happy smile. "He fills the baskets and I carries them, then I fills the baskets and he carries them. Fair's fair."

"Indeed it is, Mr Parker," I said. "And who was filling and who was carrying when you found the body?"

"He was digging," replied Barnes. "I was out with the cart, tipping in the first basket, when he yelled."

"I trod on it," said Parker in a stage whisper, his eyes wide. "I trod on the arm. Thought it was a dog – dogs is good for money, says Mr Barnes. Cats too." I nodded; fur sold well, and dustmen were always on the look-out for dead animals. "I bent down to pull it out, but it wasn't a dog. It was him." He pointed down into the dust-pit.

I looked into the hole and lying on its back, eyes open but unseeing, was the clothed body of a man.

"He's a madman," said Parker confidingly into my ear.

"A madman?" I repeated.

"Not madman," explained Barnes. "Madden. One of the men who works here came past while we were waiting for the lad to bring a constable and we asked him if he knew who it was – he said he thought it was someone called Madden."

CHAPTER THREE

Going to seed

TUESDAY 14TH JULY 1829 – EVENING

"I'm not sure I'm ready for this," said Wilson as we stood outside 88 Brook Street. It was a pleasingly proportioned building of five storeys, with tall windows on the principal floor, decreasing in height with each storey. Two small basement yards were fronted with black railings and a glossy black front door sat dignified in a pillared entrance.

"If you ever feel ready to tell parents that their son is dead," I said grimly, "there'll be something wrong with you." I pointed to the front door. "But it's as well you get the first time over and done with while I'm here."

Wilson sighed mightily then stepped forward and knocked on the door. A trim footman opened it and his practised eye quickly had our measure.

"Good evening, constables," he said, stepping to one side. We walked into the hall and the footman looked past us into the street. "Is he in a hansom? Sleeping it off?" he asked.

We shook our heads. "Is Mr Forster at home?" asked Wilson.

The footman closed the door and took our hats before indicating that we should follow him. We processed behind him and he opened the door of the drawing room for us. "I shall tell the master that you wish to see him," he said, and left the room.

Wilson hovered by the door, as was his habit, but I beckoned him forward. "You will introduce us – you've heard me do it countless times," I said. "And then just come straight out with it. Be clear: none of this fancy stuff about 'passing over' and the like. It's worse if they don't understand it straight away, if you have to explain it again."

"What if they cry?" he asked, fiddling with his collar.

"Then you pity them, lad," I said. "You're a father yourself."

The door opened and in came a man of about forty – handsome once, I daresay, but now (as Martha sometimes put it when she caught me over-indulging) going to seed, with fleshy jowls and the florid nose of a toper.

He wore a flamboyant silk banyan and black leather slippers and carried a book in his hand.

"Gentlemen," he said flatly. "As you see," he gestured with the book, "you find me at my leisure. Is this not a matter that can wait until a more public hour?" He looked first at me and then at Wilson.

"It is not, sir, no," said Wilson, clearing his throat. "I am afraid it is bad news."

"In that case I shall need a drink," said Forster, walking over to the decanter sitting on a tray on the sideboard. He poured himself a glass and turned back to us. He did not invite us to join him; we would have refused. "Continue," he said, gesturing with the glass.

I saw Wilson stiffen his back; it would certainly be easier for him to deliver his news to a disagreeable man. "I am Constable Wilson," he said, "and this is Constable Plank. We are from Great Marlborough Street police office. Could you please confirm that you are Mr Roger Forster, father of Charles Madden?"

"Stepfather, yes," said Forster, taking another swig from his glass and turning to refill it. "And if he's in debt again," he said over his shoulder, "you can tell him that the well is dry."

"What makes you think he would be in debt?" asked Wilson. It seems he had been listening, during all those visits when he stood silently at the door and took notes as I asked questions. I suddenly realised that I was falling down on my own job and quickly pulled my notebook and pencil from my pocket to jot down what had already been said.

Forster's mouth turned down and he shrugged. "The boy's a gambler. His mother spared the rod."

"Perhaps you should ask Mrs Forster to join us," I suggested.

"She's asleep," said Forster quickly. "Not to be disturbed." He saw me glance at the clock on the mantelpiece. "The lamps give her a headache and she prefers to be in bed before they are lit. And I prefer her not to have to listen to yet another complaint about her idle son's foolish behaviour."

Wilson glanced at me and I nodded. "I am afraid that it is somewhat worse than that, Mr Forster," he said. "Your son – your stepson – has been found dead. We suspect foul play."

"Dead?" echoed Forster. "Are you sure?" He drained his glass and filled it for a third time. "I mean, are you sure it is Charles?"

"Perhaps you should sit down, sir," said Wilson.

"Don't you tell me..." began Forster, and then held up a hand. "Forgive me: this is a shock, as I am sure you can see." He threw the drink down his throat and put the glass onto the tray with a clatter. He walked to a high-backed chair and stood behind it, his knuckles white as he held onto it.

"We are all but certain, sir," said Wilson. He looked at me and I leafed back through my notebook.

"The body was found to the rear of a property in St James's Street." I consulted my notes as I read aloud; I could remember the details well enough, but I find it gives people reassurance if they see you checking the record. "He had been beaten, but not badly about the face. Someone working at the property was able to identify him, and the name they gave matched a receipt we found in his pocket."

"A receipt?" Forster looked at me sharply.

I checked my notes. "For a horse – a chestnut hunter bought last Saturday at the Horse Bazaar in…"

Forster interrupted me. "In Portman Square – I know it. Charles and I went there together. But I warned him against the place – it has not been the same recently."

"In what way, sir?" asked Wilson.

"It was once a place for gentlemen, for the beau monde," said Forster bitterly. "The sort of place you could take a lady. But they let anyone in these days –

ruffians, scoundrels. You see them lounging against the walls, not watching the auction but keeping an eye on the people. Looking for easy prey. I daresay they saw Charles throwing his money about and followed him, thinking to rob him, and it went too far. My suspicion would fall on those bravos from the Horse Bazaar."

Wilson frowned. "Bravos, sir? Paid killers? So you think the intention was murder, not robbery?"

Forster blinked a couple of times. "Well, not bravos then – common thugs."

"We were wondering whether the location of the body was significant," said Wilson. "The yard of Crockford's, the club in St James's Street. It was one of their croupiers who said he recognised your son."

"That blasted place!" spat Forster.

"So you know it?" asked Wilson.

"Not personally, if that is your insinuation, constable," said Forster. "But yes, I know the sort of place it is, and yes, I knew that Charles was a – what do they call them? A member." He laughed bitterly. "A rum cull, more like."

"He was young, sir," I protested. "We all make foolish decisions when we are young."

"But not all of us make our mistakes with other people's money," said Forster. He jutted his chin at me.

"Perhaps I was wrong about the Horse Bazaar – maybe Charles had a win at Crockford's and someone decided to relieve him of it. Either way, it's no great mystery, is it, constables?" He looked meaningfully at the clock. "And now, if you will excuse me, I shall have to tell my wife." He held out an arm to indicate the door.

The footman was waiting to hand us our hats. He had doubtless listened at the door during our interview – no footman worth his salt would allow a visit by constables to go unheard – but his face betrayed nothing of his thoughts on the matter.

Once we were outside the house, Wilson looked at me.

"What do you think, sir?" he asked.

I shook my head. "No: what do you think?"

"I think it is odd that he didn't ask about seeing his son's body," said Wilson.

"Stepson," I corrected.

"Yes, but George is my stepson and I still love him. I would certainly ask to see him if he was killed," said Wilson. "And I think it is odd that he didn't ask what we were going to do about it. And did you see how keen he was that we should not meet his wife?"

"Very good," I said. "Always remember how important it is to notice the things that do not happen, as well as those that do."

Just then, we heard an anguished wail from an upstairs room. We both shivered and turned our step to Great Marlborough Street.

CHAPTER FOUR

Bright and compassionate women

FRIDAY 17ᵀᴴ JULY 1829

J
ohn Conant was standing at the window of his rooms, gazing down into the street. Having known the man for more than a decade, I knew better than to think that he was spying on someone or checking the weather: this was what he did when he was turning a knotty problem in his mind.

"Good evening, sir," I said, knocking again on the open door.

"Ah, Sam," he said, turning to me with a tired smile. "Come in, come in." He walked across to the sideboard and indicated the decanter. I shook my head, and he poured himself a modest measure. We sat in the two armchairs near the fireplace and he took a sip of his drink and then stared into the empty grate.

"Are you quite well, sir?" I asked.

He replied without looking at me. "It is the lot of the parent, Sam, to worry about a child from the day they are born until the day you die."

"I hope there is nothing the matter with Miss Lily," I said, genuinely meaning it: Lily Conant was a charming young woman, the delight of her widowed father's life and the pride of everyone who worked at Great Marlborough Street and knew first-hand how different she was from the self-absorbed, fashion-chasing ladies of society.

"Fighting fit, Sam, fighting fit," said the magistrate with a sad chuckle, "and fighting with me."

I raised an eyebrow; Conant and his daughter often butted heads, as he was proud of her quick intelligence and encouraged her to use it.

"You will be aware of the new lying-in hospital in Lambeth?" asked the magistrate. "Opened last year after moving from smaller premises."

"The grand place on York Road?" I asked.

Conant nodded. "Lily had been helping them to raise funds to cover the building of the new hospital, and now wants to continue helping in some capacity – telling people about the good work they do, soliciting more donations and so on."

"You cannot be surprised that she cares about such a cause," I said. "You have taught her to have regard for the less fortunate – she sees your example every day."

"And for this I blame myself, Sam," Conant replied. "Lily is no longer a foolish young woman – she is nearly twenty-four years old. And when proud mamas and wealthy papas look for a suitable wife for their son, this... this venture, this cause will not serve her well. If it had been the other place, the hospital for married women, it might have been better, but to be associated so closely with unmarried women – it cannot help her, Sam."

I leaned forward in my chair. "Will you permit me to speak plainly, sir?" He nodded and I continued. "I know something of the work done at the lying-in hospital at Lambeth – Mrs Plank has made sure of that, with her interest in such matters. And it sounds like an admirable place. We see the darker side of life, you and I, and we know only too well the desperate acts that an unmarried woman can resort to when she finds herself alone and expecting a child." The magistrate shook his head sadly. "This hospital gives them salvation, yes, but not at any price. Before a woman is admitted, the governors have to be satisfied that there are funds available to pay for her care and that she will not be a burden on the parish – I daresay it is these donations that Miss Lily seeks to find. An unmarried woman can be admitted only once to the hospital – she is expected to learn from her mistake. And she will be housed on a separate ward to the married women."

"Mrs Plank seems to know a great deal," observed Conant.

"She has an ulterior motive," I confessed. "She is hoping that the hospital will take girls from her school to work as servants and perhaps even nurses – she reasons that the governors will be sympathetic to the plight of her girls, many of them born into the very situation that necessitates this hospital."

"She is a bright and compassionate woman, your wife," said the magistrate.

"And so is your daughter," I replied. "I take it that you do not see the Lambeth hospital as a bad thing? You do not fear that it will encourage unmarried women to conceive simply to take advantage of the facilities on offer?"

"Of course not," he replied.

"And nor do I," I said, "and nor will many right-thinking, kind, informed young men. And," I glanced at the magistrate, "I think that this is exactly the type of husband you would choose for Miss Lily." I paused. "And perhaps her association with the hospital is actually a clever way of weeding out those, how did you put it, proud mamas and wealthy papas whose sons look merely for a decorative mother for their children, instead of an interesting, intelligent, compassionate wife."

"Like her late mother," said Conant quietly.

"Like her late mother," I repeated.

We sat in silence for a minute or two, lost in our own thoughts. The clock on the mantelpiece whirred in preparation and then struck the hour, and this served to bring us back to the present.

"Forgive me, Sam," said Conant. "You came to report something, and instead I have once again taken advantage of your sound advice. What was it you wanted to tell me?"

I explained about the grim discovery in the dust-pit and about my visit to Brook Street and the magistrate listened carefully. Word of the death had reached him, of course, but he knew none of the details.

"And the man who reported the body?" he asked.

"A dustman," I said. "From the Martin dust-yard in Paddington Basin. They have the contract to collect from the properties in St James's Street."

"So he is unlikely to have anything to do with the death," said the magistrate.

"Indeed," I agreed. "The fellow who found the body is simple, and the one who sent for us was as shocked as anyone would be to find a corpse in a dust-pit. Although he did say that he had heard of one or two in the past – topers, tumbling in in the dark, that sort of thing."

"But not this one," said Conant grimly. He stood and retrieved a piece of paper from his desk and then returned to his chair. "This is a letter from Doctor Gray. He is the family physician for the Forsters, and he was called when the body was taken home on Wednesday morning. The parents gave permission for the doctor to conduct a post-mortem and these are his initial findings." He put on his spectacles and unfolded the letter. "Let me see now…. Yes, here we are: several ribs broken on the left side, also the collarbone. A rupture of the spleen, consistent with the broken ribs."

"The spleen?" I repeated.

"Yes: here," said Conant, pointing just below his own heart.

"I know where it is," I said quickly, "but does the doctor think that the rupture killed him?"

The magistrate nodded. "Yes, he is quite clear on that point: 'With regard to cause of death, a portion of the last rib projected into the spleen – the breaking of the rib forced it into the spleen, ruptured it and caused his death.'" He looked up at me. "Murder, then – manslaughter at the least." He took off his spectacles and shook his head. "A young man – terrible waste."

"Mr Forster said he thought his stepson might have been targeted by bravos from a horse repository," I said.

"Paid assassins?" asked Conant in surprise. "And you? What do you think?" He picked up his empty glass and returned it to the sideboard, then put his hand against the side of the coffee pot that was standing there. "Not hot exactly, but not cold either – can I tempt you?"

"No, thank you," I said. "Thin Billy's coffee is only just bearable even when it's hot."

"And he takes such pride in it," said Conant with a chuckle. Williams had been the magistrate's footman for years, bearing stoically the nickname we constables had given him thanks to his gaunt frame.

"At least you know you won't be losing him to Serle's," I added. "But as for young Madden, I'd need to look into things."

"Out with it, Sam," said the magistrate. "I can tell that you're uneasy."

"Three things concern me," I said. "First, it's quite a step from the Horse Bazaar in Portman Square to where the body was found in a dust-pit at the back of St James's Street – that's what, more than a mile?"

"Considerably," agreed Conant.

"With plenty of dark alleyways and hidden corners along the way," I continued, "so if the motive was murder by assassins, why would they follow him for more than a mile rather than attacking him sooner?"

Conant nodded. "The second?"

"Wilson and I were called to the Horse Bazaar on Monday because a certain Charles Madden," the magistrate looked at me, "aye, the same man, had paid for a horse with counterfeit notes."

"Indeed," said the magistrate. "And the third?"

"The dust-tip was in the yard behind properties in St James's Street," I said. "One of them is Crockford's – and apparently Charles Madden was a member."

"Horses, gambling," the magistrate said bitterly. "When will parents realise that giving their sons everything teaches them nothing? When I think of the parade of elegant fools with full wallets and empty heads who have paid court to my daughter – I thank heavens that she is too clever for any of them."

The mention of wallets brought something to my mind. "Did the doctor make a record of what Charles

Madden was wearing?" I asked. "Anything in his pockets?"

"Was it robbery, d'you mean?" said Conant. He looked back down at the doctor's letter. "Ah: here we go: 'One gold sovereign found in right coat pocket'."

"Any thief would have taken that," I said. "In his coat pocket – not concealed at all. Even the dustman would have found it if he'd pulled the body out himself instead of calling us."

"Perhaps the thief was disturbed," suggested the magistrate.

"Or perhaps it was not a chance robbery," I said.

"A deliberate attack, you think?" asked Conant.

I shrugged. "Possibly. Mr Forster seemed to think that his stepson was being watched by some men at the Horse Bazaar, and I'd like to know who they are." I remembered something and turned back some pages in my notebook. "When we visited the Horse Bazaar and spoke to the senior clerk about the counterfeit notes and why he had called us, he said that the owner – Mr Young – is 'not a man of forgiveness'. He said it twice."

"And if such an unforgiving man were to find the rascal who had been passing counterfeit notes at his place of business…" Conant mused aloud."

◆

"And just how are you going to pretend that you know anything about horses, Sam?" Martha shook her head as she pushed past me to put the pot on the stove.

"I knew enough about them to pass muster at that watermen's stand a few years ago," I protested.

"That's caring for the beasts," she replied. "Any fool can look after an animal: feed it, give it water, and don't hurt it. A bit like looking after a husband. But when it comes to buying one, well, you'll have to ask questions about, oh, I don't know," she waved a hand in the air, "how old it is or what its parents were."

"A stallion and a mare, I should imagine," I said. "That's how these things usually happen."

Martha gave me the sort of look that tells a man his wife might be having second thoughts about her choice of husband. I played my trump card. "I thought you could come with me," I said.

"To a horse sale?" said Martha, folding her arms. "Rubbing shoulders with dealers and butchers?"

"Not a horse sale," I said, smiling. "An auction, at a horse repository. The Horse Bazaar, in Portman Square. Very elegant." Martha unfolded her arms. "They sell all sorts of things there: carriages, furniture, jewellery.

That's why they call it a bazaar – like one of those Arabian markets when you can buy anything you want. There are coffee-rooms and a refectory. And the auction room has a cupola on the top."

"A what?" asked Martha.

"A glass dome," I said. "Imagine that. And they have an exhibition of automata in the basement – musical boxes and mechanical toys. Mr Conant said Miss Lily has seen it and thought it marvellous." I know how Martha enjoyed hearing news of the magistrate's daughter and I reminded myself to tell her over dinner about my earlier conversation with the magistrate. "And you can meet a giant – Monsieur Louis, from France. Over seven feet tall, apparently. But if you're not interested, I can ask Wilson to come instead."

Martha harrumphed and turned to the stove to stir the pot. "Well, I suppose I could come, but only to help you." She turned and looked at me over her shoulder with a smile. "And to see that tall French fellow."

CHAPTER FIVE

Happy hunting

SATURDAY 18TH JULY 1829

The Horse Bazaar was almost unrecognisable as Martha and I stood on Portman Street and looked through the archway into the yard. Where Wilson and I had seen only a handful of men and one sleepy dog there was now bustling activity. Conant had advised me to arrive early, as the noon auctions were always popular, and although the clock over the doorway showed only half-past ten, we were far from the first to arrive. The uniformed grooms that I had seen on my first visit were running about the place like ants, taking hold of a bridle here, handing down a lady from a carriage there. Seeing those same ladies, Martha put a hand to her own hat.

"You have nothing to fear, my dear," I said. "You are their equal in fashion, and their superior in every other way."

"You do talk some rot, Samuel Plank," she replied, but I could tell from the tilt of her head that she was pleased. "Now, show me this glass dome and the rest."

We walked through the grand wooden doorway, past the closed door of the clerks' office, and into the main hall where the auction was to be held. It was indeed an impressive chamber: tall white walls stretched up and gave way to beautiful wrought-iron railings that girded the gallery, and almost the entire ceiling was made of glass, allowing the morning light to stream down onto us. Dozens of people were already there: the floor of the hall was busy with groups of men in smart outfits, while the gallery provided an excellent place from which the ladies could observe the fashion and the gentlemen could observe the ladies.

"Shall we head upstairs?" I asked Martha, indicating the gallery. "We can find ourselves a good vantage point for watching the auction." And for spotting Madden's alleged tormentors.

My wife took a long look around and then nodded, so we walked over to one of the two grand staircases. It was only then that I saw the sign with an arrow pointing to the upper floor: "Fancy Bazaar – forty stalls – everything for ladies of discernment and fashion".

"You'd think a constable would have noticed that sign sooner," said Martha. "Forty stalls – imagine!"

♦

Once Martha had dragged me round a dozen or so of the stalls, pointing out things that I could see perfectly well for myself – "Oh look at that brooch, and have you seen those gloves?" – I began to question the wisdom of my plan. I had thought that bringing my wife would make me less noticeable, but all advantage was lost if I had no time to observe the crowd. But, as so often, I had underestimated Martha. After sniffing an array of perfumes presented in glass bottles on a stall and deciding that none was as pleasing as the scent of fresh flowers, she turned to me.

"Sam, I'm parched," she said. "Could you go down to the coffee-room and fetch me a cordial?"

"Why not come with me?" I said. I glanced at the clock. "There's just time before the start of the auction."

She shook her head. "I will wait here – if you could take about twenty minutes, that would be best." I opened my mouth to say something but she shooed me away. "Twenty minutes, Sam."

I walked back round to the staircase and glanced over my shoulder to see Martha stopping, as though by accident, next to a pair of young ladies who were sitting and looking down into the main hall then turning to each other and whispering. Martha caught my eye and with a small motion of her head indicated that I should be on my way.

When I returned twenty minutes later as instructed, Martha and the two young ladies were chatting animatedly, their chairs pulled companionably close together. Martha held out her hand and took the glass of cordial that I had brought her.

"This is my husband, ladies," she said, placing a proprietorial hand on my arm. "This is my Samuel."

The two – no more than seventeen years old, if I had to guess, one quite pretty but the other rather plain, as is often the way with pairs of girls – inclined their heads and blushed.

"Samuel," continued Martha, "may I present Miss Roberts and Miss Foxton."

"A pleasure to meet you, ladies," I said, bowing solemnly. "Are you interested in horses?"

The two looked at each other and then at Martha, who explained, "Miss Roberts and Miss Foxton enjoy the spectacle, Samuel. They like to look around. And now," she stood and nodded her head to the two, "we shall leave them in peace. Happy hunting, ladies."

The two young women giggled and blushed again, before turning their attention once more to the hall below them.

Martha and I walked off and found a comfortable place further round the gallery where we could settle and watch the auction. I found two seats and pushed them to the railing so that we had a clear view of the proceedings.

"Who were they?" I asked. "Your new friends."

"Miss Roberts and Miss Foxton are not much interested in horses," Martha said, "but they are very much interested in the sort of men who are interested in horses." She leaned towards me. "They come here every Saturday, in their finery, and do their research. They are looking for husbands, Sam. Down there." She waved her hand to indicate the growing crowd in the hall. "They watch to see who has money, and who buys which sort of horse – after all, there's no benefit in pursuing a fellow who buys a lady's mare. And then they put themselves in the way of suitable prospects." She smiled at the look on my face. "Surely you don't think that it's the man who does the choosing?"

I thought back to our first meeting, mine and Martha's. She had been keeping house for her drunken father and four young siblings, living above his rough inn in Laystall Street, and when I strolled past as a young constable we struck up a conversation. I liked her quick humour and – there's no denying it – her pretty face and soft curves. Even at only fifteen she had more life and determination about her than any woman I had ever met.

"Surely you remember, Mrs Plank," I said, "that I was the one who wandered down Laystall Street every evening."

"And surely you remember, Mr Plank," she replied, "that we had the cleanest windows and doorstep in all of Holborn, with me outside every evening working on them, just so that your wandering wouldn't be wasted." She looked at me and smiled sweetly. "Now, if Miss Roberts and Miss Foxton are to be believed, they're the fellows to watch." She nodded in the direction of three men leaning against the wall as the auctioneer took his place. "They're here for every auction, I'm told, and they never place a bid or take much notice of the horses.

They don't even look at the ladies – all they're interested in is watching the buyers."

Just then the clock in the hall struck noon, and the auctioneer climbed onto the small, raised platform provided for him. At either side of him, a smartly dressed groom held aloft a board on which was chalked the number of the lot under auction, the barest details of the animal, and its starting price. The groom would walk slowly in a circle to ensure that his board could be read by everyone in the hall and gallery. And Martha was right: as each animal was brought forward and the auction started, the three men she had indicated showed no interest at all: instead, they turned their attention to whoever was bidding. And as the auctioneer's hammer came down, one of the three would make a note in a book while the other two had a quick discussion. Every so often, one of them would head off in the direction of the cashier's office, returning one or two lots later.

Just over an hour later, the auction finished. The auctioneer mopped his brow with a large handkerchief and climbed down from his platform to a smattering of applause. According to the programme, there would be a half-hour break before the horse sale started, when animals with fixed prices would be offered. Whether to find refreshment or for some other purpose, the three men I was watching pushed themselves away from the wall and disappeared from view.

"Look," said Martha, "down there." She pointed and I could see Miss Roberts and Miss Foxton in conversation with two young men. "The one on the right, with the moustache: he bought a hunter, I think."

"Given the plans of those two young ladies," I said, "it may turn out to be a far more expensive purchase than he realises."

CHAPTER SIX

All about the numbers

SATURDAY 25TH JULY 1829

"**D**id Mrs Plank not fancy this part of the job?" asked Wilson as we waited a week later in Portman Street.

Peering into the yard of the Horse Bazaar, I could see that it was almost three o'clock. "You could have come with us last week," I pointed out, "but you were otherwise engaged. Which reminds me: Mrs Plank says to let her know as soon as Sally is expecting, and she'll start making baby bonnets and the rest."

Wilson laughed. "The poor girl's only been married a week!"

"But you like the fellow?" I asked. Wilson had been the man of the family since he was fifteen, looking after his widowed mother and his sisters Sally and Janey. He and Alice had moved into rooms in the same building so that he could keep an eye on them and supplement the meagre income the three women made from taking in needlework.

"Well enough," he shrugged. "He's a bit serious for my taste, but then I'm not the one marrying him. He works for one of the breweries as a drayman, so that's steady work – people will always want their beer." His face softened. "And he's good to Sally – seems proper, what's that word, smitten. All moony when he looks at her." He widened his eyes and tried to look love-struck and I shook my head and smiled.

"You look more simple than moony," I said. "I hope you don't look at Alice like that, particularly not now she's in a delicate condition."

"Ha!" said Wilson. He turned his head as the clock of a nearby church struck three.

"Keep an eye out," I said. "Three of them: one tall and two shorter, and all look like they could hold their own in a fight."

Wilson stood a little more upright and straightened his coat.

"There," I said, "that's them. Coming this way."

The three were laughing as they walked towards us. One of the shorter ones was putting his notebook into his pocket, while the tall one was sucking on a pipe. Wilson and I stepped smartly into the gateway, blocking their path.

"Yes?" said the man with the notebook, whom I took to be the ringleader.

"I am Constable Plank," I said, "and this is Constable Wilson, of Great Marlborough Street." I paused, but none of them said anything. "Have you been buying horses, gentlemen?"

The ringleader spoke again. "I don't see how it is any of your business, constables, how my friends and I spend our morning."

By now, a few people were gathering behind the trio, waiting to leave the yard and craning forward to see what was holding them up.

"I leave it to you, gentlemen," I said, speaking in a clear, loud voice. "We can either discuss this matter here, until we constables have the answers we need, or you can join us in the Three Tuns for a more private conversation."

There was a moment while the man in charge weighed up his options and then he nodded once. "The Three Tuns," he said gruffly.

With me leading and Wilson bringing up the rear, the five of us turned into Portman Mews and then into the pub, which was noisy with talk of horses and carriages, bargains and swindles. I had a word with the publican and he showed us into the snug at the back, promising to send the pot boy with our drinks before pulling the curtain closed to give us privacy. We sat in silence, apart from the noises made by the tall man as he tapped, filled and sucked on his pipe. The curtain was pushed aside and the pot boy put a tray of five tankards on the table.

"Mr Sharp says there's no payment needed," he said as he turned to leave.

"Tell Mr Sharp we'll settle up on the way out," I said. "We're constables, not Runners."

The ringleader snorted. "I'd heard that you constables think you're a cut above," he said as he reached for a tankard and took a deep draught.

"Quite the opposite," I said mildly – it was an accusation I had heard before. "It's because we're not a cut above that we pay our way, and then no-one can say that constables play favourites. As for what the Runners do, well, I leave that to their conscience." I took a swallow of my own drink. "Now, gentlemen, as you're accepting our hospitality, the least you can do is give us your names."

Wilson quickly put down his tankard and took out his notebook.

"I'm Jem Sullivan," said the man in charge, "and this is Tom Dawson," he indicated the tall man, "and George Brett."

I looked at Dawson's hand as he raised his tankard. "Where'd you get those bruises?" I asked, pointing to his knuckles. "In a fight?"

Dawson glanced at Sullivan, who nodded. "Aye," said Dawson.

"A robbery that went wrong?" I asked. "Wouldn't hand it over quietly?"

Dawson looked stricken. "Robbery?" he repeated. "A robbery that went wrong? How d'ye mean, wrong?"

"A dead man has been pulled out of a dust-pit," I said. "And his family seems to think that he was followed home from the Horse Bazaar by a group of men who keep an eye out for anyone with a fat purse. I was at the auction last Saturday and I watched you – I watched you for an hour, and you didn't inspect a horse or make a bid.

But you did watch the crowd. And you," I indicated Sullivan with my tankard, "you kept careful notes of what you saw. In the notebook that you have with you today."

Sullivan put a protective hand to his pocket but said nothing.

I drained my beer and felt my own pocket for my purse. "You have the names, Wilson?" I asked. He nodded and closed his notebook. "Come," I said, standing up. "Mr Conant will be in his rooms; it will not take long for him to sign three warrants for arrest on suspicion of murder."

"Murder?" said Dawson. "Jem, please!"

I looked at Sullivan and he bowed his head. "Sit down," he said. I did so and he reached into his pocket for his notebook, which he slid across the table to me. It was dim in the snug, but Wilson shifted so that the light from the lamp on the wall behind him fell onto the table. I opened the notebook and started to read. It was a list of names, with details written alongside them – horses they had bid on, animals they had bought, friends they had met. Alongside each name was a number – "Age," grunted Sullivan when I pointed – and against some was an address. And in the margin to the left of each name was one of three symbols: an X, a mark of interrogation or a star.

"And these?" I asked.

Sullivan looked at his two companions, who nodded miserably. "As you gentlemen work in Great Marlborough Street," he said, "I take it you're familiar with Mr Crockford's establishment."

"The gambling palace on St James's Street?" I said.

"That's the one," said Sullivan. "And do you know Mr Crockford himself?" I shook my head. "Well, he's a canny businessman."

"That I did know," I said. "A fishmonger by trade, if I remember right."

Sullivan nodded. "But his real skill, Mr Crockford, is numbers. He can work out everything up here." He tapped the side of his forehead. "When he was a boy, working in the shop and the markets, his father used him as his calculator, to work out who owed him how much, interest payable and the like. That's how he made his fortune. And gambling is all about numbers." Sullivan leaned back in his seat and crossed his arms. "He's quite a character, you know, Mr Crockford. Dresses like a country farmer while he mixes with the wealthiest men in London. And holds their future in the palm of his hand." He held out his cupped hand.

Sullivan had obviously overcome his reluctance to talk and I glanced at Wilson to make sure that he did nothing to interrupt. I need not have worried: unusually for a large man, Wilson has the handy knack of knowing when to stay so still that he almost disappears from view.

Sullivan continued. "As Mr Crockford sees it, the other clubs – White's, Brooks's – waste their time pretending to be better than they are: they have secretive membership committees who vote against a fellow and he never knows why. They call themselves gentlemen's clubs and claim to offer good company and improving debate. But Crockford's is exactly what it says it is: a gambling club. Mr Crockford's sole object is to win money from his members – and they know that. That's not to say he's stingy: it's a fancy place, and the food is excellent. But a fellow goes to Crockford's to gamble – not to make friends or hear political views."

"And what is your role in this new and open way of doing business?" I asked.

"It's all about the numbers, constable," said Sullivan again. "Mr Crockford doesn't want places at his tables taken up by men who have empty purses. He wants to find men who have money and are willing to risk it. And my job – our job," he indicated his two companions, "is to find those men for him so that he can let them know that they will be welcome at Crockford's."

"And the Horse Bazaar is a good place to find such men," I suggested.

"Young men who have just come into money, or anticipate coming into it, will want a fine horse and carriage," agreed Sullivan. "We watch for them, and see how much they spend, and whether they have the air of a gambling man. A few coins here and there and someone's always willing to tell us names. And I report our findings to Mr Crockford." Sullivan tapped his finger on his open notebook. "An X is a lost cause – not much money, perhaps, or just watching the girls, or too timid in his bids. A mark of interrogation shows uncertainty – not enough information yet, but worth watching. And a star, well, that's a recommendation – the sort of fellow that Mr Crockford would want to pursue."

"How long have you kept this notebook?" I asked.

"This particular one, you mean?" asked Sullivan. I nodded and he pulled the notebook towards him, turning to the front. "I started this one on the twelfth of March, so that's four, nearly five months."

"Could you look for a name in it," I said. "Charles Madden."

"Was that the fellow who was killed?" asked Sullivan. I said nothing and he started to leaf through the pages. "D'you remember him?" he asked his two companions, who shook their heads. A few moments passed and then he stopped with his finger on an entry in the notebook. "Here he is: Charles Madden. Brook Street in Mayfair." He glanced at me. "You can always find a groom at the Horse Bazaar who'll give you information for a few coins." He read on. "Winning bid on hunter – eleven guineas. Age estimated at 22. Unmarried. Only son. No profession."

"Very knowledgeable groom," I remarked.

"Once we have the address from the groom," explained Sullivan, "we call round and have a quiet word with a footman or a maid. No secrets from them." He smiled and then quickly remembered himself and stopped.

"And what symbol did you put next to Mr Madden's entry?" I asked.

"An only son with time on his hands, living in Mayfair, no outgoings, bidding successfully at an auction?" asked Sullivan. "A star, Constable Plank – what else?"

♦

"There's been plenty of talk about the place, certainly," said Conant when I called on him that evening in his rooms. "The... professionalism of the gambling.

We're used to men wagering against each other, but this is different."

The magistrate, like his father before him, was a member of Brooks's. He rarely attended, having little stomach either for gambling or for entirely male company, but he was not above using the place to beard men of influence.

"Aye," I said, turning back a few pages in my notebook. "I asked Sullivan about that. Here it is: all wagers are between gentlemen and croupiers, who are employed by the club. Apparently Mr Crockford himself sits in the corner of the gaming room, overseeing the activity. All fair and square, with careful records kept of stakes and winnings. Professional, as you say."

"And this seeking out of members," said Conant. "We've had gulling for as long as we've had gambling, but not quite so organised – or so openly admitted to. It's certainly an ingenious approach."

"But not criminal," I said.

"Not criminal, no," agreed the magistrate. "As long as these three men are not pursuing the targets they identify, not threatening them or coercing them."

I shook my head. "Sullivan was very clear that their instructions were simply to identify and report back. He took a certain pride in his work and was almost insulted at the thought that he might have had anything to do with the body in the dust-pit."

Conant raised an eyebrow; having sat on the bench for decades and watched the best performers in the criminal world, he knew better than to take a man at his word.

"And I believed him," I added. "As Wilson pointed out, what would be their motive? If it were robbery, why would they follow and attack a man they had just seen spend almost all his money on a horse? According to Sullivan, one of the best targets for their purposes is a man who bids on a horse but does not win."

"How so?" asked the magistrate.

"Well," I said, leaning forward, "it shows that he has some money – a decent amount of money, to attend a horse auction with any hope of buying – but not enough for the animal he wants. He might be tempted to wager that money in an attempt to win more. And apparently men who like to buy at auction are similar to men who like to gamble: both are willing to go into a transaction where the final price is uncertain."

"I had no idea so much thought went into it," said Conant.

"Nor did I," I admitted.

The magistrate stood and went over to the window, pushing the curtain to one side so that he could gaze down into the street. I waited.

After a few minutes he turned to me. "Perhaps you and I should go to this club," he said.

"Perhaps," I said.

"No need for any subterfuge," he continued. "Mr Crockford conducts his business in an admirably open manner and we shall do the same. Well, almost the same." He walked back to his desk. "You can talk to some of the – croupiers, did you call them? The ones he employs to gamble with the members." I nodded. "And I shall talk to Mr Crockford about joining his club."

♦

"A gambling club?" said Martha. "What on earth can Mr Conant want with such a place? He's surely too sensible to risk his fortune."

"Indeed," I said, handing her my coat. "But Mr Crockford will not know that, and if we can encourage him to talk about his club and how it works, we might learn something to help us discover who killed young Madden and threw his body into the dust-pit."

"Why not just ask Mr Crockford what he knows?" asked Martha, laying my coat on the kitchen table and indicating for me to pass her the polish from the cupboard. She put a piece of rag behind one of the buttons, to protect the coat, spat on the polish cloth and started to rub the button. "You're a constable and Mr Conant is a magistrate – he'd have to answer your questions."

I sat at the table and watched her move onto a second button. "Aye," I said, "but then we'd have to know exactly what questions to ask him. I'm not sure what we suspect at the moment – it may even be a complete coincidence that the body was dumped in that particular dust-pit." Martha looked up at me. "I know: that's not likely, but it's possible. But the fact remains that if you ask someone a question, they give you an answer to that question. If you have a conversation with them, you never know what they might say."

"I'll bear that in mind," said Martha, bending down to inspect one of the buttons. "This one here: there's a dent in it. Shall I replace it? Or is it not worth it now?"

She looked up at me, her face soft, and I knew we were both thinking of that day not too far in the future when I would no longer wear the coat of a magistrates' constable."

CHAPTER SEVEN

Three hundred thousand bottles

TUESDAY 28TH JULY 1829

What with one thing and another, it was not until the following Tuesday that John Conant and I visited the gambling club. It was a fine evening and we decided to walk; the magistrate was once a naval man and retains the liking for physical exercise common to that breed. It was another reason why he had so little tolerance for spending hours in clubs; after a day in court and his rooms, he preferred to be outside. As we crossed Regent Street and walked along Maddox Street, he took deep breaths and swung his arms, keeping up a smart pace.

"I'm not too sure about that place," he said, indicating St George's Church. "To my eye it looks more like an exchange than a church – the pillared area at the front looks perfect for moneychangers. The portico – that's the word."

"I'm no expert," I said, "but I should imagine that a fair amount of business is conducted in its pews – there's plenty of money around here."

We walked through the churchyard and stopped at the front of the church. He was right: the grand pillars looked more boastful than a house of God should be.

"That's true," said Conant. "John Copley lives in one of these houses – the Lord Chancellor."

"Lord Lyndhurst, you mean," I said.

Conant smiled. "Of course. I knew him best when he was a humble Attorney General – how the mighty are risen."

We reached the junction of Conduit Street and Old Bond Street.

"We can turn left," I said, "which is the most direct route. Or shall we make a slight detour to see the gardens in Berkeley Square?"

The magistrate sniffed the air. "Gardens, I think," he said. "From what I know of gambling clubs, we won't see much daylight or breathe fresh air once we're inside, so let's take our fill now."

♦

The clocks were striking eight by the time we turned into St James's Street. The St James's Club, which no-one called anything but Crockford's, was an impressive pale building on the right, the width of five of its neighbours.

"There you are," said Conant, pointing. "More columns. They go together: columns and money."

We walked up the wide, shallow steps and as we approached the double front door it swung open, a uniformed doorman bowing on each side. I let the magistrate precede me into the magnificent entrance hall, which had large doorways leading off into chambers left and right. Ahead of us was a sinuous staircase, winding up to a landing supported by four elegant columns. I tilted my head back and saw a ceiling with panels of stained glass that glowed even in the dimming light of evening. In the centre of the glass panels was a beautiful dome and hanging down in the middle of it was a lantern containing a magnificent chandelier.

"The committee at Brooks's will have to increase their subscriptions to keep up with this," said Conant at my side.

Just then a man approached us. His eyes flicked down towards my coat. "Constable," he said smoothly. He looked at the magistrate. "Sir," he added. "Welcome to Crockford's. How may I help you?"

"I am Constable Sam Plank of Great Marlborough Street, "I said, "and I would like to speak to the croupier who identified the body of Charles Madden in your dust-pit." The fellow looked around quickly to see if anyone had overheard. I continued. "When I mentioned my proposed visit to Mr Conant, one of our magistrates, he expressed an interest in accompanying me."

Conant leaned forward as though to share a confidence. "I'm not interested in the body," he said. "At least, not yet – the constable will let me know if there's anything to concern me. But I am interested in this place." He waved a hand around. "Might it be possible for me to have a word with the owner? I'm at Brooks's at the moment but," his voice dropped further, "the play is a little tame. Not a criticism I have heard levelled at your establishment."

I might have been mistaken, but I think the magistrate winked.

"Mr Conant," said our new friend with a smile, "I am sure Mr Crockford would be very pleased to show you just how different our establishment is. If you would like to take a seat in the reading-room," he indicated one of the large doorways, "I will ask him to come and speak to you."

The magistrate nodded and walked off towards the reading-room. "I shall see you tomorrow, constable," he said without looking back at me.

The smile disappeared from the face of the man at my side. "And you can come with me," he said. He led me past the grand staircase and through a small door. Although Crockford's had been built at great expense and with every luxury, the back rooms were as plain and cramped as in any grand house. A slim young man in black trousers and coat hurried past and my companion caught him by the sleeve.

"Is Beech in yet?" he asked.

"Yes," said the young man. "He's changing his shoes – he'll be along in a minute." He looked at me, frowned slightly and then walked off.

"Is Beech the man who identified Mr Madden's body?" I asked my host.

"I can see why they give you that uniform," he said. He looked down the corridor and beckoned to someone.

"Here he is. Beech, this constable wants to talk to you about the body. We'll go into my office."

Beech was slightly older than the other man I had seen but dressed in an identical outfit. I held out my arm to indicate that he should follow his boss and the three of us walked back down the corridor until we reached a closed door with "Inspector" written on it in flamboyant gold script. The inspector went into the room; it was surprisingly large and elegant, with a desk set in front of a tall window looking over the yard behind the building. There was a low wall at the end of the yard and behind that, I guessed, was the dust-pit. The inspector walked towards his desk.

"I was wondering, sir," I said, "whether I could be permitted to speak to Mr Beech on my own. I am sure you have plenty to do – plenty to inspect."

The inspector looked at me with narrowed eyes. I am sure he was about to refuse when there was an urgent knocking at the door and a head appeared around it.

"Mr Guy," the man said, "you're needed out front. I think we'll need to open the upstairs room – a gentleman has arrived with a large party."

The inspector flapped his hands at the newcomer. "Go, go – I'm on my way." He looked at me. "You may speak to Mr Beech, constable, but for fifteen minutes only – he is on duty." He walked to the door and opened it. "Fifteen minutes, Mr Beech, or I shall dock your pay." He left.

I took one of the two chairs that were placed in front of the desk and indicated that the croupier should take the other. He sat on the very edge of the seat, bolt upright.

"Mr Beech," I said, opening my notebook. "And your Christian name?"

"Leonard," he said. He watched me write it down. "Did I do something wrong, constable?" he asked.

"What do you mean, Mr Beech?" I asked in response.

He shrugged but I could see from the way the knuckles of his clenched hands were white that he was far from relaxed. I said nothing.

"With the body," he said eventually. "It was just a coincidence that I was the one the dustman found when he came in."

"Mr Barnes," I said. "The dustman. And why did he find you, Mr Beech?"

"I was early for work that day," he said, shifting in his seat. "Mr Guy likes us here for half-past ten, ready to open the room at eleven. But Edie and me, we'd had a row – Edie's my wife," he said. "And I thought it would be best if I just cleared out for a while. So I came here. I like to read the newspapers if I have time."

"So that you can have intelligent conversation with the members?" I asked.

Beech barked a laugh. "The croupiers don't converse with the members," he said.

"But you do know who they are?" I asked. "After all, you identified the body – you knew it was Charles Madden."

He shrugged. "Of course: we're silent – not stupid." He looked stricken. "Forgive me, sir – I did not mean to sound impertinent."

I held up my hand. "There is no need to apologise, Mr Beech," I said. "I would rather you were honest than polite. Perhaps you could explain to me exactly what a croupier does."

"Are you familiar with the game of hazard, sir?" asked the young man, visibly relaxing now that he was on familiar ground.

"I know that it is played with dice," I said, "and that fortunes can be won and – probably more regularly – lost."

The croupier leaned forward in his seat and gestured with his hands as he explained. "The player – known as the caster – chooses a number between five and nine inclusive, which is called the main. He then puts two dice into a cup and casts them onto the table. If he rolls the main he nicks – which means that he wins. If he rolls a two or a three, he throws out – he loses. If he rolls an eleven or a twelve, the result depends on the main – he may nick or he may throw out. If he neither nicks nor throws out, the number thrown is called the chance and so he casts the dice again. If he rolls the chance, he nicks. If he rolls the main, he throws out. And if he rolls neither the chance nor the main, he keeps casting until he does roll one of them – winning with the chance and losing with the main." He smiled at the blank look on my face. "It becomes second nature when you have watched it a few times."

"And your role in the game?" I asked.

"In many places, the caster will be betting against other men, but here at Crockford's the caster always bets against the house," said Beech. "It is more professional, says Mr Crockford, and makes the gentlemen feel that they have some control over the game."

I looked up from my notebook. "But of course they do not."

Beech shook his head. "It is a simple matter of mathematics," he said. "Anyone who studies the fall of the dice and works it out knows that an honest game will give the house a profit of between one and two per cent."

"And does Crockford's run an honest game?" I asked.

The croupier looked suddenly serious. "It does, sir, yes," he said. "This is not my first job as a croupier – I have worked in other establishments – and I can assure you that the play here is fair. At each table there is a croupier. Our job is to watch the game and the stake; we call out the numbers as the dice fall, and we declare the result of each game so that no-one can be misled. The stake must be placed on the table in full view of all, and at the end of the game the croupier uses a rake to push the winnings to the caster or pull them to himself, on behalf of the house. We then make sure the dice are passed on quickly, rattling them in the cup to stir the blood."

"A responsible job," I said. "It must be tempting…" I left the question unasked.

"You are talking about what happened at Watier's, I suppose," said Beech, frowning.

"I know that Mr Crockford lost money in that establishment," I said, "and I believe that the dishonesty of some of his employees contributed to that."

"Whether that's true or not," said the croupier, "Mr Crockford has learned from it. As well as a croupier on each table and the calling out of scores and results, we have the inspector – Mr Guy – sitting on a high chair in one corner of the room, and Mr Crockford himself sitting at a desk in the opposite corner."

"Every night?" I asked.

Beech nodded. "Every single night. He says it makes the members feel safe, but we know he's watching for cheating – by anyone." A clock on the mantelpiece chimed a pretty tune and the croupier stood. "And now, constable, you must forgive me if I leave you – Mr Guy was serious when he said he would dock my pay. Crockford's is always serious about money."

♦

"Was it as magnificent as you expected?" asked Martha as we settled into our chairs after supper. She bent over and sorted through some items in her sewing basket, eventually pulling out a pillowcase which she draped over the arm of the chair while she carefully threaded a needle. She glanced up at me before she began stitching. "The gambling palace?"

"It was very fine," I said. "Crockford certainly knows his business."

"Gambling?" asked Martha, peering at the pillowcase and adding another few stitches.

I shook my head. "Seduction." Martha's eyebrows went up in surprise. "Enticement, perhaps. Tempting people into his club." I described the grand entrance hall and repeated to her what Conant had told me about the reading room and dining room. "Crockford employs a French chef called," I cleared my throat, "Eustache Ude – or something like that. Mr Conant knew the name – apparently he cooked for Louis XVI in France."

"Mr Conant cooked for a French king?" asked Martha with wide eyes. She laughed.

"You can laugh," I said with mock sternness, "but this cook is paid two thousand pounds a year."

Martha's mouth fell open. "Two thousand pounds?" she repeated. I nodded. "But Mr Conant's cook would be paid, what, thirty pounds a year?"

"At the most," I confirmed. "And that's part of Crockford's plan. With that Frenchman in the kitchen whipping up fancy dishes better than anything the members can get at home, is it any surprise that some gentlemen choose to dine at the club every night?" I leaned forward in my chair and pointed at the floor. "And underneath the club, stretching out under St James's Street, is the club's wine cellar – with three hundred thousand bottles in it." Martha shook her head in disbelief. I sat back again. "Once those members have dined and supped, well, of course their thoughts turn to the dice."

"And I daresay it gives the place an air of respectability," said Martha, biting off her thread and shaking out the mended pillowcase before folding it. "Fine dining, good wines, elegant surroundings – the sort of place where a mother might not mind her son spending his evenings."

CHAPTER EIGHT

Those unsettling eyes

FRIDAY 31ST JULY 1829

The black door of the house in Brook Street had a mourning wreath on it and the footman who opened it was wearing black gloves and a black ribbon around his sleeve. He inclined his head in recognition.

"I am here to see Mr Forster," I said.

"The master is out," he replied. This was no surprise to me; I had waited around the corner until I had seen Roger Forster climb into his carriage and head off towards Regent Street.

"Ah," I said. "In that case, I am afraid that I shall have to disturb Mrs Forster – it is a matter of some importance concerning her son."

The footman stood to one side, took my hat and showed me into the drawing room, closing the door silently as he left. The curtains were half-drawn and this, combined with the black crêpe draped across the pictures and mirror, made the room almost unbearably gloomy. I shuddered.

The door opened and in came a tall, dignified woman. She was dressed in full mourning but her outfit was still assembled with care. She wore a simple black dress with no embellishment, of course, but her mourning bonnet was made of fine stuff through which I could see her fair hair. And as she held out her arm to indicate that I should sit, I saw that she was wearing an elaborate bracelet, with a woven silver band and a large black lozenge.

"Constable Plank," she said in a clear, rather beautiful voice, "do sit."

I bowed and sat on the over-stuffed sofa behind me, while Mrs Forster sank gracefully into the high-backed chair that I remembered from my previous visit. She glanced at the footman who was hovering by the door.

"Tea, please, Robert," she said.

She turned once again to look at me and it struck me that she was one of those women who can make a man feel that he is the only person in the world. When Martha asked about Mrs Forster, as she surely would, I would concentrate on the dress and the bracelet and leave out any mention of those unsettling eyes. "I understand that you wish to speak to me about my boy," she said. On the last word she hesitated and swallowed delicately. "About Charles. How may I be of assistance?"

"Mrs Forster," I said, "I am not sure how much your husband has told you about the circumstances of your son's death." I paused but she said nothing. "It is of course possible," I continued, "for a young man to die of natural causes – a sudden illness, perhaps, or a seizure. Others are taken by accidents and misfortune."

"But not my son," she said in that clear voice.

I shook my head. "Not your son, no."

"You believe he was killed by someone," she said.

"We do, madam, yes," I said. "We did consider whether it was an attack that went too far, a robbery – sometimes when a young man is challenged, he will fight back and things can end badly."

Mrs Forster glanced down at her hands, clasped in her lap, and then back up at me. "But you do not think that this is what happened to Charles," she said.

I shook my head. "He had money in his pocket when he was found. Robbers would not have been so careless."

"Indeed," she agreed, looking steadily at me. "If it was not an illness or an accident or a robbery gone wrong, then you are telling me that my son was deliberately killed, constable. That he was murdered."

"That is what we believe, madam," I said.

"Then you must find whoever did it," she said.

"And that is one reason for my visit today," I said. Mrs Forster frowned but said nothing. "We have spoken to the men who found your son, and to people living and working near where he was found, and none of them saw or heard anything that might identify your son's attacker. It is possible that he was not killed where he was found – that his body was moved in order to hide it, or to protect the guilty. In cases like this, we have to start at the other end: not with the death, but with the life. In short, madam, the more we know about your son, the better will be our chances of finding who is responsible for his murder."

There was a light knock on the door and the footman entered with a tray. He placed it on a low table near Mrs Forster and asked her quietly whether she wished him to serve. She waved him away and he left us, closing the door silently behind him.

"Tea, constable?" she asked, indicating the pot.

"Yes, please," I replied and she poured me a cup. As she handed it to me, my eye was caught again by the mourning bracelet on her fine wrist.

"I bought that nearly ten years ago," she said conversationally, pouring her own cup of tea and holding it in one hand while extending the other arm to allow us both to inspect the bracelet. "My first husband fell from his horse – a great shock to the family. He survived the best efforts of Bonaparte to kill him at Waterloo, and then died on an early morning gallop in Hyde Park." She withdrew her arm to take a sip of tea. "Charles was twelve. A difficult age for a boy. Do you have children, constable?"

"I do not, no," I replied. "My wife and I were never blessed with them."

"They are a mixed blessing, you know," she said. "Charles and his father were very close – both headstrong, both impatient, both obsessed with horses. Perhaps it was the similarity between them..." She put down her cup and straightened her back, as people will do when gathering their strength. "When I was widowed, I was cast adrift. My own parents were dead, my brother was killed on the battlefield and my sister lives in Porto – her husband is a wine merchant. My husband's family had never approved our match. They had someone else in mind for him but he refused – headstrong, you see. And when he died they saw no reason to change their opinion of me, or of my son. Charles was like his father in character but in appearance he was almost entirely mine – and they found that hard." She smoothed down her skirt and took a breath. "So there we were, just the two of us – Charles and me. Well-meaning friends told him that he was the man of the house and his duty was to take care of me, and I encouraged him to believe it; I thought it would distract him from his grief and keep him from temptations, if he felt he had responsibilities. And, I will admit to my shame, I needed his company and his consolation."

"I see no shame…" I started, but Mrs Forster held up a hand and I fell silent.

"I put too much responsibility on young shoulders," she continued. "I let him believe that he was a man, and my equal. By the time he was sixteen, my authority was completely gone. I should have been stronger, constable – for his sake and my own." She shook her head. "And then there was the money."

"Would you mind if I made a note or two?" I asked, putting my cup onto a side table and reaching into my coat pocket. "I find in matters of money it is always best to keep careful notes."

"Very sensible," she said. "My first husband, William Madden, came from a well-to-do family – not landed, but very comfortable. Although his father threatened to cut him off when he married me, his grandfather thought differently – he was a sentimental old gentleman and said that I reminded him of his own first love. When the old man died, he left most of his fortune to William, which allowed us to set up in some style." She waved her hand to indicate our surroundings. "And when William died, I assumed that he would have left instructions but he died without a will – intestate, I am told it is called." She looked enquiringly at me and I nodded.

"He was a young man still," I said. "I daresay he thought he had plenty of time for making such arrangements."

"We always think we have time, constable," said Mrs Forster quietly. She sat for a moment, lost in her thoughts. "The lawyer explained that when a man dies intestate, there are standard rules that are applied: one third of his estate is passed to his widow, and the remaining two-thirds are divided equally between his children. Charles, being an only child, therefore inherited a sizeable fortune. And, being headstrong and rudderless, he set about spending it."

"He would not be the first young fellow to follow that path," I observed.

"I don't doubt it," she said, smiling sadly. "When I met Roger – Mr Forster – I hoped that an older man's influence would steady him again. But on the contrary, it seemed to make him angrier and more determined."

"How old was Charles when you married Mr Forster?" I asked.

"Nineteen," she said. "And before you say it, yes, I know that it can be difficult for a boy to see his father replaced in his mother's bed. Ha! Do not look shocked, constable – do you think women are not as aware as men of the central contract of marriage?"

"Not shocked, madam," I said, "but simply wondering why you are so certain that jealousy was the cause of your son's animosity towards Mr Forster."

"You think it was something else?" she asked, tilting her head in enquiry.

"I cannot know," I said, "as I have met your husband only briefly and your son not at all, but there could be other reasons for them to fall out. Different characters, perhaps, or money." I turned back in my notebook.

"When Constable Wilson and I spoke to Mr Forster on the day your son was found, he said that Charles was a regular visitor to the Horse Bazaar, and that he liked to gamble."

"Well, there, you see," said Mrs Forster. "Two things that they had in common. It was Roger who first took Charles to the horse sales here in London, and Roger who accompanied him to Crockford's. A young man must have his diversions, he said, and better he should indulge under careful supervision." She sighed. "And yet Charles disliked him."

"And did he dislike Charles?" I asked.

She shook her head. "Roger blamed me for giving way to Charles, for not disciplining him. He warned me that Charles had rogues as friends, that he was taking reckless chances. His only thought was to protect my son." She grasped the arms of her chair and leaned forward, fixing me with those unsettling eyes. "It is my fault, constable," she said fiercely, "and I will carry that guilt to my grave."

CHAPTER NINE

Calculating the odds

TUESDAY 4TH AUGUST 1829

I was just lifting the first forkful of pie to my mouth, the smell of rabbit tantalising me, when there was a smart knock at the back door. I rolled my eyes at Martha and she sighed as she stood to answer it. I looked over my shoulder when she opened the door and standing there was a young lad. I turned back to my meal.

"Message for Constable Plank, missus," he said.

"From Great Marlborough Street?" she asked.

"No, missus," he said. "From Mr Beech at Crockford's. He's paid a farthing, but it's a long way."

I wiped my mouth and stood, reaching into my coat pocket. "It is a fair step, lad," I agreed, passing him a coin, "but you're young and fit. And if you play your cards right, Mrs Plank might find you a piece of pie to keep you going."

Martha was already bending over the pie dish. She scooped out a decent wedge and wrapped it in a piece of cloth. "It's hot, mind," she said as she handed it over. "And if you rinse through the cloth afterwards, it will serve as a kerchief."

"Thanks, missus," said the lad, lifting the pie to his nose before scarpering off into the night.

"I'm not sure he appreciated your gambling pun," said Martha, sitting down again.

"Perhaps not," I said, "but you did."

"Well, it's part of a wife's job," she said. "Now, who's Mr Beech?"

♦

An hour later I was pushing open the door of the Cock and Harp on Jermyn Street. As requested by Beech in his note I was wearing plain clothes, and he was obviously looking out for me as he waved as soon as I entered and beckoned me over to the small table he was occupying in a dark corner of the room. Although the room was warm and I took off my coat, he kept his on.

"Thank you for coming, constable," he said. "Will you take a drink?"

"If the purpose of me wearing my own clothes and you hiding your uniform beneath your coat is to convince others that we are simply friends meeting in a tavern, then it would make sense," I said.

The croupier flushed and nodded. "We could have met somewhere else," he said as I caught the sleeve of a passing pot boy and asked for two tankards. "But I don't go into taverns as a rule, and at least I knew this one. The landlord's brother works in the kitchen at… where I work." He turned his hands nervously in his lap. The pot boy leaned past me and put two tankards on the table. I reached into my coat pocket but Beech was faster and put some coins into the boy's hand.

I raised my tankard. "Thank you," I said, and took a drink.

"Edie – my wife – said I should pay," said the croupier, drinking from his own tankard and wincing slightly.

"Was it her idea that we should meet?" I asked.

"Does that make me sound hen-pecked?" he asked in response.

I shrugged. "It probably comes down to whether you think she's right," I suggested.

The croupier put his tankard down and leaned towards me. "The truth is, I haven't been easy since you came to... since we last met. It shook me, seeing that body, and then to have the constables involved, talking about murder." He glanced over his shoulder and then leaned even closer. "I took this job because I'm good with numbers, and because the wage is steady. I've never been strong and working outside doesn't suit me. But I don't agree with gambling – or at least, not what it does to men when it has them in its grasp. The last place I worked, I saw someone lose everything he had and the next we heard he'd hanged himself – and he had a wife and six kiddies. I was going to leave after that, but then Mr... my employer said he was setting up a new place, going to do things differently."

"Differently?" I asked.

"More..." he waved a hand as he sought the word, "more openly. In other places, they give the gamblers the impression that they can win – that it's a fair competition. But then the house will load the dice and mark the cards and do everything they can to skin the players." He took another drink and shook his head – perhaps at the memory of the cheating, perhaps at the taste of the ale. "Mr... my employer, he's different. He knows that there's no need to cheat. He's a numbers man, like me." In an echo of Jem Sullivan's gesture, the croupier tapped the side of his head. "It's simply a matter of calculating the odds, constable. Hazard, for instance: using completely fair dice and following the rules of the game, over time the house will make a profit of one and a half per cent. We even tell the players if they ask, tell them that in the end the house always wins, but they always think they're different, that they've been blessed with good luck, or have some sort of control over the dice. They don't: it's all down to the numbers."

"And you approve of this approach?" I asked.

"I do, yes," said Beech. "A man can join our club for an annual subscription of twenty-five pounds. For this he can dine at reduced cost, or for free when he's playing, and come to the club as often as he likes. You've seen our dining room and the reading room – very elegant. If he chooses to gamble, he knows that he will play against the house – never against another member – and that the house will eventually take its profit. It's a charge for the entertainment. All clear and open. Honest. Or it was."

He paused. I waited, but it was as though he simply could not find the words.

"Are you being asked to load the dice and mark the cards?" I asked.

"No," he said quickly. "The house is still honest. But some of those who work there..." He closed his eyes to gather his strength. "I have heard rumours that some of the croupiers are taking winnings from players and exchanging them for counterfeit notes."

"How?" I asked.

"The caster is handed the dice and puts his stake on the table in full view of everyone. This stake is matched by the house. At the end of the game, the croupier rakes the stake towards him and then either pays out to the caster or puts the money in his pocket to deliver later to the supervisor. All of this the croupier calls out, so that the caster, the spectators and the supervisor know what is happening. But some croupiers have counterfeit notes in another pocket, and they are keeping the sound notes and paying the counterfeits to the supervisor."

"Surely the supervisor would spot the counterfeits," I said.

The croupier shook his head. "These are masterful forgeries, constable." He dropped his voice. "I have seen one myself, and you cannot tell."

"So when you say you have heard rumours, you are understating the matter," I observed.

"I am trapped, sir," said Beech. "I am an honest man, but I work with shavers. If I report them to Mr Guy they will make my life intolerable – and he is a man of quick temper and may well think that I am trying to save my own skin. If I leave, where else can I work? Not another gambling hell, and I need my wage. We have children, constable."

"And so you came to me," I said.

"It was Edie's idea," he admitted. "When I told her that you had been... that we had met, she said that you were obviously suspicious already and if I told you, you could say that you had uncovered it yourself during your..."

"During my enquiries," I suggested.

"Yes," said Beech. "Edie said I should speak to you before you found out who the murderer was, otherwise you would stop asking questions. And when I heard Mr Forster say earlier today that you had been to see his wife, I decided to ask you to meet me before it was too late."

"Where was Mr Forster when he said this?" I asked.

"At my table," said Beech, puzzled. "He visits the club most days." He looked over his shoulder at the clock on the wall. "And now I must go to work."

"Mr Guy values punctuality," I said and the croupier nodded. "But before you leave, Mr Beech, I need one more piece of information from you." He looked at me warily. "If I am to find a way to bring the matter of coun-terfeiting to Mr... to your employer's attention, I need to know who is involved. I need names, Mr Beech." I looked down at my notebook. "You said that 'some of the croupiers' are swapping genuine notes for counterfeits."

"Yes, that's right," he said.

"Now, Mr Beech," I continued. "We have two ways forward. Either I can go into your place of work and tell Mr Guy that I want to see each croupier in turn, to ask about rumours of counterfeit notes being circulated. He may well then start his own enquiries to find out the source of the rumours – and he will remember that you and I spent some time together not so long ago. And you can be sure that the guilty men will soon get wind of my interest and do everything they can to cover their tracks. Or," I leaned forward and looked Beech in the eye, "you can simply tell me the names of the men you know to be involved."

♦

As I walked along Great Marlborough Street I could see a light in the rooms above the police office. Martha would be asleep by now and my mind was busy with what I had learned, and so I knocked on the magistrate's door. Thin Billy answered, putting a hand to his mouth to cover a yawn.

"He's awake, then?" I asked, indicating upstairs with my head.

The footman nodded wearily. "Far be it from me to wave a voucher from Almack's under his nose," he said, "but I do sometimes wish he had a warm wife waiting for him, so that I could get to my own bed."

"You can turn in now, Billy," I said. "I'll keep him company."

"He shouldn't need anything more," said Billy, closing the door and yawning again. "I've left a pot of coffee and some cheese out for him – enough for you too, if you're minded."

I knocked quietly on the door of Conant's room and went in. The magistrate was sitting in his armchair, his back to me.

"No more coffee, thank you, Billy," he said.

"It's Sam, sir," I said. "I've sent Billy to bed – he looked done in."

The magistrate turned with a smile. "And what are you doing out at this time of night?" he asked. "Come: I need a distraction from these tedious papers." He indicated the pile on his lap.

I sat in the other armchair and told him about my meeting with Mr Beech, and what he had said about Roger Forster.

"And you're certain that Forster told you he was not a member of Crockford's?" asked Conant.

"It's here in my notebook," I replied, taking it out of my pocket and turning to the relevant page, which I had marked. "He called it 'that blasted place' and said that he did not know it personally – quite indignant at the suggestion, I recall."

"I can understand a man not wanting his wife to know that he spends his days – and his money – in a gambling hell," said the magistrate, "but Crockford's has an altogether different reputation."

I nodded. "Mrs Forster told me that she knew her husband took her son there – she did not seem upset about it."

"Indeed," agreed Conant. "Granted, the majority of Crockford's members are gamblers, but then there are some who do not indulge, such as the Prime Minister."

"He does not gamble?" I asked. "He cannot be a cautious man by nature."

"He was a gambler in his youth – the first time he proposed to his wife, her family chased him off because of it – but nowadays hard work and ambition give him all the excitement he needs," said Conant. "I imagine he seeks congenial company and good food at Crockford's."

"Surely most men would be proud to boast that they are a member of the same club as the Duke of Wellington," I said. "But Forster was quite clear that he wouldn't set foot in the place. And now we find that he is not merely a casual visitor, but a member. Why would he seek to conceal that from us?"

"Perhaps he realised how hypocritical it would sound, to lambast his stepson for gambling and then admit to being a member of a gambling club," suggested the magistrate. "Sadly for Mr Forster, it has served instead to make you mistrust everything he has said. You hold the rest of us to a very high standard, Sam."

"Someone has to," I replied, smiling. "As I explained to Mr Beech, he who lies down with dogs, rises with fleas."

CHAPTER TEN

The face of an angel

THURSDAY 6TH AUGUST 1829

Armed with Beech's description, Wilson and I waited in the alleyway alongside Crockford's, close to where I had met the dustmen when they found Charles Madden. Although it had been a pleasant summer's day the night was cool, and we both fidgeted as we tried to keep warm.

"You'll be doing more of this, in the new force," I commented. "Out at night."

"Aye," said Wilson. "There are to be two shifts: first night relief from six in the evening until midnight, and second night relief from midnight until six in the morning. Half of us will be out on the beat during the first shift, while the other half is back at the station to deal with the charges brought in."

"Does Alice understand that you will be from home six nights a week?" I asked.

Wilson gave a quick smile. "She says I snore like a warthog and she'll be glad of the quiet."

"All the same," I said, "it will be a change for you both."

"Are you sure you're not tempted to join the new police, sir?" asked Wilson. "With your experience, you'd not be a lowly constable like me."

I was grateful that he was distracted at this moment by the opening of the gate in the wall; my thoughts on the matter of the new police were still very much my own. As we'd previously agreed, Wilson walked away towards St James's Street while I waited by the gate as the croupiers whose shift had ended at two o'clock started to leave the club. They came out singly or in pairs, glancing at me as they walked past, but schooled well enough not to be too curious about anyone they might find loitering outside a gambling club. When ten minutes had passed and I had almost given up hope of spotting our man, the gate creaked open once more and there he was – unmistakably as Beech had described him. I had thought it an exaggeration when Beech said it, but the young fellow really did have the face of an angel. His face was round and open, his dark uniform showing his pale skin and blue eyes in sharp contrast, and light blonde hair curled around his head. I stepped in front of the young croupier.

"Thomas Sedley?" I asked.

He smiled innocently. "Yes," he said. "How can I help you?"

"My name is Constable Sam Plank of Great Marlborough Street..." I had no chance to say more because Sedley dodged past me and took to his heels. I watched him hare away up the alleyway and disappear into St James's Street. I walked after him and as I turned the corner I saw him being held in front of Wilson, his arm twisted up behind his back, and the innocent smile replaced with an angry snarl.

"Mr Sedley seems reluctant to talk to us out here, constable," I said to Wilson. "He may be more interested in answering our questions back at the police office. Handy for the magistrates in the morning, too."

♦

John Conant had sensibly chosen a room at the back of the building as his bedroom, knowing that when we constables bring someone in during the night we have to hammer on the door of the police office to wake the night keeper. Tom Neale ruled the roost during the day but – however reluctantly, given the chilly reception he knew he would receive from the fearsome Mrs Neale – he went home at night. And taking his place for the few hours he was away from his counter was Old Isaac.

Old Isaac had been in and around police offices most of his life – although of course he wasn't always known as Old Isaac. Decades as a rum diver saw him make close acquaintance with several of London's gaols; when age caught up with him and his fingers and legs were no longer nimble enough for that work, he took to the booze. Finally tiring of a husband who was either behind bars or under them, his wife threw him out. And soft-hearted Tom persuaded the magistrates that having someone sleeping on the premises was a good precaution. Old Isaac asked for little in return; I think he took wry amusement from the reversal in his fortunes.

As Wilson kept hold of Sedley – who had made several attempts to break free as we walked from St James's to the police office but had finally realised that his guile and wheedling were no match for Wilson's strength and determination – I banged on the door with my fist.

"Isaac!" I called. "Constable Plank here – we have a prisoner." I banged again.

After a minute, I heard the bolt being dragged back and the door was hauled open. Old Isaac peered out, pulling a shawl around his shoulders as he looked first at me and then at Wilson.

"Just the one scoundrel is it, constables?" he asked, standing to one side so that we could squeeze past him into the front office. He pushed the door closed again, secured the bolt and then reached across the counter for the ledger. "You'll be wanting this." Old Isaac had never seen the use of reading or writing; the only time he'd ever had to deal with paper was when he was released from gaol, and then a simple mark was all he needed to make. I wrote Sedley's name and time of arrival, and in the neatly drawn column for "offence", I wrote "uttering counterfeit banknotes".

"Do you want me to add assault, Constable Wilson?" I asked. "For the kick in the shins and the attempt to bite you?"

Wilson shook his head. "I've had worse from George," he said, "and he's not even a year old yet."

"There's no hot water, sir," said Old Isaac. "I could get the fire going if you like."

"There's no need, Isaac," I said. "We're just going to take Mr Sedley down to the cells and tuck him up in there while Constable Wilson and I go home for some kip."

"You can't do that," protested Sedley. "You can't leave me here – I'm expected at home."

"Now you see, Mr Sedley," said Wilson, "if you'd stopped and talked nicely to Constable Plank instead of hiking off like you did, you wouldn't be here at all. But you didn't and you are, so there's an end to it."

CHAPTER ELEVEN

Queer screens

FRIDAY 7TH AUGUST 1829

Six hours later Wilson and I were back at Great Marlborough Street. Tom Neale had collected Sedley from the cells for us and stowed him in the back office. The croupier looked considerably less angelic this morning, with his uniform crumpled and his eyes shadowed with fatigue. However, his night in the cell had obviously given him time to plan his strategy and he was politeness itself as we walked in.

"Good morning, constables," he said, rising to his feet.

We hung our coats next to his on the pegs and sat down. Sedley remained standing until I indicated his chair; I caught Wilson rolling his eyes at this exaggerated but mock show of respect. Wilson reached for the pot of tea that Tom had left on the table and poured three cups, pushing one towards Sedley. The croupier took it gratefully.

I took out my notebook and laid it on the table. "Now, Mr Sedley," I said. "I understand that you are a croupier at Mr Crockford's establishment. Have you been with him since the club opened?"

Sedley put down his cup of tea. "Not since the very start, no, but I joined soon after that."

"And how did you get the job?" I asked.

Sedley narrowed his eyes momentarily – the question was unexpected. "I know someone who worked there and he recommended me," he said.

"And his name?" I asked, pencil poised above my notebook.

"He's no longer working there," said the croupier.

"I see," I said, "but wherever he is now, I assume he still has a name."

"Chambers," said Sedley. "John Chambers."

"And why did Mr Chambers recommend you?" I asked. "Did he know you for a skilled croupier?"

Sedley shook his head. "This is my first job as a croupier. John – Mr Chambers – and I were friends. Childhood friends."

"And where was that childhood?" I asked.

Sedley looked at Wilson and then back at me. "Constable Plank, I am not quite sure..."

"Mr Sedley, your understanding of my reasons for asking these things is of no concern to me at all," I said firmly. I waited.

"Whitechapel," he said eventually. "I grew up in Whitechapel."

"You're a long way west, Mr Sedley," I commented. "What has brought you all the way to St James's?"

"I told you," said Sedley. "I was recommended and I took the job. For the money."

Wilson reached forward and the croupier flinched. Wilson smiled and picked up the teapot, refilling my cup and his but ignoring Sedley's.

"Ah yes, Mr Sedley," I said, as though the thought had only just occurred to me. "The money. Now, as you've shared some information with us, let me share some with you. We know that when you're working at a table and you rake in the stakes at the end of game, you put genuine banknotes in one pocket. We know that when you report to the supervisor to hand over the winnings from your table, you give him counterfeit banknotes from your other pocket. We know that you then steal the genuine banknotes. And," I held up a finger as Sedley was about to protest, "we know that the penalty for forgery is death."

Sedley's eyes widened.

"Aye," I continued. "Did no-one mention that to you? Not pretty, is it, Constable Wilson – death by hanging?"

Wilson shook his head. "Well, it can be quick, if the hangman knows what he's about, but if he calculates the wrong length for the rope, it takes an age to finish you. Or it tears your head clean off. Either way, it's a nasty way to go."

Sedley shifted in his seat. "But I'm no forger, sir," he said. "Those notes – they're given to me by someone else." His eyes followed my hand as I wrote in my notebook. He looked up at me and a cunning look flashed across his face. "I had no idea they were queer screens."

"Now Constable Wilson," I said conversationally, continuing to write in my notebook, "if you were to go home this evening to your good lady wife and tell her that you had a queer screen in your pocket, would she have any idea what you were talking about?"

"I doubt it, sir," replied Wilson.

"Nor mine," I said, "and she's been a constable's wife for nearly three decades now. And yet Mr Sedley here, who claims to be entirely innocent of anything to do with forgery, knows exactly what a queer screen is."

The croupier leaned forward on his elbows and spoke urgently. "Listen," he said. "I'm a croupier in a gambling hell. I spend my life surrounded by banknotes. We're used to taking and collecting and counting them, and we're warned to look out for queer screens, so, yes, I know what it means."

"But you deny switching real banknotes for counterfeit ones between the table and the supervisor?" I asked.

"I do," said Sedley, sitting back and folding his arms, as though that were the end of the matter.

I closed my notebook. "Well, I think that's all we need for now, Mr Sedley," I said. "Constable Wilson, could you pass Mr Sedley his coat?" As Wilson stood and took hold of the coat, I held up a hand. "Mr Sedley, are you saying that if Constable Wilson were to go through your pockets now, he would find nothing out of the ordinary – no stashes of banknotes?"

Sedley's face fell. I nodded at Wilson and he put the croupier's coat on the table so that we could all see what he was doing. He emptied each pocket in turn, and at the end of it there were four one-pound banknotes, three two-pound notes and four five-pound notes on the table.

"If that's your pay for working at Crockford's, I'm in the wrong job," I observed. "It takes me about six months to earn that much, Mr Sedley." He said nothing. "As I see it," I continued, "there are two possible explanations: you have stolen the money for yourself, or it is money you have switched for counterfeit notes, and you now have to pass it on to whoever supplied those." Still he said nothing. "Both could lead to the scaffold, Mr Sedley, so I advise you to do what you can to avoid it."

"But that's not right, constable, surely," said the croupier, a wheedling tone in his voice. "If I didn't make the counterfeit notes, I cannot be charged with forgery."

"So you are admitting that there are counterfeit notes?" I asked, opening my notebook again.

Sedley looked from me to Wilson and back again, and his shoulders slumped. "It's just as you said," he replied. "All I did was swap the good notes for bad ones."

"And when you passed the bad ones to the supervisor, did you know that he would assume that they were good notes?" I asked. I turned back a page in my notebook. "Because – as you said – you are used to taking and collecting and counting banknotes and you're warned to look out for queer screens. So your supervisor would expect you to know the difference."

Sedley shrugged.

"Mr Sedley," I asked, "did you tell the supervisor that the bad notes you knew you were handing to him were counterfeit?"

"No," he replied.

"Then that, I am sorry to tell you," I said, "is a plain example of the offence of uttering – of presenting a counterfeit in order to deceive. And uttering is as serious an offence as the forgery itself, Mr Sedley. We're back to the hangman's noose, I'm afraid."

Sedley put his head into his hands, then leaned back in his chair and took a deep breath.

"What do you need to know, constables?" he asked.

"That's more like it, Mr Sedley," I said. "We have a few more questions for you, and then I'll need you to bring me one of those counterfeit banknotes."

CHAPTER TWELVE

The other judges

SATURDAY 8TH AUGUST 1829

No matter the weather, Newgate presented a forbidding face to the world. I had enjoyed my walk after breakfast, turning my face to the warm sun and watching the gentle procession of wispy clouds across a sky as blue as any I had seen. But I swear that as I walked along Skinner Street towards the prison I felt a bite in the air and when I stood in front of the gate, waiting for the turnkey to answer my knock, I shivered.

"Constable Plank," said the young turnkey as he peered around the door. "Good morning to you."

"And good morning to you, Mr Grant," I said. "I would like a word with Mr Wontner, if you please. I am afraid I have no warrant."

The young man smiled as he hauled the door open. "As it's you, sir," he said, and he made an extravagant bow.

♦

John Wontner, keeper of Newgate, was sitting at his desk. He had removed his coat and rolled up the sleeves of his shirt, and indeed the room was stuffy and airless. With only one small window high in the wall, there was little chance for a cooling breeze to make its way in.

"Thank you, Grant," he said to the turnkey, who nodded and left us.

I took off my own coat and draped it over the visitor's chair, removing the inevitable pile of papers from its seat before sitting down. "It's our compromise," I said, "Mr Grant and me. He lets me in without a warrant, and I let him escort me to your door in case I lose my senses and indulge in mischief along the way."

"He's a good lad," said Wontner. "He's been here for six months now, and the other turnkeys are gradually knocking the edges off him. And he's been a good influence on them too. Rather like you and Constable Wilson in the early days." He smiled and reached for the jug of barley water that he kept on the shelf behind him, pouring a tumbler before topping up his own. We raised them to each other and I took a drink.

"Goodness," I said, as I tasted the barley water and a sharp tang hit my throat. "That's different."

"Grace has been experimenting again," he said, raising an eyebrow. "This batch has ginger in it, I'm told."

"Mrs Plank is the same," I said. "As soon as I grow fond of something, she decides to change it. What's the use of living in the trading capital of the world, she says, if we don't take advantage of it." I took another drink. "But I think this might be a success, this ginger. Certainly a great improvement on the lavender."

The keeper leaned back in his chair. "I shall be sure to tell her," he said. "Now, Sam, I doubt you're here simply to sample my wife's latest experiment with barley water. I have had a trying morning and could do with a good story – I'm relying on you."

"I'll do my best," I said. "Are you familiar with Crockford's?"

"Well, I'm familiar with its line of business," replied Wontner, "and I have heard and read plenty of stories about Mr Crockford – some admiring, and some more critical. But I am not a member, unsurprising as that may be." He smiled at the idea and then turned more serious. "We've both seen what gambling can do to a fellow, Sam."

"Aye," I said, "but my concern today is not with the gambling at Crockford's. Some weeks ago we found a young man dead in the dust-pit behind the place, and I am beginning to think that it's all tied up with counterfeiting."

One of the joys of a long friendship is the assumptions it makes. Wontner did not expect or need me to explain my reasons, but said simply, "Ah, now – counterfeiting."

"I have spoken to a croupier from Crockford's and he admitted that he takes banknotes from the players and then pays in counterfeit notes instead, pocketing the good notes," I continued. "And once I had explained about uttering and where it can lead, he was most helpful."

Wontner nodded. "A sniff of the scaffold can have that effect," he said drily. "But here's a riddle for you." He smiled like a schoolboy. "Why is a forged banknote like a whisper?" I shook my head. "Because it is uttered but not aloud."

"Very good," I said, laughing. "I shall try to remember that for Martha." I took another sip of the fiery barley water. "And talking of whispers, I'm hoping that you'll be able to help me find out who is creating the counterfeits, and at whose command. From what I understand about the business of forgery, they are rarely the same person. The first is the artist, and the second the merchant." Wontner nodded. "Sedley – the croupier – told us that the banknotes are delivered to him by a young lad. He doesn't know his name, but he says it's the same boy every time. Aged about eight, he thought."

"Anything else? Any more description?" asked the keeper.

I opened my notebook and checked what I had written during my discussion with Sedley. "Dark hair," I said, "polite, clean, wearing boots and in winter a felt hat."

Wontner frowned slightly. "A well-cared for boy," he said. "Not a street child or a beggar. And it's unlikely that Sedley is his only customer: he may well be making deliveries to other croupiers, maybe at other gambling clubs. This could be a grand scheme."

"That was my very thought, John," I said. "I haven't seen any of the counterfeit notes myself yet; Sedley had only the genuine ones with him, ready to hand back to his master, but they must be quality items. Crockford is no fool, and his supervisor is a canny fellow – they would spot second-rate forgeries in a wink. If the notes are good enough to pass muster with them, they have been made by an expert."

"And then there is Crockford's banker," pointed out Wontner. "Crockford will be paying his takings into his bank, and they do their own checking."

"An excellent thought, John," I said, making a note in my book. "I shall visit Freame and ask him what checks the banks are doing."

"And how is our Quaker friend?" asked the keeper.

"I hear news of him mainly through Martha," I said. "He calls in at her school once a month so that he can report back to his charity. A touch of gout, apparently, but otherwise in good form."

"I am pleased to hear it – he is a good man," said Wontner. "So – did your croupier tell you the name of the counterfeiter?"

"Not exactly," I said. "He said he knows him only as 'the German' – and I believe him. There's no reason he would be taken into anyone's confidence. But he told me enough. He said that the man is German, an artist, and that he was a gaolbird."

"But no longer?" asked the keeper.

I shook my head. "Sedley was quite animated on that point. He said that the fellow had been sent to trial and found guilty – but something was wrong with the process and the 'other judges' set him free."

"The 'other judges'?" said Wontner. He frowned and then his face cleared. "Did he mean the Twelve Judges?"

"That was my thought," I agreed. "Chances are the fellow would have been one of yours – can you remember anything? Or find anything in those folders of yours?" I jerked my head at the over-stuffed shelves behind the keeper.

Wontner was silent for a moment and then smiled. "Of course," he said, standing up and turning to his shelves. He sifted through a couple of piles, pulling out a few files and stuffing them back in before turning back to me, a folder held aloft with triumph. "Mr Ernst Kaufmann," he said. "But he was Austrian, not German, I think." He opened the file and nodded as he read from it. "Yes, here it is – born in Vienna. Convicted of forgery in July 1828, released in November of that year. Saved by an administrative oversight: the forged instruments were produced at the trial in German only, not in English translation. Ten judges heard it and eight of them decided that the judgement should be arrested." He looked up at me. "I remember him now: a quiet fellow, scared of his own shadow." He closed the folder and handed it to me. "If you'd asked me at the time, I'd have said that one narrow – and extremely lucky – escape from the law would have taught him his lesson."

"Unless there is something that frightens him more than the law," I said, shrugging on my coat.

CHAPTER THIRTEEN

Mr Nutt's spiced biscuits

MONDAY 10TH AUGUST 1829

Just as the stark face of Newgate had chilled me, the pale walls of the banking house of Freame and Company lifted my spirits. Here I would find order and welcome and generosity of spirit. Over the past few years elegant merchants had taken over the surrounding buildings and now the slim banking house near the corner of Cheapside and Milk Street found itself at the heart of a bustling and fashionable district.

Not that Edward Freame cared about that; a Quaker by birth and by nature, he sought only to provide a reliable service to his customers and to make a modest profit that would be entirely given over to charitable works. But he was no pigeon: he had a sharp commercial brain and a full understanding of how harsh the world could be. Martha helped at a school funded by Freame and his Quaker friends, for young girls who would otherwise fall into bad ways, and she told me that she had never seen him shocked by any story he heard of their maltreatment or misbehaviour – saddened, yes, but never shocked. I had a great deal of time for Edward Freame, and I am proud to say that he felt the same about me.

I stood aside to allow a smartly dressed gentleman to leave the bank, tipping his hat to me as he did so, and then walked into the banking hall. As always, the senior clerk Mr Harris was sitting on the stool nearest the door that led through to the parlour and other back rooms. He had been at least sixty when I first met him, more than five years earlier, but he showed no signs of leaving the bank. He glanced up and smiled when he saw me, then slid off his seat and disappeared through the door before returning a moment later and beckoning to me.

"Mr Freame is in the parlour," he said. "He said to ask whether you would like some refreshment."

"From the question, Mr Harris," I said, "can we assume that Mr Freame is a little peckish himself?"

The clerk inclined his head with a smile. "His wife made some biscuits at the weekend," he confided, "and allowed him to bring some into the bank on the proviso that he eats them only with visitors. And no-one has yet called on him. I shall send in Stevenson with some tea."

I knocked on the door of the parlour and Edward Freame opened it, a wide smile on his face.

"Samuel," he said warmly. "What a pleasure to see you. Please, do take a seat." And he stood aside, waving me towards one of the armchairs. "Harris is arranging tea. Why, whatever are you doing?"

I ignored him and continued my search, lifting the cushions of both chairs, and even dropping to my knees to look under them. Finally I took my seat. "I give up," I said. "The *Morning Chronicle* ran a little piece about the delivery of a new batch of Mrs Freame's incomparable biscuits and I raced over immediately, but sadly they are nowhere to be seen."

"Hah!" said the banker, clapping his hands. He was as far from the dour Quaker of lore as can be imagined and retained a childlike pleasure at silliness which endeared him to everyone, but particularly to the young girls at his school who delighted to find an adult laughing along with them. "I see that Harris has let slip my little secret. Did he also tell you that I am not permitted to be alone with the tin?" I nodded. "And that I am so untrustworthy that the tin is kept under Mr Harris's bench?"

"That I did not know," I said.

Freame shook his head sadly, then looked at me with an impish grin. "I am ashamed of myself, Sam – but you will forgive me the instant you taste these biscuits."

There was a knock on the door and in came Stevenson. He was finally growing into his limbs and had carefully cultivated a seriousness that he thought suited his role as junior clerk in the banking house of Freame and Company – a role of which he was enormously and justifiably proud. He was one of Edward's great successes, and repaid the faith shown in him with absolute loyalty and touching affection.

"Constable Plank, Mr Freame," he said solemnly, nodding at us in turn. He put his tray onto the table and carefully poured us each a cup of tea. With a flourish, he removed the napkin that was covering the plate of biscuits. Then he bowed and left, shutting the door silently behind him.

"Young men have such dignity," said Freame. "They take themselves enormously seriously in the hope that everyone else will."

"Whereas we square toes have long since given up the fight," I said. "Now, tell me about these biscuits."

Taking the hint, Freame held out the plate for me to take one. The pale brown biscuits were lozenge-shaped, very thin, and studded with slices of almond. I took a sniff.

"Spiced biscuits," said Freame, "from a recipe by Mr Nutt. My wife is working her way through his book, and I am enjoying her endeavours enormously." He patted his stomach. "Now, these are meant for dipping – into sweet wine if you're a young man of fashion, or into tea if you are a more mature banker or constable." He demonstrated, taking a large bite from his own biscuit and rolling his eyes with pleasure. I copied him – both the dipping and the rolling. "And so, Sam, you can see why I am not to be trusted with them."

"They are delicious," I said, reaching for another. "Could Mrs Freame be persuaded to write out the recipe for Martha, do you think?"

"She will be relieved to have proof that I didn't eat them all myself," said the banker. "It is one of the – many – great mysteries of women, that they cook us such delights and then tut when we grow rounder." I laughed. "And now, Sam, we should turn our minds to business. As we have not reported a crime today, I assume that you have need of me and not the other way round."

"I do, Edward, yes," I said, brushing crumbs from my lips and then reaching into my coat pocket for my notebook. "I wanted to ask you about counterfeit banknotes."

"Ah," said Freame, shaking his head sadly. "The bane of the banker's life."

"You see them often?" I asked.

"Often enough," he replied grimly. "Thankfully we have the inestimable Mr Harris – his sharp eye has saved this bank hundreds of pounds. But of course the real concern is not with the banks."

"No?" I asked, looking up from my notebook.

Freame shook his head again. "Harris is exceptional, yes: he is experienced and loyal and sees it as matter of personal and professional pride to protect our house from being cheated. And all banks are aware of the dangers and will instruct their clerks to be alert and to check the notes carefully when they are presented. But banknotes in circulation, well, therein lies the problem. A bank clerk knows what to look for, but what about a jeweller, or an innkeeper, or a baker? Crooks will present counterfeit notes to pay for items, or will ask the local grocer or publican to break a note for them." He put his head on one side and smiled at me. "But I am not telling you anything new, Sam – your pencil is still."

"It is always good to be reminded of what I once knew," I said. "But you're right, Edward. What I hoped you could tell me is something about their technique – how counterfeiters work nowadays. Clippers and coiners I know about, but counterfeiters of banknotes, well, that's specialist work."

"Artists is what they are, Sam," said Freame.

"It's funny you should say that," I said. "Do you know the name Kaufmann?"

"Ernst Kaufmann?" said Freame. "Of course." His face became serious. "But I thought he had gone home to Germany. Do you mean he is still here in London – still working as a counterfeiter?"

"It's possible," I admitted. "And it was Austria – he is Viennese. I have spoken to John Wontner at Newgate about him, and I know that he was found guilty and then freed by the Twelve Judges." I turned to the right page in my notebook. "Here it is, copied from Wontner's file: found guilty, but judgement respited and reserved to the Twelve Judges. Forged instruments produced to court in German only, not in English translation. Ten judges heard the appeal – eight decided judgement should be arrested on this point." I looked up at the banker. "There were four months between the trial and the appeal – during which time Kaufmann sat in Newgate. His case was reported widely in the papers. Anyone who wanted a talented counterfeiter would know where to find him."

Freame shook his head. "If it is Kaufmann's work," he said, "it will be the best quality. The instruments he produced before weren't banknotes, were they?"

I checked my notebook again. "No: they were promissory notes from the Prussian treasury. Never intended for use in London – he made them here, engraving the plates in his workshop in Shadwell, but they were to be sent back to Berlin. He told the printer that they were admission tickets and asked him to print ten thousand copies. The printer knew no better – everything was written in German – but Kaufmann was so impatient and so demanding that the printer became uneasy and mentioned it to a friend who happened to work at a bank. He showed the friend one of the tickets."

Freame nodded vigorously. "I remember that: the clerk recognised the German word for treasury note. The clerk showed the note to his senior clerk, who reported it to Mr Christmas at the Bank of England, and Mr Christmas reported it to someone at the Prussian treasury, who gave evidence at the trial."

"Mr Christmas?" I asked.

"Mr Charles Christmas," confirmed the banker. "He is an investigator of banknotes at the Bank. Very able." He held out the plate once more and after a polite pretence at reluctance I took a final biscuit. "In fact, he is exactly who you need to speak to."

CHAPTER FOURTEEN

Whitehall Place

TUESDAY 11TH AUGUST 1829

I made sure to be early, already sitting at a table in the George and Dragon with two tankards in front of me by the time Wilson arrived at our agreed time. A young father setting up home, with another little one on the way, has no money to spare for ale. He hailed me from across the room, pointing to the back yard to indicate that he needed to relieve himself first, and a few minutes later joined me at the table.

"That's a welcome sight," he said, nodding at his tankard. "Thank you."

I lifted mine and we drank in unison.

"It's a thirsty step from Whitehall Place in this warm weather," observed Wilson.

"Whitehall Place?" I echoed. "So they held the examinations there?"

Wilson nodded. "Number four: the offices are on the first two floors, with an entrance at the rear of the building, and Commissioner Rowan is living in an apartment upstairs."

"Smart fellow," I said. "Keeping an eye on things. I believe he's a bachelor, so no wife to object. Mr Conant has always believed in living above the shop when he can." I caught the eye of the pot boy and pointed to our tankards. "Did you meet Commissioner Rowan?"

Wilson nodded. "He's examining each applicant himself, if you can believe that. Nearly nine hundred of us, I hear."

"And how did you find him?" I asked.

"Upright, sober dress, about your age," replied Wilson. "I asked Mr Conant about him before my examination." He looked a little embarrassed to admit this.

"Now that's clever thinking," I said, draining my tankard. "Know your enemy. He served with distinction, I understand."

Wilson was distracted by the arrival of our drinks; he took another deep draught before replying. "Waterloo," he said, wiping his mouth. "And his were field promotions, not purchases."

"Do you think he will adapt to life out of uniform?" I asked. "No-one wants an army on the streets of London."

"He spoke about that when he addressed us," said Wilson. "There were twenty of us there, and he spoke to us as a group before we went into a side office and met him one by one for a few minutes. He said that after selling his commission he served as a magistrate in Ireland, so he knows about civilian courts as well as courts martial. And then he said that Sir Robert Peel has declared that senior uniformed ranks would be filled from below – not brought in from above."

"Good prospects, then," I observed.

"And I took your advice," said Wilson, leaning forward. "When I was alone with him, he asked about my situation – what work I had been doing, whether I was married. And then he asked about my plans for the future, and I did as you said: I told him that I want to make my life with the new police, to start as a constable and learn my trade, and then move up the ranks. And I told him that as I had been a constable at Great Marlborough Street for years and had served under Mr Conant, I expected to move up quite quickly." He sat back again.

"Well, you certainly set out your stall," I said with a smile. "How did he react?"

"He noted it on the piece of paper that I had filled in earlier, shook my hand and said that I would be an asset to the Metropolitan Police," said Wilson, smiling broadly.

"Well done, lad," I said, lifting my tankard to salute him. "Mrs Plank will be delighted – she said she never had any doubt. Commissioner Rowan would be a fool not to take you, was how she put it, and that man is far from a fool."

CHAPTER FIFTEEN

Tiny imperfections

THURSDAY 13TH AUGUST 1829

The Bank of England always stirs a conflict in me. When I see its pale columns, elegant pediment and imposing green door at Tivoli Corner, I am filled with pride. The money flowing from this very building has financed our national interests, conquered territories around the world and even beaten Napoleon. But then I reflect on the misery that has come from all those endeavours – and I recall that I have not once met an employee of the Bank of England who was anything but self-satisfied and rude. And despite Edward Freame's recommendation, I held out little hope for Charles Christmas being any different.

The doorman at the entrance to the bank in St Bartholomew Lane had obviously been selected for his size rather than his manners. He stared at me blankly as I explained my business, and reluctantly told me where to find Mr Christmas, adding sullenly that the investigator would almost certainly be too busy to see me without an appointment.

I walked through the vestibule into the transfer office, where sunlight streamed down onto us from the wonderful dome above, which was circled by windows and elegant statues. John Conant had once told me that it reminded him of the basilicas he had seen in Rome, and certainly the golden light brought an almost religious quality to the mundane business taking place in the office below. I passed through the golden space into another vestibule and repeated my business to another guard. Like his fellow, he looked at me with undisguised dislike, but indicated with his arm where I should go. I could feel him watching me as I walked along a corridor and then passed through a doorway into the less exalted, more ordinary area of the bank. A secretary sitting at a grand desk outside the Directors' offices rose to his feet as I approached, but he at least seemed to respect my uniform and refrained from sneering as he summoned a junior clerk to accompany me on the final part of my journey, through the accountants' office and to a door in the corner. On it was a plaque: "Investigators' Office". The clerk knocked quietly, and then a little more loudly.

"Enter!" said a voice, and the clerk opened the door gingerly and put his head around it.

"I have a Constable Plank here," he said softly, "to see Mr Christmas." He stepped back from the door and nodded at me. "Mr Christmas will see you," he said, and then scurried off in the direction we had come. I pushed open the door and went in.

The Investigators' Office was, to be frank, a mess. A large square desk took up much of the centre of the room, and the shelves and boxes that climbed up two of the walls were filled to overflowing with papers. On the far side of the desk stood a rotund fellow with a shock of red hair; behind a pair of thick spectacles, his eyes looked enormous. He held out his hand and I picked my way around the desk to shake it. More boxes of paperwork were on the floor, pushed under the desk and stacked against the walls. It was a very light room: one wall had three tall windows looking to the outside – although I knew from experience that the outside would be an internal courtyard, as the Bank of England had been designed to look inwards only and to turn a blank face to the world – and the wall opposite had a matching trio of tall windows, this time looking into the printing room.

"Charles Christmas," said the man with a shy smile. "Blank, did he say your name was?"

"Plank," I replied, "like the wood."

"And I'm Christmas, like the celebration," he said. "Come, sit – yes, just put those on the floor," he added as I looked behind me for a chair and found one piled with yet more papers. "Have no fear: there is a system and nothing will be lost. My wife despairs of me at home but here, I am the ruler of my own kingdom and will keep it in the manner that suits me. At least when Mr Foy is not here." He smiled that shy smile again.

"Mr Foy?" I asked, taking my seat.

"My esteemed colleague," he explained. "But he is away from London today – his mother is taken ill on the south coast. But you are not here to discuss the health of the elderly Mrs Foy." He put his head on one side, like an inquisitive bird – a robin, perhaps.

"I am not, no," I agreed. I reached into my coat pocket and took out the counterfeit two-pound bank-note that the croupier Thomas Sedley had reluctantly delivered to me at Great Marlborough Street. I smoothed it out on the desk and pushed it across to

Christmas. He peered at it where it was for a long minute, leaning so low over it that his nose all but touched
the paper. He then picked it up and turned to hold it to
the light and spent another minute examining every inch
of the banknote. Finally he put the banknote back on the
desk in front of him. He looked at me.

"Where did you find this, constable?" he asked.

I explained a little about the croupier and Crockford's, but mentioned nothing of Charles Madden or his
fate. "It is definitely a forgery, then?" I asked.

"Oh yes," said Christmas.

"And this one?" I asked, this time handing him one of
the one-pound notes I had been given by the clerk at the
Horse Bazaar.

The investigator went through the same movements
with this note – the peering, the holding up to the light,
the close examination.

He nodded. "Another forgery," he confirmed. "Both
excellent examples. In that I mean they would deceive
most people."

"And are they by the same hand?" I asked.

Christmas smoothed both notes again and placed
them side by side in front of him. Then he opened a
drawer in the desk and took out a large magnifying glass
with a worn wooden handle. He leaned close over the

notes, this time peering through the glass at them. "Ah yes, it's unmistakable. Still going strong, then." He looked up at me, blinking, and passed one of the notes and the magnifying glass to me. "Some of the note is printed by the gentlemen labouring next door – the name of the Bank, the promise to pay and so forth." He pointed to the windows overlooking the printing room. "These elements of the note are simple to copy – anyone with a printing press and the same plate can do it."

"The same plate?" I asked, surprised. "But surely you cannot just buy these plates?"

"Not openly, no, constable," said Christmas, "but if someone were to borrow a plate from the printing room and take it to a printer to have it copied, well... We do our best to make sure that only honest men are employed here, and they are searched whenever they leave the bank, and we have the Picquet, but we cannot be entirely certain that no plate is ever removed and then returned before it is needed again in the printing room."

"The Picquet?" I asked.

"The nightly guard," explained Christmas. "You will have seen them, I am sure, in their dashing red coats, marching from their barracks to the bank. Very reassuring for our depositors."

"I have seen them, yes," I replied, "but had no idea of their name."

"A military term, I believe," said the investigator. "French, I suppose – ironically." He smiled his quick, shy smile again. "As I was saying, there are elements of the note that could be forged by anyone with the right plate. The handwritten parts – the date, the payee, and the signature of the clerk – might seem easier to forge, but for we investigators, they are the key. And both these notes, they have something I have seen before. Take the glass, constable, and look at the clerk's signature."

I did as instructed. "G Munro," I read aloud. I looked up at the investigator, who had risen from his seat to retrieve a leather-covered folder from one of the overstuffed shelves. "Is Mr Munro one of your clerks?"

"He is indeed – George Munro," said Christmas, extracting a sheet of paper from the folder and handing it to me. "And this is his signature, as agreed on his appointment. Compare the two. Use the glass."

Again, I did as instructed. I looked between the banknote and the specimen signature, back and forth, peering closer each time. Eventually, I looked up at the investigator and shook my head. "I cannot see it," I said. "They look identical."

"It's an excellent example, constable – and a disturbing one," said the investigator. "Look again, and this time look at the u in Munro. What can you see on the banknote?"

I bent to my task, and there it was. I looked up at the investigator and smiled. "There's a little dash above the u," I said. "I thought it was an imperfection in the paper, but it's definitely ink."

Charles Christmas clapped his hands and smiled widely, like a child being handed a cake. "Bravo, constable," he said. "Now look at the other note." He pushed it over to me and I did so. There it was again – the dash above the u.

"So we are certain that they are forgeries, and by the same hand," I said. "And you said, 'still going strong'. What did you mean by that?"

The investigator sat back and again tilted his head like an inquisitive bird. "It is just that the man who made them, I thought he had gone," he said. "Or rather, I wished him gone – for our sake, and for his too."

"You know who made these notes?" I asked.

"Of course," said Christmas. "Clumsy forgers, the amateurs, their work is easy to spot – there are so many errors and inaccuracies. The paper is too thick or too thin, the ink too dark or too light, and the lettering rough and inelegant. But the professional ones – the artists, we might almost say – well, you have seen for yourself the quality of their work. But even they, constable, even they are not perfect, and if you can learn the specific tiny imperfections of a forger," he leaned forward, pinching together his thumb and forefinger to suggest precision, "well then, you can identify his work wherever you see it."

"And this dash above the u is one such imperfection?" I asked.

"Have you heard of Kurrent script, constable?" asked Christmas in return. I shook my head. "It is the script taught to children in school in Germanic countries. Their alphabet is very similar to ours, but they use accents as well – you may have seen the dots above some letters in their writing." This time I nodded. "One other difference is that the minuscule n and the minuscule u are identical to each other, except that the latter is distinguished by having a small dash above it – as in our Munro." He pointed at the banknote.

"And this tells you that the forger was taught Kurrent script?" I asked.

"The way we are taught to write as children stays with us, constable," said Christmas. "It becomes tidier, perhaps, but the urge to add a dash to a minuscule u would be almost irresistible for someone taught to add it as a child."

"Which means that the forger of these notes is of Germanic origin," I continued.

"Indeed he is," said the investigator. "Mr Kaufmann is from Vienna."

"You are saying, Mr Christmas, that the man who created these banknotes is the forger Ernst Kaufmann?" I asked.

"Of course," said Christmas, as though it were obvious. "I am sorry to hear that the poor fellow is still in London – or at least, still working in the London market. The notes might have been made in Vienna and sent over here. I hope for his sake that this is the case. I met him, you know – Kaufmann. A quiet fellow – a true artist, who in kinder times might have made a living that way." He shook his head sadly. "I thought his spell in Newgate would have taught him a lesson – he certainly told me that he wanted to return to Vienna and live an honest life. But I suppose every criminal tells you that, constable."

"We do hear it quite often, yes," I agreed. "A criminal pleading for his life will promise the moon and the stars. But the keeper of Newgate said the same as you, that he genuinely believed Kaufmann would mend his ways.

And he's not a man to fall for gammon." The investigator looked at me questioningly. "For false promises and deceit," I explained.

"Indeed not," said Christmas. "The keeper of Newgate must have heard gammon from every swine in the land." He smiled delightedly at his own joke.

CHAPTER SIXTEEN

Three premises

FRIDAY 14TH AUGUST 1829

Knowing that Mr Young would give me short shrift if we interrupted him on an auction day, Wilson and I returned to the Horse Bazaar on a Friday. The busyness Martha and I had seen on our visit was a memory, and once again the yard in front of the entrance was all but deserted. We could hear the soft neighing and whinnying of horses in the stables, and a lad appeared from the stable door on one side of the yard, staggering under the weight of a large bucket in each hand. He looked across at us, no doubt taking note of our coats, but said nothing and disappeared into the stable block opposite.

As we had done on our first visit, Wilson and I walked through the yard and pushed open the heavy

wooden door leading into the building. Almost immediately we heard a man shouting; the sound was coming
from the clerks' office to our right. The door was flung
open and whoever was shouting flung a final volley back
over his shoulder. "If I have to come in here again to
check, Mr Duke, it'll be the worse for you!" And out into
the hallway barrelled a tall, well-built man, a high colour
to his face. His dark hair, going grey at the temples, was
swept back, and he ran a hand through it with impatience. He stopped short when he saw us, and barked,
"Well?"

I looked at him levelly, feeling Wilson draw himself
up to his full height at my side.

"Mr George Young?" I asked. The man frowned and
then nodded.

"I am Constable Samuel Plank," I continued, "of
Great Marlborough Street, and this is Constable Wilson.
We would like to talk to you about the counterfeit banknotes that have been found on your premises." Behind
him, someone unseen in the clerks' office silently pushed
the door closed.

"On my premises?" repeated Young. "If you're insin-
uating…"

I held up my hand and he stopped. "We do not insin-
uate, Mr Young," I said carefully, "we establish. Now, is

there somewhere we can discuss this matter, or would you prefer to stand here in the hallway, in full sight of any visitor who may arrive?"

♦

Mr Young's office was on the floor above, with windows overlooking the entrance yard. There was a compact desk in the corner of the room, with a pile of ledgers upon it, but otherwise the office more closely resembled a gentleman's sitting room, with one large, comfortable armchair pulled up close to the fireplace, and two smaller chairs on either side of a low table. I revised my initial poor impression of the man when he insisted that I take the armchair while he perched on one of the smaller seats; Wilson, as ever, indicated that he would prefer to stand by the door. No sooner had Young sat down than he jumped up again to offer us refreshments.

"Coffee? Tea?" he asked. "A fruit cordial? The kitchen can send up anything you like, gentlemen – nothing alcoholic, of course, but still refreshing."

"Thank you, no," I said. "Nothing alcoholic, you say?"

Young sat down again and shook his head. "I used to permit it, but there are those who do not know when to stop, and the ladies were complaining. I want this to be a place for families, constable – somewhere a man can bring his wife and not worry that she will be exposed to rowdy behaviour. And the grooms – well, they like a drink, and it seems sensible not to put it in their way. Now, you wanted to talk to me about counterfeit bank-notes. And about time too."

"Constable Wilson will be taking notes as we talk," I said. "Am I to understand that you have had concerns for some time?"

"You and I are of an age, Constable Plank," said Young. "And we know what rough places sale yards can be. Rogues trying to sell near-dead animals, ruffians scheming to get a decent animal for a pittance. When I took over this place, I wanted it to be different. After all, a fine horse is a handsome animal – a creature of elegance and beauty. Add to that the graceful lines of a barouche, or the workmanship in a gentleman's saddle, and you have the makings of something special. It's been hard work – harder than I thought it would be – but, by God, I think I've achieved it. Three premises, sir: this one, and branches selling harness and saddlery at Cornhill and Lombard Street. And I'll be damned if I'll let it all be ruined by slips of paper passed over the counter by smashers." Young stood up and turned to the fireplace, grasping the mantelpiece with both hands, his knuckles turning white. "But now, as I feared, it's brought the constables to my door."

"So you are aware of counterfeit banknotes being presented here?" I asked.

"More than aware, constable," he said, turning to face me. "Since the beginning of the year, we have had more and more of the blasted things offered to us. The first couple of times we were duped and were the losers as a result. But we have learned from our mistakes. Thankfully my chief clerk is a canny fellow and makes sure to check all the notes that are presented." He folded his arms. "But he won't need to do that for much longer, constable, I can assure you."

"What do you mean, Mr Young?" I asked. "I must warn you against taking the law into your own hands."

Young laughed. "Ha! Quite right too, constable – warning noted. Little good it would do me to rid myself of the forgers and smashers, only to swing from a rope for it." His expression turned serious again. "No, I mean to be cleverer than that." He touched the side of his nose. "There are some gentlemen whom I employ to ensure that any rowdy behaviour is nipped in the bud. And when they are not keeping an eye on things here on auction days, they make themselves useful by asking questions and encouraging people to answer." He raised an eyebrow and I nodded. "And these gentlemen tell me that many of the counterfeits that are presented to us have found their way into our customers' pockets at Fishmongers' Hall."

"You mean Mr Crockford's gambling club in St James's?" I asked.

"Club!" sneered Young. "It's nothing more than a common gambling hell. The fishmonger may have pretensions to elegance these days, but his business stinks as much as it ever did."

"It is some years since Mr Crockford sold fish," I said mildly. "Are your informants certain about the connection with his establishment?"

Young leaned forward in his seat. "As I said, the first couple of times, we were stuck with the queer screens. But then we were on our guard. We refused them and kept a note of who had presented them. In exchange for not being hauled off to the magistrate, people were happy to tell us where they had acquired the notes – and the same place came up again and again."

"Do you think those presenting the notes knew they were counterfeit?" I asked.

Young shook his head. "Perhaps one or two of them weren't surprised," he said, "but most were horrified. Scared, too – uttering's a serious crime, constable."

"So I am told," I said. "Now I am going to propose an exchange of my own, Mr Young."

"Are you indeed?" said my host, amused. "Go on then, constable."

"We are aware of one occasion on which Mr Duke did not spot some counterfeit notes, and they were accepted as payment," I said. "Eleven pounds in counterfeit notes – the shillings were sound." Young opened his mouth to speak but I held up a hand to stop him. "The sum is being repaid gradually; indeed, if I had not mentioned it you would never have known of it. And if you give me your word that you will not raise this matter with Mr Duke – who has taken responsibility for the repayment – I will tell you why Constable Wilson and I are here." Young said nothing. "Alternatively, Mr Young," I continued, "I can refer the matter to the inspectors at the Bank of England. As you say, uttering is a serious crime."

"You would make a fine auctioneer, constable," said Young with a laugh and a shake of his head. "You know how to push a man to the limits of what he can offer. Very well: I shall leave it to Mr Duke to make good on the eleven pounds. And now you can tell me your interest in the matter."

"The young man who presented the counterfeit eleven pounds," I started, "was found dead the next day, beaten, with your receipt in his pocket. His father is of the opinion that he was robbed and killed by," I reached into my coat pocket and took out my notebook and turned in it to my record of my discussions with Roger Forster, "ruffians and scoundrels, who likely saw him at the Horse Bazaar, flush in the pocket, and followed him. Would these ruffians and scoundrels be the gentlemen whom you employ to ask questions, Mr Young?"

Young's expression hardened. "Let me be sure that I understand you, constable," he said. "A man brings counterfeit banknotes to my establishment. He exchanges them for a horse, which is my property – in other words, he steals from me. And when this thief is found dead, you accuse my associates of his murder."

"Mr Young, you go too far," I said sternly. "If you prefer, we can leave this matter to be heard before a magistrate, who will be informed of the dead man's visit to your establishment in the hours before his death. You can attend the hearing and explain your connection to him. There are often newspaper men in the court who are interested in such things. Or you can control your temper and help me to work out what happened, so that the magistrate need not be troubled."

Young deflated. "Well, perhaps I was a little intemperate," he admitted. "But a murder – you can understand why I wouldn't want my establishment dragged into it."

"Indeed," I said, "and you can understand why I cannot allow you to accuse Mr Madden of being a thief. As far as we can tell, he thought the banknotes were genuine – you said yourself that you were initially fooled by the counterfeits, and he was much less familiar with banknotes than you are." I stopped when I saw the look on Young's face – the colour had drained from it and he put a hand to his throat.

"Did you say Madden?" he asked. "Charles Madden?"

I nodded. "Did you know Mr Madden?" I asked. Of course Mr Duke had told me that Charles and his mother and stepfather had all visited the Horse Bazaar, but I had no plans to tell Young of our meeting. Young stared at me and blinked several times. "Did you know Mr Madden?" I asked again.

Eventually, Mr Young responded. "Yes. Mr Madden bought a horse from us earlier in the summer. But before that he had accompanied his parents on several occasions." He stopped but I knew there was more. "Dear heavens, are you saying that Charles is the man who was killed?"

"Mr Young," I said, "what is it that you are not telling me?"

Young stood and turned away from me. He seemed to be battling with himself, and after a long minute he turned back again. "I have a daughter," he said. "Sophie. Nearly eighteen years of age. A pretty thing – takes after her late mother in that – and fond of clothes and amusements. When Charles Madden and his parents came to collect their new carriage, Sophie and Charles fell to talking, and it seems they formed an attachment. I did not object – after all, a house on Brook Street would be quite a step up for her. And I liked the lad: he was lively, and quick to laugh."

"Were they promised to each other?" I asked.

Young shook his head. "Mrs Forster – Charles's mother – was in favour of the match," he said. "She could see that Sophie made her son happy, and that was all that mattered to her. But her husband – the stepfather – well, he was set against it. I couldn't fathom why. Perhaps he had someone else in mind for Charles. A more profitable alliance." He shrugged. "We heard that Charles had died, of course. Mrs Forster sent a kind note to Sophie, saying that she was sorry they would not be family after all. Sophie has been grieving – as much as can be expected of an almost-engaged girl of eighteen.

But the note said nothing of a violent death. We assumed a fever of some sort." He shook his head. "The poor woman." He walked over to the sideboard, opened a cupboard and took out a decanter. It seemed that his prohibition on alcohol stopped at the door of his own office. He pulled the stopper from the decanter and turned to me with raised eyebrows, but I shook my head. He poured himself a generous measure, and the decanter clattered against the glass. He threw the drink down his throat and immediately poured another, drinking that one just as quickly. He turned to face me once more.

"I should have told someone at the time," he said. "But it was something and nothing, and with Sophie being sweet on young Charles..." He sat down again, but looked smaller, diminished.

"Should have told someone what, Mr Young?" I prompted.

"About six weeks ago," he started, "one of my men came to see me. One of the men who keep an eye on things. Tom Dawson."

"Tom Dawson?" repeated Wilson. Young looked surprised to hear him speak, and I turned to Wilson and widened my eyes, warning him to stay quiet.

"Aye," said Young. Why – do you know him?"

"What did Mr Dawson tell you?" I asked.

Young paused for a moment, looking from me to Wilson and back again, and then continued. "He said that he had been approached by a man who asked whether he would be interested in earning a bit of money using his fists. Pugilism, Dawson thought at first – he's won a few bouts in his time. But it wasn't that: the fellow wanted him to waylay someone and hush him."

"Hush him?" I repeated. "You mean – kill him?"

"Aye," said Young miserably.

"And did he say who he wanted your man to murder?" I asked.

"Not at first," said Young. "But Dawson thought perhaps I could be the target, or someone else working at the Horse Bazaar. When you're as successful as we are, you make enemies. And Dawson is a loyal old dog. So he pretended to be interested, sounding the man out. And the fellow was a boaster, trying to be a hard man, and soon gave it away." Young looked even more miserable. "His target was Charles Madden."

"Just to be clear, Mr Young," I said. "Six weeks ago, a man asked your employee Mr Dawson to kill Charles Madden. And neither you nor Mr Dawson thought to report this matter, or to warn Mr Madden."

"Tom Dawson did report it – he reported it to me. And if I believed every threat of violence that came to my attention, constable, I'd have to set up camp at Great Marlborough Street," said Young. "Selling horses can be a rough game, which is why I employ the likes of Mr Dawson." He paused. "But I do regret not saying anything this time." He shook his head. "Aye, I do regret it."

"Is Tom Dawson here today?" I asked.

"He should be," said Young. "He'll be in the main hall, I should think – he's sweet on a woman who works in the coffee-room, and he wanders around hoping she'll notice him. He's a bit slow, is Dawson."

I turned and nodded at Wilson, who slipped from the room.

"He's a good-sized fellow," observed Young. "Constable Wilson."

"If you're thinking of offering him a job," I said sternly, "you can put the idea from your mind. He's joining the new police, and with a wife and baby and another on the way, I'm happy to see him in steady work. Good work."

"You're like my clerk Duke, with that useless son of his," said Young with a laugh.

"Useless?" I asked. "Surely just learning his trade."

"And taking an age about it," said Young. "Don't think for a moment that I can't guess who accepted those counterfeit banknotes, constable. Still, loyalty is worth something, isn't it?"

Before I could answer, the office door opened and in came Tom Dawson, ducking slightly. I doubt he had been upstairs in the building before: he stood in the doorway, turning his hat in his hands, and gazed around at the fine furniture, the paintings on the walls – mostly of horses, but one of a severe-looking woman in an unflattering dress – and the rich rugs on the floor.

"I'm told you want to see me, sir," he said softly. I looked at him. It was the same man we had met in the Three Tuns. Big, quiet, with bruises on his knuckles. No doubt Wilson had had a word with him, and he made no indication that he recognised me.

"Not me, Dawson, but Constable Plank here wants a word with you." Young looked at me and I looked back silently. "Ah," he said after a moment. "Perhaps you would prefer me to leave."

"If you wouldn't mind, sir," I said.

Young looked rather as though he would mind, but he nodded and rose from his seat and walked to the door. Dawson stood to one side, shoulders hunched, and closed the door quietly once Young had left. Wilson indicated that Dawson should move further into the room and he stepped forward reluctantly. I pointed at the chair that Young had vacated but Dawson shook his head and I could see his point – his knees would be round his ears if he sat there. I stood so that I would not be craning my neck to look up at him.

"So, Mr Dawson," I said, "you are a man with two masters – three, if you're married." The poor fellow looked so nervous that I felt obliged to try and put him at his ease. He gave me a weak smile.

"It was Jem's idea," he said softly, clearing his throat.

"To work for both Mr Crockford and Mr Young?" I asked.

He nodded. "He said it made sense. They both wanted the same thing, he said, and what we find out at Crockford's we can tell Mr Young and what we find out here we can tell Mr Crockford. He said we wasn't doing nothing wrong." He leaned forward and dropped his voice, like a child sharing a secret. "Mr Crockford never asked if we was working for Mr Young. And Mr Young never asked if we was working for Mr Crockford. So we never lied."

"How do you know Jem?" I asked.

"He's married to my sister Betsy," he said. "They look after me, Jem and Betsy."

"I'm sure they do," I said gently. "And in return you help Jem with his work."

Dawson nodded. "Sometimes people laugh at me, but Jem never. I can be pudding-headed, on account of being hit in the head so much when I was a fighter," he held up his hands, which were enormous, with the knuckles misshapen from too many breaks, "but I can still help Jem."

"Was Jem there when that man asked you to attack Charles Madden?" I asked.

Dawson's face fell. "I remember now: that's what you asked about in the Three Tuns," he said miserably. "I promise I never done it." He looked desperately at Wilson and then again at me. "If Betsy thinks I hurt someone she'll be angry. She said I sometimes hurt people when I'm not meaning to."

"We know it wasn't you, Tom," I said, and his face cleared again. "Mr Young told us that a man asked you to attack Mr Madden – to kill him, Tom – but that you said no."

Dawson nodded vigorously. "That's right: I said no."

"Did this man tell you his name, Tom?" I asked.

"No," he said sadly. "He knew my name, but when I asked him what he was called, he just touched the side of his nose, like this." He demonstrated with one huge hand.

"And was his nose big? Or small?" I asked.

Dawson considered. "About like yours, I think. But he was younger than you, and taller. Very neat and tidy, and clean. He smelled like soap." He looked across at Wilson, who was writing down what he said. "Am I in trouble?" he asked.

"No, Tom," I said. "You know how Jem has a notebook, where he writes down things about people so that he doesn't forget?" Dawson nodded. "Constable Wilson does the same, with his notebook. Now, tell me a bit more about this fellow who wouldn't tell you his name. Would you recognise him again?"

"Oh, yes," said Tom, looking at me seriously. "I'm good with remembering faces. I can't write in a notebook but I can remember. Faces stay in here." He pointed at his head.

"What about his clothes?" I asked. "Was he wearing a smart outfit, or workman's clothes?"

Dawson tilted his head as he tried to remember. "He had a coat on," he said. "Like his," he pointed at Wilson, "but longer, and the buttons weren't that fancy." He paused and then smiled. "And he swore when he trod in some dung in the yard – he splashed it on his stockings."

"Stockings?" I repeated. "Not breeches?"

Dawson nodded. "Light stockings – like Betsy wears. Black shoes with big buckles and light stockings. Silly things to wear in a stable."

"Indeed," I said. "And what did the man say when you told him you wouldn't do what he asked? Was he angry?"

"He was rude," said Dawson sadly, his smile disappearing. "He laughed at me and called me soft. He said I didn't know a good offer when it was made, and that he knew plenty of others who would take the money."

"How much did he offer you, Tom?" I asked.

"Five pounds," he said. "That's a lot, isn't it?"

"Aye," I said. "But what shall it profit a man, if he shall gain the whole world and lose his soul?"

Dawson smiled broadly. "I know that – Betsy taught me that one. It's from the Bible."

"Your sister Betsy sounds like a very sensible woman," I said. "Now, Tom, I think we have everything we need from you – I shall tell Mr Young how helpful you have been. I shall not tell him about your other work, but you be careful, Tom. And if you see this man again, the one who offered you that five pounds for a very wicked thing, send word to me at Great Marlborough Street police office. Remember my name: Constable Plank, like the wood."

♦

"It can't be easy," said Martha that evening, her back to me as she stirred a pot on the stove and I told her of our visit to the Horse Bazaar. "Having a grown man who's like a child in his head. Thank goodness he has a sister to care for him."

"While her husband takes advantage of him," I said grimly.

"Still," said Martha, handing me a plate and pointing to the bread on its board, "she's taught him right from wrong – he was offered five pounds to do something bad and he turned it down. There's plenty who wouldn't."

I cut three slices of bread, putting two on my own plate and one on Martha's. She lifted the pot from the heat and spooned stew from it, rolling her eyes when I held out my plate for more but adding another spoonful anyway.

"That's tasty," I said, dipping my bread into the stew.

"Did Mr Dawson's description of the man sound familiar to you?" asked Martha, putting the pot back onto the stove and taking her seat.

I shook my head. "Too general," I said. "A clean-smelling man who was younger than me, and taller.

Wearing a dark coat over light stockings, and black shoes with big buckles."

"That sounds like an indoor uniform to me," said my wife. "What do the croupiers wear at Crockford's?"

A fragrant experience

MONDAY 17TH AUGUST 1829

The next Monday I was sitting in the back office at Great Marlborough Street when there was a knock at the door and Tom Neale's head appeared.

"Visitor, Sam," he said. "A Mr Christmas. Natty." And he looked pointedly at the coat I had removed and hung on the hook. "Shall I bring him through?" I glanced around the room, making sure that it was tidy, and nodded.

A moment later, the office-keeper appeared again, this time with Charles Christmas in tow. He showed the investigator into the room and asked whether we would like tea.

"Constable Plank has a couple of slices of walnut loaf, brought from home, hidden in his coat pocket, if you're peckish," he added mischievously.

"Just tea will be fine, thank you, Mr Neale," said our visitor.

When Thomas had disappeared, Christmas shook my hand and sat down. "I see that your Mr Neale knows everything that goes on," he said. "We have one just like him at the Bank. Invaluable – but unsettling, I always think."

"Aye," I said. "Every young constable who joins us thinks that he will be able to outsmart Thomas Neale, and it's yet to happen."

Just then the door opened and the office-keeper re-appeared with a tray. He set it on the table, poured two cups, and left us.

"Now, Mr Christmas, how can I help you?" I asked.

"It's rather the other way round," said Christmas, taking a sip of his tea. "After we met last week, I became curious about Mr Kaufmann. The more I thought about it, the more likely I thought it was that he is still here in London."

"You said you thought he might be working back in Vienna, and sending the counterfeit banknotes to England," I said.

"And that is indeed possible," agreed Christmas, "but it would be quite a coincidence, for a counterfeit created by Mr Kaufmann to makes its way from Vienna to London, and then to me. And so I called on a man I know – please don't ask me his name, as I cannot tell you. We investigators at the Bank sometimes have to rely on the help of men who are not strictly, well, perhaps we should call them unprincipled."

"A useful word," I said, "and very apt. I shall not ask you to give him up."

"Thank you," said Christmas. "And he was indeed useful: he confirmed that Ernst Kaufmann is still in London. And," he reached into his coat pocket, "this is where he is living."

I took the scrap of paper that he handed to me and read it. "I shall call on Mr Kaufmann today," I said.

Christmas drained his cup and stood. "I am very sorry that he is still in England," he said. "I thought the trial would finish him off – he looked so frightened most of the time, almost ill with fear. And when he was released – unexpectedly, but I could not find it in my heart to be sorry – I was sure he would race back over the

Channel and we would never hear of him again. I cannot imagine what has possessed him to stay, and now to risk his neck again."

♦

"Alice keeps reminding me that there won't be many more times for us, like this," said Wilson. He looked across at me and quickly looked away again. "Not once I'm properly sworn in."

"Aye," I said. "Things will be much more... regimented, I should imagine. With Commissioner Rowan being a military man, I mean. You won't be able to disappear off to the ends of Whitechapel without good reason."

"Not that anyone would want to," said Wilson, neatly sidestepping a pile of excrement.

"It's a fragrant experience, I'll give you that," I said as we passed the leather factory on Deal Street. "But look at these buildings – it's almost as though we're in Germany."

We stopped and craned our necks to look up at the row of weavers' cottages on Pelham Street. Three or four storeys high and flat-fronted, they had windows on their upper floors that were wide rather than tall, made with small diamond-shaped panes, and designed to allow in as much light as possible for the weavers to do their work. As if to complete the illusion, two women bustled past us, arms linked, talking nineteen to the dozen in what I guessed to be German. No wonder Ernst Kaufmann had chosen to live here.

I looked again at the slip of paper that Charles Christmas had given me. "Here we are," I said, "Hunt Street. Next door to the Ship." We stopped opposite the address indicated on the paper. Like the houses in Pelham Street, this too was tall, brick-built, with long windows on the upper two storeys. It occurred to me that a forger might also welcome good, clear light by which to do his work.

As we looked up at the building, the front door opened and a lad of about ten came out. He was carrying a packet wrapped in paper – about the size of a brick – and he put it between his knees as he turned and used both hands to haul the door closed. He then retrieved the packet and tried unsuccessfully to tuck it into the waist of his trousers before sighing mightily and setting off down the street with the packet under his arm.

I looked at Wilson.

"Let's see where he goes," he said, "but if he starts running I'm not chasing him – he'll be like a whippet at that age."

Thankfully the lad seemed in no hurry and we followed him as he turned right into Pelham Street and then left into Brick Lane. The sweetish smell of the mash from the breweries mixed with the less pleasant aroma of the livestock in the market. As we squeezed through the crowds, Wilson rising onto his toes to keep the lad in his sights, a plump woman wound about with a woollen shawl and wearing the clogs of a farmer's wife stepped into my path and waved a chicken in my face, its legs held in her dirty fist as it dangled upside-down, flapping its wings and squawking with outrage. At her feet were several baskets, all filled with chickens, and behind her stood a weary-looking donkey, dozing in the shafts of the barrow that he had hauled in that morning. I wondered whether Martha would welcome an unexpected chicken and decided against it. I shook my head and stepped around the woman, who was already offering the indignant bird to the fellow behind me.

At last we burst clear of the market, just in time to see the lad pulling open the door of the Three Compasses. Wilson looked at me and smiled.

"That's another thing that will change," I said. "Once you're with the new police. No drinking while in uniform."

"Then I'd better make the most of it while I can," he replied.

We crossed the road towards the pub. Just as we reached the door it swung open and a fellow was pitched out headlong into the street. The burly innkeeper who had sent him on his way wiped his hands on his apron and stood aside to let us pass.

"Gentlemen," he said, inclining his head. His sharp eyes took in our coats but he said nothing. I looked over my shoulder and the drunkard was staggering to his feet.

"His wife tells me to do it," said the innkeeper. "If I don't send him on his way, he'll spend every penny he earns on his stall on my ale."

"An innkeeper turning down money," I said. "That's not something you see every day."

The innkeeper smiled. "And I don't do it for everybody," he agreed. "But his wife is my sister and there's a pack of kiddies at home. Now, constables, what can we get you?"

"A dark table and no more talk of constables," I said.

The innkeeper touched the side of his nose and led us inside. He pointed at a small table tucked away in a corner and Wilson and I took off our hats, turning our backs to the room to hide our distinctive buttons, and pushed through the gloom to our seats. The room was crowded: with the market and the breweries and the brickworks, there were plenty of thirsty men in Brick Lane. But as a small group of them threw back the last of their drinks and moved towards the door, we caught sight of the lad from Kaufmann's house. He was standing with his back to us, in front of someone sitting at a table, and we could see from the movement of his arms that he was handing over the packet he had been carrying. I leaned more to the side, and now I could see him taking something in return – money perhaps – and this was small enough for him to tuck it into the waist of his trousers. He paused for a moment more, listening to whoever was sitting at the table, and then turned to leave. As he made his way to the door, and before the crowd closed again in his wake, I caught a glimpse of the man at the table. Or more particularly, I caught a glimpse of his waistcoat. Even in the dim light, I could see that it was a bright canary yellow.

◆

John Conant turned from the fireplace to look at me. "And you are sure it was the same man?" he asked. "Not just someone else with a fondness for a fancy waistcoat?"

"Papa," said his daughter, "we are going to be late."

"I'm sorry, Miss Lily," I said. "I would have waited until morning if I had known you had an engagement this evening."

The magistrate's daughter took off her evening coat with an exaggerated sigh. "To be honest, Constable Plank," she said with a smile in her voice, "both papa and I would be relieved to miss this particular engagement. One of mamma's friends has made it her mission to see me married and arranges these gatherings so that I can see her latest find – and he can see me. But as her idea of a suitable gentleman is someone with plenty of money and very few brains, I have yet to be tempted by any of them." She walked across to her father and leaned up to kiss his cheek. "I am afraid that my clever papa has quite spoiled me for lesser men."

Conant's eyes shone as he looked at his daughter. "Then that is my failing, Lily," he said. "A woman should have a household and children of her own – look at the joy you brought your own dear mother."

"And look at the misery of being married to a dull man," parried Miss Lily. She threw herself onto the couch in a mock faint, the back of her hand to her forehead. "Imagine the tedious conversation at breakfast. The dreary silence at supper. No, papa: I am quite determined." She sat up and looked at me. "So, Constable Plank, please continue: your man in a canary waistcoat sounds ten times more interesting than any of the dull fellows Aunt Alicia will be lining up for me tonight. Why are you so alarmed to see him again?"

Conant indicated one of the two armchairs and we both sat. I glanced at him and he nodded. "Well, Miss Lily," I started, it was a few years ago now – the summer of 1825, I think." Another nod from the magistrate. "Constable Wilson and I were looking into some very sad cases – a young lawyer who killed himself, a schoolteacher who was stealing from charitable funds – and we uncovered a gang of rogues who were encouraging the gullible…"

"And the greedy," added Conant sternly.

"And the greedy," I echoed, "to invest their money in schemes that turned out to be…" I twirled my hand in the air.

"Empty?" suggested Miss Lily.

"Precisely," I said. "Empty schemes. Fraud. People lost their own money and, to save their skins when the rogues came calling, would entice others into the same useless schemes. The misery just grew and grew. And at the head of it all, planning the schemes and directing the rogues, was our fine fellow in his yellow waistcoat. You'd think he'd want to avoid drawing attention to himself, but no: he and his crew wore their bright waistcoats as though daring us to notice them." I shook my head, remembering. "The damage he has done over the years, it hardly bears calculating."

Miss Lily shivered. "And this is the man you saw today?"

"Without a doubt," I said. "Constable Wilson and I both recognised him. The surprising thing is that he's running his own errands; after all, he took over from his boss Georgie Mac four years ago now, and from what I hear has made even more of a success of duping people out of their money than Georgie did. I saw him earlier this year, in a nasty incident near Drury Lane, and he was quite obviously the captain, with underlings jumping to do his bidding and him keeping his own hands clean. So what's he doing waiting in a pub in Brick Lane, taking deliveries from an urchin?"

I sat pondering. We had never caught this man with his bright yellow waistcoat – and the swagger and arrogance that went with it. Indeed, I did not even know his name, or anything about him beyond his criminal activities – and it rankled that I had never managed to arrest him, let alone see him brought to justice. I was irritated, too, that present circumstances meant that I had not been able to grasp his wretched elbow and arrest him there and then in the Three Compasses. Maybe now, after all these years – perhaps I could end my time as a constable with no loose ends left flapping? I sighed. I knew only too well that life was rarely that obliging.

The magistrate frowned slightly as a thought occurred to him and he leaned forwards in his seat. Most magistrates contented themselves with the official limits of their job: they listened to hearings, decided which cases should be sent to the judge, and passed sentence on lesser offences. But with his quick mind and lifelong concern with justice, John Conant had always been more interested in why people turned to crime. Indeed, it was this shared fascination that had turned our working relationship into a friendship.

"We now have two men, seemingly connected to each other, who are acting inexplicably," he said. "There is Kaufmann who, having escaped the noose by the skin of his teeth last time, should have fled England for Vienna as fast as his legs could carry him. And yet here he is, still in London, still engaged in the very crime that so nearly cost him his life. And now there is your canary waistcoat fellow, who by all accounts should be sitting at the very top of his organisation, but instead he is collecting packages in a grimy public house." He leaned back and steepled his hands – a clear signal to those who knew him that he was enjoying a mental puzzle. "What would entice both men to take such chances?"

"Perhaps Kaufmann needs the money," I suggested. "Or felt he could not return to Vienna without having made his fortune in London. And my information about the man in the canary waistcoat could be outdated – perhaps his power is waning. Although he is a young man still, and that waistcoat – a man on the way down would surely ditch something so recognisable, so full of arrogance."

Conant and I sat in silence. After about five minutes Miss Lily came and stood in front of us, her hands on her hips. "Has neither of you considered the most obvious explanation?" she asked. "What makes a man change his behaviour? Take unnecessary risks? Stay where he is in danger?" She looked at us in turn. "Good heavens – it is as well that I am here. Love, gentleman. You can be sure that love is at the heart of this." And she smiled with satisfaction at her pun.

♦

"She's as smart as a whip, that's for sure," said Martha, laughing as I told her what Miss Lily had said. She sat on the edge of our bed, taking the pins out of her hair and shaking out the curls. I had watched the same actions almost every night for nearly three decades and I never tired of seeing it. I have never been a jealous man or a possessive one, but the thought that I was the only man in the world to see this gave me great satisfaction. Martha felt me watching her and turned to look at me. "What are you staring at, Constable Plank?" she asked.

"I'm staring at you, Mrs Plank," I replied, holding up the bedding so that she could slip under the covers. She tutted but it was all for show, and she kissed my cheek before settling down with her head on my chest. After a moment or two she turned to look up at me. "She's right, of course," she said.

"About it being love?" I asked.

"Perhaps not love – simple love," said my wife, "but some sort of emotion. You men think you are logical creatures and that women are the silly ones, ruled by feelings, but the real difference is that we talk about them. You men still have them." I don't know whether she was aware of it, but as she spoke she moved her hand until it was resting over my heart. "You don't talk about them very often, but they come out in your actions. If there's no logic to a man's actions, it's his feelings at work." She sighed and closed her eyes. "The first thing you should do is find out about these men's private lives – their families. That'll be why they're doing what they're doing." She stopped talking and I waited, but she said no more.

"And what's the second thing I should do?" I asked.

"I thought you'd never ask," she said, smiling. "You should kiss me, of course."

And so I did.

CHAPTER EIGHTEEN

A life outside the law

TUESDAY 18TH AUGUST 1829

The next day Wilson was sent out on an early warrant and so I returned to Hunt Street alone. I knocked on the door and waited. There was no response and I knocked again, louder.

"I come, I come," replied a voice on the other side of the door, and a scrap of a girl appeared, red in the face and wiping her hands on her apron, then using her wrist to push a damp curl away from her forehead. "In kitchen," she said, pointing to the floor in explanation. "Herr Kaufmann?"

"Yes," I nodded vigorously. "I would like to see Herr Kaufmann."

"Come," she commanded, and beckoned. I followed her into the hall. She used her hip to push open the door to her left and then shooed me into the room. As though suddenly remembering something she had almost forgotten, she dropped a quick curtsy and smiled.

"Danke," I said.

The girl looked up at me and grinned. "Bitte," she said, before backing out of the room and pulling the door closed. I could hear her running up the stairs, her boots thudding on the bare wooden steps. I looked around the room, which was dark with heavy furnishings. A portrait of an austere-looking man – a clergyman, perhaps, from the plainness of his garb – glared down from the chimney breast. I could hear someone coming more slowly down the stairs – someone heavier, older. The door opened and in came a man of indeterminate age; his stooped back and pale skin suggested a housebound invalid, but his face was almost unlined and his eyes were bright blue behind their spectacles. He held out his hand to me.

"Good morning," he said pleasantly; there was a definite accent to his words – goot rather than good.

"Good morning, Herr Kaufmann," I said. "I am Constable Sam Plank of Great Marlborough Street. I work for the magistrate Mr John Conant."

"You like coffee?" asked Kaufmann. I suspected that he was giving himself time to think. He smiled shyly. "Proper coffee – not like in cheap coffee house."

"In that case, Herr Kaufmann," I said, "it would be a pleasure."

Kaufmann went to the door and called out. "Birgit – zwei Kaffees bitte!"

He closed the door and then turned back to me and indicated the two high-backed chairs near the window, with a low table between them. We sat down.

"Now, constable," he said. "What do you want?"

His question was blunt, but his gentle demeanour suggested that this was simply a difference in language rather than any impatience with me.

"Herr Kaufmann," I said, "your direct question deserves a direct answer. I know your history." I took my notebook from my coat pocket and opened it to the page I had marked before my visit. "In July of last year you were found guilty of forging promissory notes from the Prussian treasury. You spent four months in Newgate before the Twelve Judges decided that an error of process had been made and you were released. You told the keeper of Newgate that you intended to turn your back on crime and return to Vienna." I closed my notebook.

"And yet here you are, Herr Kaufmann – still in London and still creating counterfeits."

There was a noise at the door and Kaufmann jumped up to open it. The maid Birgit came in with a tray; on it were a tall coffee-pot, two cups and a plate of biscuits. She put the tray on the low table and left, pulling the door closed with a bang.

Kaufmann looked at me wryly. "She is not angry – she is a country girl, from a farm. All day long it is bang and crash. But her cooking... I cannot do without it." He poured two cups from the pot and handed one to me, then held out the plate of biscuits. "Gingerbread," he said, "but like in Vienna." I took a biscuit and bit into it; the crust gave way to a soft middle, almost like a pudding, with the kick of strong ginger mellowed by other flavours I did not recognise. Kaufmann watched me intently. "Good, no?" he asked.

I nodded, chewing carefully. "Very good," I agreed.

Kaufmann sat down with his own coffee and took a piece of gingerbread. "And so the banging and the crashing, they do not matter so much," he said.

I put my cup down on the table. "Herr Kaufmann," I said, "you seem to be an intelligent man. You are a talented artist. Both Mr Christmas at the Bank of England and Mr Wontner at Newgate thought that you had learned your lesson and would make the most of the second chance you had been given. But if I were to go upstairs to that well-lit room at the top of this house, I would find counterfeit banknotes. And this time, there would be no Twelve Judges – the Old Bailey does not like to be robbed of the same prey twice, I can assure you."

Kaufmann said nothing, but his cup rattled as he put it in the saucer and he had to use both hands to steady it.

"Herr Kaufmann," I said again.

Kaufmann took a deep breath. "Do you have children, constable?" he asked. "In particular, do you have a daughter?"

"There is a young woman who treats me like a father," I said. "My wife and I were not blessed ourselves."

"And this young woman like a daughter," continued Kaufmann, "you do everything you can to make her happy?"

"Herr Kaufmann," I said, "are you saying that you are counterfeiting banknotes because of your daughter?"

Kaufmann's shoulders slumped even further. "You know I spend four months in Newgate. Horrid place. Rats, so dirty, always hungry, so much noise." He shuddered at the memory. "My daughter Johanna, every day she visit me. She try to bring food, but other men, they steal it, they say bad things, they try to touch her. And one day it changes. They move me to my own cell – small, but clean, with food every day."

"So someone was paying your garnish," I said.

Kaufmann nodded. "I ask Johanna how she pay for it. My heart," he put his hand on his chest, "was heavy, constable – so heavy. Did she sell herself for my comfort? But she promised me no. A man was paying, yes, but because he wanted to marry her." I must have looked disbelieving, because Kaufmann laughed. "Yes – I looked like that too, when she tell me. But she bring him to me, the man. Older than Johanna, but younger than me. Polite, respectful. Good clothes. He said that he loved Johanna and asked to marry her."

"And you agreed?" I asked.

Kaufmann shook his head. "Not at first. I wanted a nice Austrian boy for Johanna, someone who speaks the same language as me. But then I think: I am in prison. I will die on scaffold. Johanna will have no father, no mother, only her little brother – perhaps she should have husband." Kaufmann sighed. "I am not a fool, Constable Plank. I know this man is not inside the law. He has money to protect me, but he know many of the men in prison with me – he is not gentleman. And so I say no to Johanna."

"What did she say?" I asked, caught up in the story despite myself.

"Johanna is seventeen years, constable – for her the world is like this," he raised his hand as high as he could, "and then it is like this." He stooped down and put his hand to the floor. "She tell me she will die – die! – without this man. She tell me she love him like I love her mamma – which is very much, constable." He shook his head, remembering. "And then she tell me about the baby."

"Ah," I said.

"Ah," repeated Kaufmann. "And so the man, he come to see me again. In his best clothes – blue trousers, very fancy yellow waistcoat."

I looked up sharply from my notebook. "A yellow waistcoat?" I asked.

He nodded. "Very fine – good cloth." He rubbed the fingers of one hand together, to signify quality fabric. "He say again that he want to marry Johanna – and this time I say yes. And then the judges say that I can go home. Now that Johanna will be married, I think, I can go back to Vienna with Gregor. He is my son – good boy, do well at school, clever like his mother. Johanna will be sad that we leave, but she will have husband and baby in London." He sighed. "But Johanna, she have brains, constable. She tell Mr Fraser that she will not have a husband who is outside the law."

"Mr Fraser?" I asked. "That is the name of the man who visited you in Newgate – who wants to marry your daughter?"

"Yes," said Kaufmann. "Edward Fraser. Next month they marry in St Georgeskirche. And so we agree: I work for Mr Fraser until baby arrive, we save money, and then we all go to Vienna: Johanna, Edward, baby, Gregor, me."

"Why not go straight away?" I asked.

"Johanna too sick – just like her mother with babies," he explained. "Every day being sick."

"And this work that you do for Mr Fraser," I said. "Is it counterfeiting banknotes?"

Kaufmann looked miserable but nodded.

"Does Johanna know?" I asked.

Again he nodded. "We promise her: just until we leave England, to make money for new home and new baby. I have been in Newgate, constable, and everyone read in the newspapers about Kaufmann the forger – who in London will give me a job?"

"It is hard for a man when he loses his good reputation," I agreed. "But the fact remains that you are forging

banknotes. And what has brought me to your door today is that some of your banknotes were used by a young
man who was murdered shortly afterwards."

Kaufmann looked stricken. "Murdered?" he repeated. "Killed?"

I nodded. "He used the counterfeit banknotes – un-
knowingly, we think – to buy a horse. Hours later his
body was found in a dust-pit. He had been beaten to
death. Perhaps the person who was cheated by the banknotes took their revenge, or perhaps someone saw him
spending large amounts of money and thought to rob
him of whatever he had left. Whatever the motive, Herr
Kaufmann, your counterfeit banknotes and his murder
are linked."

"What are you going to do, constable?" asked Kaufmann. "Will you take me to Newgate?" He sat more upright in his seat, as though preparing himself.

I shook my head. "Herr Kaufmann, I cannot simply
take you away. I am only a constable. I need to present
my information to the magistrate, and if he thinks you
should face an accusation, he will issue a warrant for
your arrest." I closed my notebook and stood up. Kaufmann likewise stood. "If I may offer some advice, Herr
Kaufmann," I said. "I know that you will be tempted to
run. But if you do that, this life outside the law will never

be over, not for you and not for your family. I have an
idea that may help, but first I need to meet the man who
is to be your son-in-law."

CHAPTER NINETEEN

Something clean and bright

FRIDAY 21ST AUGUST 1829

"**A** criminal coming here?" said Martha with indignation. "In the yard, maybe, and up to the back door," she flicked the cloth she was holding towards the yard, indicating dismissively the limits of her tolerance, "but never have you asked me to entertain a criminal at my own table, Samuel Plank. To offer him our food and hospitality." She turned and put her hands on her hips. "Fancy telling a criminal where we live, Sam."

"Any criminal worth his salt can easily find out where we live, Mar," I said. "He can follow me home from the police office – I'm hardly in disguise, am I?" From the high colour that rose in Martha's cheeks I could tell that I was on the wrong track. "If I summon Fraser to Great Marlborough Street," I said, "Tom Neale will need to be told, and the other constables may recognise him. And if I meet him in a pub or on the streets, we will be on his territory, not mine. And," I spoke quickly as I could see Martha about to object again, "I need your opinion. I need you to meet him." My wife took her fists from her hips and looked at me appraisingly. "Fraser has been a criminal for years – he bested Georgie Mac, so we know he's clever and determined, and he's certainly feared. According to Kaufmann, he is mending his ways. But that could all be gammon. And I know no-one better than you at seeing the truth in people." I held out my hand and after a moment Martha took it. I pulled her onto my lap. "Honestly, Mar," I said, "I need to know what you think of him."

My wife leaned back so that she could look at me. "Are you getting soft in your old age?" she asked teasingly.

"Not soft: just smarter," I replied. "If I go to Mr Conant, he'll talk about the law. John Wontner's been fooled by too many repentant prisoners to fall for it again. Edward Freame goes the other way: he sees only good in everyone. But you, Mar: you've seen the best and the worst in people. You say that it's being a constable's wife that's taught you, but you were already wise when I first saw you – I've just given you plenty of chances to practise what you already knew."

Martha looked at me for a long minute and then kissed me – not a quick peck but a proper kiss. I was just beginning to hope that it might lead somewhere when there was a sharp, confident knock at the back door.

I opened the door. Edward Fraser and I looked at each other. He was tall, aged about thirty, with a thin, handsome face. He held out his hand.

"Constable Plank," he said in a low voice.

"Mr Fraser," I said in return. I stood aside to let him into the kitchen, and as he caught sight of Martha he quickly removed his hat and bowed his head.

"It is kind of you to allow me into your home, Mrs Plank," he said. "Not many would be as welcoming."

"And with good cause, Mr Fraser," said Martha, taking his hat from him and hanging it on the hook. "Your actions have caused a deal of misery for many people, I have heard."

Fraser turned to me with a wry smile. "I see now why you asked me to meet you here," he said.

I raised an eyebrow. "My wife is an excellent judge of character," I said. "If your desire for reform is just a pretty story, she will sniff it out."

"It seems that we have both been lucky in our choice of wife, constable," said Fraser. "We are no match for these determined women, and yet it is their very strength that draws us to them."

"If you hope to flatter me, Mr Harris..." said Martha warningly.

"I tell only the truth, Mrs Plank," he replied. "I have spent a lifetime telling people what I think they want to hear, to persuade them to open their purses to me. And sometimes I told them what I wanted them to hear, to make them do my bidding. But now..." He shrugged. "Now, with Johanna, I have a chance to do things right. For the first time in a long time, I actually want to do things right." He shook his head as though he could hardly believe it himself.

"Don't just stand there, Mr Fraser," said Martha, moving to the stove. "Have you eaten?"

Fraser looked at me and I nodded. He unbuttoned his coat and I saw his familiar yellow waistcoat as he took his seat.

"The man with the canary waistcoat," I said. "That's what we have called you."

Fraser laughed. "Yes: once upon a time I fancied my-self quite the macaroni. Yellow waistcoat, tight blue breeches, hat at a jaunty angle." He put his hand to his head to suggest this. "We all wore them, in my swell mob. It's my criminal uniform, I suppose." He glanced at Martha, who had turned to stir a pot.

"Mrs Plank is hard to shock, Mr Fraser," I said. "But easy to disappoint."

Fraser's face turned serious at once. "You know that I took over from Georgie Mac." He stopped and seemed to be considering something. "You know that I bridged Georgie."

I nodded. "I had known Georgie for years – since I was a boy. I wasn't sorry when I heard that he had died."

"Sam," said Martha, reaching up to the shelf for an extra plate, "it's wrong to speak ill of the dead."

"What's wrong is to pretend that dying undoes all the evil that someone has done," I said. "If a man spends his life selfishly, harming others for his own benefit, he can't be surprised if people rejoice when he is gone." I looked at Fraser. "Which brings us to why I asked you here this evening, Mr Fraser."

Martha leaned across me and put a plate in front of Fraser. "Haddock with potatoes and leeks," she said.

"And polite conversation only while you eat my food, please, gentlemen. Business can wait until later."

♦

"That was a very tasty meal, Mrs Plank. Thank you," said our visitor. "Johanna is an excellent seamstress but for cooking she relies on Birgit – the maid. More's the pity: Birgit has set her cap at a young porter from Smith-field market and I fear won't be with us for much longer. The fellow may be poor but with all that meat and then Birgit for a wife, he'll eat like a king."

"Pass me your plates, please," said Martha, standing to clear the table. "There is a pear pudding to come, but perhaps we should leave that for afterwards." She looked at me and I nodded. As Fraser handed her the items from the table, I reached across and retrieved my notebook and pencil from my coat pocket. After Martha had stacked the plates and covered the pot, she returned to the table and sat down.

"Now then, Mr Fraser," I began, "you do not deny that you have been involved in crime for several years." I looked at him and he shook his head. "And you do not deny that you were the one who suggested to Mr Kauf-

mann that he take up counterfeiting again, after his re-
lease from Newgate." Another shake of the head. "Why
did you do that, Mr Fraser?"

Fraser sighed. "It was a selfish thing to do, I know,
but I could think of no other way to keep Johanna close
to me, while I, well, while I wooed her." My eyebrows
shot up. Fraser leaned forward, his elbows on the table.
"I was calling on someone I knew in Newgate." He
closed his eyes for a moment, as though remembering
the scene. "One of my drovers. I wanted to make sure
that he wasn't telling tales about me – to remind him to
keep his mouth shut. And as I walked along the corridor
I saw her. I saw Johanna. She was visiting her father –
taking him food, which is madness as a soft fellow like
Kaufmann would never be allowed to keep hold of it.
She had a basket on her arm and wore a pale blue dress
with a white shawl. In that God-forsaken place she was
something clean and bright." He smiled at the memory.
"And just then – you'll think me cork-brained for saying
this – the light shone in through those grimy little windows and onto her golden hair, and she looked like an
angel."

I glanced at Martha; I had some sympathy for Fraser's predicament. I remembered that night so long ago,
when I had been walking along one of the rougher

streets in Holborn and had stopped to talk to a little girl who was crying on the steps of a public house and her older sister had come out. Martha. Not an angel exactly, with her dark hair and wise eyes, but I was lost from the moment I saw her.

"And what did this angel think of you, Mr Fraser?" asked Martha.

"To begin with, she was not impressed," said Fraser. "I offered to carry her basket and help her find her father, and then I said I could make sure that the food she had brought would not be stolen." He shook his head. "That was a mistake. It made me sound..."

"Threatening?" suggested my wife. "Boastful?"

Fraser nodded. "I was showing off. I wanted to impress her. But angels are not impressed by strength: they value kindness and gentleness and consideration for others." He smiled sadly. "Not my usual calling cards, Mrs Plank."

"I should imagine not," said Martha. "And do you expect us to believe that you had a Damascene conversion right there in Newgate," she looked at me to check that she had the right word and I nodded, "and put your life of crime behind you?"

Fraser sighed. "No, Mrs Plank – I wish I could say that's what happened. But once Johanna had sent me on my way, I tried to forget about her. If anything, I threw myself with even more energy into," he waved his hand in the air, "well, your husband knows my line of work. But she was always there, in my head, and my heart. I knew plenty of people in Newgate and through them I found out about Mr Kaufmann and what he had done, and I thought that if I used my... influence to make him more comfortable, then Johanna would know that I wasn't just fine words and fancy clothes. I paid his garnish, to get him a cell on his own, with decent bedding. And once he was settled I would visit, and take him newspapers, and play chess with him – and talk to Johanna. She could see that her father was happier and safer, and she liked me for it. And when he was set free he gave me permission to call on him, and I met Gregor and Birgit."

"Is Gregor the boy you use to deliver the counterfeit banknotes?" I asked. Fraser's tale was veering into self-congratulation and I wanted to remind him of the role he was playing in keeping this family tied to a life of crime.

A spark of anger flared in Fraser's eyes and then he remembered where he was. "Yes," he said. "He's a smart lad, quick to learn. Johanna says he should be in school, but, well, you know what boys are like: they want excitement, not the classroom." He smiled apologetically at Martha, but his smile faded when he saw the stern look on her face.

"I teach in a school, Mr Fraser," she said in a tone that always put me on warning when she used it on me. "We teach girls how to make an honest living and we show them how to avoid the pitfalls – the tempting, easy pitfalls – of a life outside the law. It is a great shame that you have not seen fit to use your influence to do the same for this young lad. Perhaps when you told Mr Kaufmann that you would mend your ways, you were thinking only of winning over his daughter. Perhaps you are lying to us as well, Mr Fraser."

Fraser glanced at me and I raised my eyebrows. He looked shamefaced.

"You are right, Mrs Plank," he said, "but only about Gregor – I should have thought of him first, rather than seeing what he could do for me. As for the rest, I was not lying to Mr Kaufmann and I am not lying to you. I want to turn over a new leaf – I have to turn over a new leaf." He took a deep breath and sat up straight. "Johanna is going to have a baby. My child."

"Then you will soon be a husband and a father, Mr Fraser," said Martha decisively, "with weighty responsibilities."

"I will, Mrs Plank," he replied. "And I have worked out what we will do, Johanna and I."

♦

I sat up in bed, leaning against the pillow, while I watched Martha. She sighed deeply as she always did when she removed her stays, and rubbed her hands over the indentations in her skin before shrugging her nightdress over her head.

"I should sell tickets," she commented, catching my eye in the small looking glass.

"I'd pay everything I have," I said – cleverly, I thought.

"Flatterer," she replied, but I could see her smiling in her reflection. Once she had removed all her hairpins and shaken her curls loose, she pinched out the candle and climbed into bed, tucking herself up next to me.

"Do you believe him?" she asked.

"Well, what he said makes sense," I said. I heard Martha's sharp intake of breath and corrected myself. "It makes sense of what he has done: it doesn't mean that he has made the right decision."

"Indeed not," said Martha. "Making counterfeit banknotes and selling them may well make them a deal of money, and fast, and Mr Fraser may well have resolved to use that money to take them all to Vienna to start a new life, but Sam, it's not right that people should make money from their crimes."

"What would you have me do, Martha?" I asked. "Tell Mr Conant and have Mr Kaufmann and Mr Fraser swing for their crimes, with Gregor left an orphan and Johanna and her child thrown onto the streets?"

Martha sat up, pulling the blanket around her. "What choice do you have, Sam? You're a constable."

"Not for much longer, Mar," I said mildly. "And what this grizzled old fellow knows – which would have surprised the handsome young devil who first spied you in Laystall Street – is that choices are rarely simple. I have had an idea about how we could make some good come of all of this." Martha raised an eyebrow at me. "But I want to talk to Mr Freame about it first: I can rely on him to tell me whether we have the balance right." I kissed Martha's cheek. "I notice you didn't object when I called myself a grizzled old fellow."

"No," said my wife, wriggling down under the covers and yawning. "But then nor did I correct you when you remembered your young self as handsome."

CHAPTER TWENTY

Silence in court

WEDNESDAY 26TH AUGUST 1829

Perhaps unsurprisingly, Edward Fraser looked decidedly uncomfortable. He had forsworn his usual smart clothing and was wearing an altogether more subdued outfit, almost the same colour as the stone wall against which he leaned. I crossed Old Bailey and hailed him.

"No canary waistcoat today?" I asked. "Worried that the judge might recognise you?" The flush that rose in his cheeks told me that I had hit my mark. "You're not the first to find the old fortress a bit alarming," I said more gently. "Come: we'd better go in, or all the seats will be gone." I held my arms out to shepherd him ahead of me and, taking a last look behind him, he reluctantly passed through the narrow gateway in the wall.

The yard was already busy with people. Prisoners and their guards, awaiting their turn before the judge, mixed with witnesses looking almost as nervous as the accused. Friends and family members steeling themselves for what they might see rubbed shoulders with the light-hearted crowd who had come for a day of drama and entertainment. Between them squeezed peddlers selling pies and other foodstuffs from trays on their heads; anyone who managed to secure a seat in the court would be reluctant to leave it, and in the short breaks between trials the public seating took on almost a carnival air as people unpacked their provisions and chattered about what they had seen. I indicated one of the piemen but Fraser shook his head.

"Are you sure?" I asked. "There's no guarantee our fellow will appear before noon."

Fraser shook his head again. "I can't imagine being able to eat," he said, swallowing hard.

"How much worse it must be for Mr Robertson," I said.

We pushed our way through the crowd to the door of the main courtroom. It was still blocked by a guard, but he recognised my coat and stood aside with a respectful nod to allow us to pass. Fraser walked ahead of me and then stopped. I have attended the sessions court so often that I forget the impression it makes on people who see it for the first time. It was an overcast day, so the curtains were pulled back from the tall windows to allow as much light as possible into the room. The bench and the lawyers' table were still empty, as was the jury box, but a few favoured spectators had already gained access to the gallery and were shifting along the benches to gauge their preferred location for the day's viewing. I put my hand on Fraser's shoulder and indicated a place at the end of one of the lower rows in the gallery; I had no intention of spending my whole day here.

We were only just in time; a few minutes later a clock chimed the hour and the guard opened the door. A clerk had taken up his position just inside and took the fee from each spectator who entered. Some obviously had their favourite place to sit and headed for it without hesitation, while others gazed about the room, assessing its potential. Once the gallery was full the door was shut – we could hear protests from those still in the yard just before the door was closed on them – and the business of the court began. The lawyers gathered at their table, their clerks bringing in their books for them and stacking them in piles within easy reach. The jury filed into their box. And finally the judges took to their bench. As these stern men arrived, taking an elevated position from which they could survey the whole courtroom, the uncompromising sword of justice on the wall behind them, I felt Fraser shrink a little beside me. If he had had his hat on his head rather than in his lap, I had the distinct feeling he would have pulled it lower over his eyes. I resisted the urge to say anything comforting to him; his discomfort was part of my plan.

The senior judge, sitting in the centre of the bench, was Mr Justice Park. His long nose had become bonier and more pronounced over the years I had known him, and now gave him the appearance of a bird of prey looking down from his eyrie. He was a stickler for formality and rules, which one might expect in a judge, and fair and sensible in his findings, which in my experience was rather rarer.

The first three trials followed the same pattern; two pickpockets and one manservant were found guilty and sentenced to transportation. The manservant's master spoke angrily in the witness box – outraged that the fellow could no longer be sent to the scaffold. The fourth trial was the one I had wanted Fraser to see, on the recommendation of John Wontner, who had sent me word the previous day. As soon as the manservant had left the dock, his place was taken by a tall, pale man of middle years, who placed his hands on the ledge of the box –

even from a distance, we could see that he was shaking. The mirror angled above his head reflected the milky light onto his face, so that the judges could see him more clearly. He looked up to the gallery, behind us, and I turned to see a woman staring at him, rigid in her seat.

The clerk who stood at a lectern at one end of the lawyers' table looked down at the paper in front of him and in a voice devoid of all emotion read aloud. "William Robertson, you stand indicted, for that you on the 11th of August, at St James, Clerkenwell, feloniously did dispose of and put away a forged and counterfeit banknote (number 10880, for five pounds, dated the 17th of May 1829, signed G Munro) with intent to defraud the Governor and Company of the Bank of England, well knowing the same to be forged and counterfeit. You also stand indicted for that you did feloniously offer to Abigail Levin a like forged and counterfeit banknote, with a like intent, knowing it to be forged and counterfeit. You also stand indicted of intending to defraud Aaron Levin." The clerk now looked up at the man trembling in the dock. "William Robertson, how say you? Are you guilty or not guilty of the said felony?"

The accused looked once again at the woman behind us, and then at the clerk. He studiously avoided looking at the judges, or at the gilt sword behind them. "Not guilty, sir," he said.

"How will you be tried?" asked the clerk.

"By God and my country," replied Robertson.

"William Robertson," responded the clerk, raising his arm to point at the jury, sitting in three tiers in the box to his left, "these good men are to pass between our Sovereign Lord the King, and you, life and judgment."

At these words, the spectators shifted in their seats, nudging any neighbours who had dozed off. Transportation was one thing, but seeing a man fight for his life, well, there was sport.

It was a year or two since I had watched the prosecution lawyer John Bosanquet at work. He retained the untidy look of a country gentleman called unexpectedly to the courtroom, his wig jammed on over his curly hair, but that hair was now thinning and greying. He still, however, smiled easily, and it was with what sounded to me a tone of regret that he called the first witness, Abigail Levin. She climbed the steps to the stand, in a tidy green frock and neat hat, and inclined her head to the judges. But when she spoke, there was a tremor in her voice that suggested she was not as composed as she wanted to appear. She confirmed that she was indeed Abigail Levin, wife of Isaac Levin, a clothes salesman, and that they lived above their shop at 29 Holywell Street, near the Strand. I knew the alleyway well; its cramped, overhanging buildings and dingy courts were home to radical thinkers – many who had fled from France – and publishers of books of a dubious nature, and seemingly a haberdasher as well. Bosanquet then asked her about what had happened on Tuesday 11th August.

"On that day," started Mrs Levin. Bosanquet smiled at her and made an upward motion with his hand, and she spoke more loudly. "On that day, a man came into the shop, with a young woman."

"Can you see that man here today?" asked Bosanquet, indicating with a sweep of his arm the entire courtroom.

Mrs Levin looked behind her, to the prisoner in the dock and pointed at him. "He is there."

"Thank you, Mrs Levin," said the lawyer graciously. "And what did this man want in your shop?"

"The young woman asked for some cloth to make a pelisse," replied Mrs Levin. "She had seen a pattern she liked and Mr Levin took down the bolt for her. I asked her how much she wanted and she asked how much it would take, and I said two yards and a half. She then said she wanted a matching cape, and I said a yard more would do. Then she turned to the man and he said that he would have a waistcoat off the same cloth, and I might as well cut four yards and a half, and I did."

"And how much was the cost of the four yards and a half, madam?" asked Bosanquet. "For those of us who are neither haberdashers nor seamstresses." He glanced at the bench and was rewarded with a very small smile from Mr Justice Park.

"Two pounds and nine shillings," she replied. "The man put a five-pound note on the counter and said, 'Here, give me change of this.' I suspected it to be forged."

Here Bosanquet put up a hand to stop her. "Why, Mrs Levin? Why did you suspect it to be forged? Was it a poor-quality counterfeit?"

The witness shook her head. "No, not at all – the note itself seemed good. It was more the manner of the man and the woman. They didn't seem like husband and wife – a married couple would have decided before what they were going to buy, but these, well, it was like they were finding ways to spend money. And what man wants a waistcoat made of the same material as his wife's pelisse?" At this, a few men in the courtroom laughed. "And when he put down the note, he was nervous. I could see it in him. And she looked at me, not at the note or her husband or the cloth – at me."

The lawyer paused for a few moments to let the jury digest what they had heard and then asked, "What did you do next, Mrs Levin?"

"I asked the man for his name and address. He said Whitfield, 218 Tottenham Court Road, which I wrote on the note, along with my husband's initials AL."

"Is this the note?" asked Bosanquet, picking up a banknote from his pile of papers and passing it to Mrs Levin.

She looked at it. "Yes, here it is written – Whitfield, 218 Tottenham Court Road, AL." She handed the note back to Bosanquet, who passed it to a clerk, who walked to the bench and reached up to hand it to the judge. Bosanquet indicated to Mrs Levin that she should continue.

"I said that I would have to send my son out to get change. I called him – Joseph, he's nine – and told him in Yiddish to take the note to my brother-in-law and to ask him to come to the shop. Samuel – my brother-in-law – works for a jeweller in Hatton Garden and knows more about these things. When my husband came down, I explained to him in Yiddish what had happened. After about a quarter of an hour, the man said, 'I cannot stop for the change' and told the woman, 'You wait for it and take it and I will meet you by and by', and then he left, and my husband followed him. After another quarter hour or so, Samuel and Joseph arrived. And Samuel said to the woman, 'This note is forged – what do you know about it?'. And she pushed past him out of the shop and ran off."

"Thank you, Mrs Levin," said Bosanquet. "You have been admirably clear in your evidence. You may go."

The woman once again inclined her head to the bench and walked down the steps of the stand. Her place was taken by her husband, whose story confirmed everything his wife had said, up to the point where the accused had left the shop.

"Now, Mr Levin," said Bosanquet, "your wife has told us that you followed the prisoner when he left your shop."

Aaron Levin was, like his wife, dressed in elegant clothes – which surprised me less now that I knew their line of work. And, like her, he spoke softly until reminded to keep his voice up. "I did, yes," he confirmed. "I followed him down towards St Clement's church, then he turned back towards Holywell Street but did not go along it; instead he went into a public house in the Strand and came straight back out with another man. They crossed over to Somerset House. I ran back to the shop to see if my son had returned, and when Abigail told me that the woman had gone, I ran back to Somerset House and saw the... the prisoner and the other man standing at Somerset House gateway." He looked at the lawyer, who nodded. "I went up to the prisoner and said he must come back with me because there was something not right in the change of the note. He said he would come back in a quarter of an hour and I said he must come back straight away, and he said, 'If I must', and came quietly with me. The other man said nothing to me and walked off. By the time we returned to the shop, a constable was waiting with Abigail and took the prisoner away."

"Did the prisoner attempt to get away?" asked Bosanquet. "Did he run from you, at Somerset House or as you walked back to the shop?"

Mr Levin shook his head. "No. Once I insisted, he was quiet and did what I told him."

"Thank you, Mr Levin," said the lawyer. "You may leave the stand."

Mr Levin walked down the steps of the stand and looked around for his wife. She was standing near the door and beckoned to him.

Bosanquet turned to the bench. "We have several more witnesses, my Lord, but their evidence is less detailed than that of Mr and Mrs Levin." And so it proved.

Thomas Corbett confirmed that he was a bookseller, living above his shop at 218 Tottenham Court Road, that no-one of the name of Whitfield lived at his address, and that he had never seen the prisoner before.

Joel Cox told the court that he was a court stationer, with a shop in Liquor Pond Street. In the first week of August – he could not be sure of the date – a man who resembled the prisoner had come into his shop and tried to buy some skins of parchment. When Mr Cox had asked his name, he said he was buying them for a Mr Price in St John Square and offered a five-pound note in payment. But Mr Cox became uneasy at his manner and turned him away.

John Price was then called and said that he had lived at 5 St John Square some nine years previously, but now lived in St James's Walk in Clerkenwell. He looked sadly at the prisoner in the dock and said that he had known him, some years ago, but had not seen him recently and was sorry to see him in this situation. He confirmed that no, he had not sent the prisoner to buy those items for him from Mr Cox's shop.

I looked at William Robertson in the dock. All the colour had drained from his face and he was now not so much leaning on the ledge as slumped against it. I nudged Fraser and pointed at the prisoner. "You see

how it affects him," I said quietly. Fraser nodded wordlessly.

"My Lord," said Bosanquet, turning to the bench, "we
shall now hear from Mr Munro, of the Bank of England."

"I am a clerk of the Bank of England," confirmed
George Munro, "and it is my duty to sign one-pound and
two-pound banknotes."

"Not five-pound notes?" asked the lawyer.

"No, never," replied Munro.

"And so not this five-pound note, which," Bosanquet
took the banknote from the clerk, who had just retrieved
it from Lord Justice Park, and examined it dramatically,
"I see bears the signature of G Munro." He handed the
note back to the clerk, who walked around the desk and
passed the note to the witness.

Munro looked carefully at the note, turning it over
and then back again. He shook his head. "It's a good
job," he admitted, "but that is not my signature. I do not
sign five-pound notes."

There was a general sighing and tutting in the courtroom. Munro left the stand and Bosanquet turned once
again to the bench.

"My Lord," he said, "you have heard all the witnesses
for the prosecution. The prisoner uttered a counterfeit

banknote in the shop of Mr and Mrs Levin, fully knowing it to be counterfeit and intending to defraud both them and the Governor and Company of the Bank of England. The prisoner offers no defence, save to deny that he was aware that the banknote was counterfeit, but offers one witness as to his character."

Robertson looked up as the door to the witness room opened and a man was led to the stand. The new arrival gave Robertson a warm glance and then turned to face the bench.

"I am John Chew," he replied in response to prompting from Bosanquet. "I live in Carnaby Street, Golden Square, and I have known Will... the prisoner for fifteen years. His father lived near me some years ago, and we became acquainted. In all that time I never knew a stain on his character."

"What has been his business during the last year?" asked the lawyer.

"He was once a schoolteacher, but then he became unwell," said Chew, "and now I do not know his employment. I suspect he has none. He called on me a fortnight before this incident, and appeared distressed, and asked for relief. I gave him a shilling. I wish that I had given him more." The witness shook his head sadly. "He told me he should be happy to take a pot boy's place, and that he had not broken his fast for twenty-four hours."

"Would you say that he was a desperate man, Mr Chew?" asked Bosanquet.

"Without a doubt, sir," said Chew. "I should have been a better friend, and for that I ask forgiveness."

Chew left the stand and Bosanquet turned to the bench. "That, my Lord, concludes the case for the prosecution," he said, and bowed his head.

Mr Justice Park nodded at him and looked at the papers in front of him, on which he had been making occasional notes. He then lifted his head and looked across at the jury. "Gentlemen," he began, "the prisoner before you is indicted for disposing of and putting away a forged and counterfeit banknote with intent to defraud the Governor and Company of the Bank of England, well knowing the same to be forged and counterfeit. He is also indicted for offering a forged and counterfeit banknote to Abigail Levin, with a like intent, knowing it to be forged and counterfeit, in other words, uttering, and for intending to defraud Aaron Levin. What you have to decide is this. First, was the banknote forged and counterfeit? We have heard from Mr Munro that it was, and so this first point is proved. Second, did the prisoner dispose of and put away the banknote, and offer it to Abigail Levin? You have heard from both Mr and Mrs Levin that the prisoner is the man who came into their shop and offered the banknote, and that the banknote was marked by them as he did so. And so the second point is proved. Finally, did the prisoner at the time of offering the banknote, know it to be forged and counterfeit?" The judge paused and the foreman of the jury nodded to show that they were paying attention.

Mr Justice Park continued. "We have heard from Mrs Levin that what concerned her was not the banknote but rather the behaviour of the prisoner." He glanced down at his notes. "The manner of the man and the woman, she said. We have heard that the prisoner gave Mrs Levin a false name. And he made some attempt to escape – although the fact that he returned, when his female companion did not, should count in his favour. And we heard from Mr Cox that someone resembling the prisoner had attempted to offer him a banknote about which he was uneasy. Mr Cox could not be certain in his identification of the prisoner, but the prisoner did say that he was buying items for a Mr Price, who confirmed that he had once known the prisoner – who would therefore have known Mr Price's line of business and his address. It is for you to decide whether this all suggests that the prisoner did know when he offered the banknote that it was forged and counterfeit, when he claims that he did not." The judge stopped talking and nodded curtly at the foreman of the jury.

As the twelve jurymen leaned towards each other to confer, I turned to Fraser. "Do you recognise Mr Robertson?" I asked.

"The prisoner, you mean?" asked Fraser, looking over at the dock. He shook his head.

"He works for you," I said.

"For me?" said Fraser with surprise.

"Oh, you wouldn't know him," I said. "You have dozens, maybe even hundreds – who knows? Mr Robertson is one of those poor fellows who, finding himself out at heels, is catmint for your recruiting sergeants. Once respectable and desperate to be so again, he's offered an easy way to make a few shillings. Just buy a few things with this banknote and bring us the change. No trouble at all for an honest-looking fellow like you. But best not to use your own name, just in case. Tell me, Mr Fraser, how much do you pay a person for uttering one of your counterfeit banknotes?"

The man on the other side of Fraser caught this last question and looked at us with interest, nudging his wife to pay attention. Fraser shifted in his seat but stayed silent.

"And when it goes wrong, Mr Fraser," I continued, "when the poor fellow is found out and brought into this," I gestured around the courtroom, "and when his very life lies in the hands of twelve strangers," I nodded towards the jury box, "where are you and your lieutenants?" I saw several of the jurymen sitting back in their seats as the foreman smoothed down his waistcoat. "Here we go, Mr Fraser: will it be the rope for your man?"

Fraser looked at me, his face a picture of misery.

The foreman of the jury rose to his feet and the clerk called out, "Silence in court."

Mr Justice Park looked down from the bench at the foreman. "How say you?" he asked. "Are you agreed upon your verdict?"

"We are agreed," said the foreman, a meaty fellow with generous jowls and what Martha called prosperous whiskers.

"Is the prisoner at the bar guilty or not guilty?"

"Guilty of uttering a forged and counterfeit banknote, knowing it to be forged and counterfeit."

Fraser leaned forward, gripping the rail in front of us with a white-knuckled hand. Behind us, the woman I had seen earlier – Robertson's wife, or perhaps sister – sobbed quietly, her hand to her mouth.

The judge nodded as he made a note. "And are there any recommendations to mercy?" he asked.

Bosanquet stood. "I recommend the prisoner to mercy," he said, "on account of his previous good character, as testified to by Mr Chew, and on account of his distressed situation."

The foreman of the jury then spoke. "We recommend the prisoner to mercy for the same reasons."

Mr Justice Park now addressed the prisoner, who was weeping. "Mr Robertson, you have heard the verdict of the jury, and the recommendations to mercy. Have you anything to say to me before I pass sentence on you?"

William Robertson steadied himself against the front of the dock and stood a little more upright. He took a handkerchief from his pocket and wiped his face.

"Thank you, sir," he said. "I am grateful. My tears are not for myself, but for my wife and my children and the shame I have brought upon them." He looked up at the gallery behind us and then back at the bench. "I was a schoolteacher once, but medical expenses – we lost two children.… I was desperate, sir – I did not know where to go for help. But should not have done what I did, and

I ask humbly for the forgiveness of the court and of God Almighty."

"Mr Robertson," said Mr Justice Park, "I have some sympathy for your situation. But as an educated man – a schoolteacher, no less – you know right from wrong. We cannot allow such attacks on our currency to go unpunished, if trust is to be retained by ordinary men in the worth of our banknotes. Uttering is rightly a capital offence," I heard Fraser take a sharp breath, "but in light of the applications to mercy made by both Mr Bosanquet and the jury, and your own evident remorse, your sentence is commuted to transportation for a period of twenty-one years."

Fraser looked at me, bleakly. "It's as good as death for a man like that," he said. "And what of his wife and children? If they were struggling before, what of them now?"

"What indeed, Mr Fraser?" I asked.

CHAPTER TWENTY-ONE

Different ambitions

FRIDAY 28TH AUGUST 1829

As Edward Fraser and I walked into the banking hall, everything went silent. I doubted Freame had told his clerks who his visitor was, but information like this is hard to keep quiet, and the eyes of Harris the senior clerk followed us as we walked towards the door leading to the parlour. The junior clerk, Stevenson, slipped from his stool and walked noiselessly to meet us.

"Constable Plank," he said solemnly, bowing his head. He glanced at Fraser and then away. He took our hats and then went before us to knock on the door of the parlour.

"Your visitors, sir," he said, opening the door and then stepping back.

I went first and shook the banker's hand. His face did not break into its usual smile of welcome, but he courteously held out his hand to Fraser.

"Samuel," he said, "and Mr Fraser. A pleasure to see you both. Please, come in." He indicated two chairs; the third, with a newspaper draped over its arm, was his own, and in the middle of the group was a table with cups, saucers and a covered plate already on it. "The teapot, if you would, Stevenson," he said to the clerk, who nodded and withdrew, closing the door.

Fraser took a seat and then looked around him, but not in an impertinent way. "I have never been invited into a bank like this before," he said. "A respectable place, I mean."

"But you have been into other banks?" asked Freame. "Disreputable places?"

Fraser smiled. "Disreputable is probably going too far," he replied, "but certainly catering to a different sort of customer."

"Criminals, Mr Fraser?" asked Freame.

Fraser nodded. There was a quiet knock on the door and Stevenson came in with the teapot. At a look from Freame, Stevenson bent over the table and, biting his lip in concentration, slowly filled our cups from the pot. When he had finished, without spilling a drop, and had put the teapot onto the table, without clattering it, he stood up straight and smiled broadly before remembering and looking serious once more.

"Thank you, Stevenson," said Freame. "And please do thank your mother for the fruit loaf."

Stevenson nodded and left the room, again closing the door behind him.

"In all honesty," said the banker with a smile, "Mrs Stevenson's fruit loaves can be a little dry, but with a cup of tea, we will manage. If a gentleman ever finds a way to suggest improvements to a lady's cooking without risking life and limb, he will make a fortune by sharing his secret." He took the napkin from the plate and passed it to us, and we each selected a slice. After a few moments of silent chewing and sipping, we began the business of our meeting.

"Mr Fraser," said Freame, wiping his mouth with a napkin and putting his cup and plate onto the floor beside his chair, "I will be honest and say that I never expected to entertain a fraudsman in my bank. Your crimes strike at the very heart of my work, and although I would certainly not want to see you hang for them, I would find it hard to argue against a long stay in Newgate."

Fraser nodded. "And I am grateful to you for agreeing to meet me, Mr Freame," he said. "Constable Plank tells me that you are a Quaker."

"I am, yes," said our host.

"As I understand it, sir," said Fraser, putting down his own cup and leaning forward, "one of your beliefs is that there is something of God in everyone."

Freame raised an eyebrow. "You have been learning about Quakers?" he asked.

"It is an old habit, sir," replied Fraser. "You called me a fraudsman, and you are right: for many years, I ran schemes to part people from their money. And as Constable Plank can tell you, the most successful fraudsmen are those who study their victims: the better you know a man, the easier it is to fool him." He caught sight of a look on the banker's face. "I am not boasting, sir. I am ashamed of my past. But you wondered how I knew about your faith."

"I did," said Freame, leaning back in his chair and looking at Fraser appraisingly for a few moments. "Why are you ashamed of your past? Or more precisely, why have you just now become ashamed of your past – I certainly agree that being a fraudsman is shameful."

Fraser blinked in surprise; perhaps he had not believed me when I told him that Freame, despite his soft heart and deep faith, was a realistic man who had spent his life in a city with crime and despair on every corner. "Yes, sir, it is," said Fraser when he had recovered himself. "But for many years I did not think so, because the world in which I lived had different standards. Different ambitions. My father was a thief, my older brother too – and when I had brains enough to be a fraudsman instead of dipping my hand into people's pockets, they were proud. And when I became a good fraudsman and ran my own mob, they were prouder still."

The banker nodded. "We learn our values from those around us, it is true," he said.

"Aye," agreed Fraser, "and that is what has changed." He looked at me. "You have told Mr Freame about Robertson's trial?" I shook my head and he turned back to Freame. "The day before yesterday, Constable Plank took me to see a trial. A man called Robertson, accused of uttering a counterfeit banknote. He worked for me, only I didn't know it. A schoolteacher fallen on hard times – my men know how to sniff out such people." He shook his head sadly.

"Do you expect me to believe that you never once thought of what your... organisation was doing?" asked Freame.

"Only in terms of money," admitted Fraser miserably. "The money it made for me. And to see that poor fellow, and his wife – he won't survive the voyage to Van Diemen's Land, let alone what awaits him there." He fell silent.

"You have every reason to be sceptical, Edward," I said to Freame. "We've both heard every tale in the book. But I've been following Mr Fraser for years now, and I'm minded to give him the benefit of the doubt. And so is Mrs Plank."

Freame looked at Fraser appraisingly; I knew the banker had a great deal of respect for my wife and her opinions of people.

"To be completely honest, Mr Freame," said Fraser, "I'm not being entirely selfless. There's something I want now more than money, and the only way I can get it is by mending my ways. The woman I want to marry – Johanna Kaufmann."

"Kaufmann?" repeated the banker, looking from Fraser to me.

"The daughter," I confirmed.

Fraser's face softened as he spoke. "Johanna is a simple girl. I don't mean stupid – I mean that for her the world is clear. There are good actions and bad actions, and she knows that she wants nothing more to do with the bad ones. When her father went to Newgate, she was a dutiful daughter – and thank heavens for that, otherwise I would never have met her. But having seen the poor wretches in there, and their wives and children brought low through no fault of their own, she resolved that for her own husband she would choose only a good man." He paused and looked down at his hands, which were clasped in his lap almost in prayer. "And I was not a good man, Mr Freame. I never felt the need to be a good man – until now." He looked up again. "Johanna knows about my past – well, most of it. But she also believes that a man can change. And I have promised her that I will change."

"And yet, here you are, Mr Fraser, encouraging Johanna's father to break the law again," said Freame. "That is not the action of a man who wishes to change."

"But I had a good reason for it," said Fraser.

"A good reason for breaking the law?" asked Freame, raising an eyebrow.

"A good reason for the counterfeiting," said Fraser. "It wasn't only to make money." He sat forward in his seat. "I think gambling hells are evil. And I thought that if word got out that you cannot trust the banknotes that they hand out, then it might make people keep away."

The banker looked at me and I shrugged.

"I am interested, Mr Fraser," said Freame. "What makes a fraudsman take against gambling? Both fraud and gambling are designed to separate a man from his money."

"Aye," said Fraser, "but a man will fall victim to a fraud once, perhaps twice, whereas once gambling enters his blood, then it rules his life – and he will fall victim to it every day. And yet this activity is legal – encouraged by the government. It makes no sense." He shook his head. "And Crockford's is the worst of them all. The others – White's, Brooks's – restrict their membership: you have to be wealthy to belong. And a wealthy man losing at the tables is not often ruinous. But the fishmonger – he welcomes everyone. Anyone can gamble at his hell – and they do. Men of modest means, losing everything. While Crockford himself grows fatter and richer."

"So you thought that if you could infiltrate his establishment with counterfeit banknotes," said Freame, "word would spread and his custom would drain away."

Fraser nodded.

"Well, it's an interesting theory," said the banker, "but I am not convinced that the ends justify the means in this case. Even if your scheme were to work, you would simply replace the harm caused by gambling with the harm caused by counterfeiting – not least to Mr Kaufmann, who once again will face the scaffold for his actions."

Fraser's shoulders slumped. "I see now that it was not a wise course of action, and you have little reason to trust me, Mr Freame," he said, "but I had hoped that if I came to see you with Constable Plank, and explained my plan and how I hope to make amends…"

"Ah," said the banker. "Hence your reminder that we Quakers find something of God in everyone. Very well, Mr Fraser: what is your plan?"

"To go to Vienna with Johanna and our baby, and her father and brother," replied Fraser promptly, "and to make an honest living there. Herr Kaufmann is a talented artist but he lacks business sense. And I know all about persuading people to buy. There is much call for portrait painters in Vienna and we shall set up a family business: Herr Kaufmann will paint and teach his son Gregor, and I will find customers. Johanna tells me that Vienna is very popular with visitors now that the wars are over, and I think we will start Gregor on painting little landscapes, small pictures of important buildings in the city, for people to buy to take home as a keepsake."

"All very laudable, Mr Fraser," said the banker. "But we cannot escape the fact that you will be starting your business with tainted money – money made from fraud, from other people's misery. And from counterfeiting."

I looked from one man to the other with interest: they seemed matched in intellect but one had turned his gift to the good and the other had chosen a darker path.

Fraser sat forward in his haste to reply. "No, we cannot, Mr Freame. Johanna said much the same when I suggested it to her. But Constable Plank has thought of something, and we would need your help."

◆

Wilson looked at me, weighing up what I had told him. "But what about Mr Conant?" he asked.

"I called on him this morning, straight after my meeting with Mr Freame and Mr Fraser," I said, "and explained my idea. I told him what Fraser told us, that he conceived of the counterfeiting as a way to force Mr Crockford out of business, but that he had nothing to do with the murder of young Madden."

"And you believe him? You believe a fraudsman – someone who makes his living from deceiving people?" asked Wilson, picking up his tankard and putting it down again, disappointed to see that it was empty. The observant pot boy appeared at my elbow and I signalled for two more drinks. Martha would have something to say about it, but there wouldn't be many more evenings when Wilson and I could meet like this. A second child would be arriving soon, and I knew that his determination to do well in the new police would swallow every minute of time that he was not with his family.

"I do," I said. "I'm no Quaker, seeing God in everyone, but I have seen enough people turn away from a bad path to know that it's possible. And if someone wants to try, genuinely wants to try, then we should do everything we can to encourage them."

The refilled tankards arrived and we both took a drink.

"You mean Alice," said Wilson.

"I was not thinking of Alice," I said truthfully, "but yes, look at the wonderful changes she has made to her life." We both fell silent, thinking back to the bedraggled creature I had found all those years ago, cowering in a filthy yard, giving birth to a scrap of a baby fathered by God knows who. And now she was a young wife and mother, proudly and devotedly married to Wilson, who in turn would gladly walk to the ends of the Earth for her.

Wilson spoke first. "Things are changing, you know. With the new police. Arrangements like this," he swirled his tankard in illustration, "well, it won't be the same.

We'll have to account for everything – make a record of it all. Every arrest, every charge, every person spoken to."

"And so do we, officially," I said. "But the new police will soon learn what we learned – that there are some arrangements," and I swirled my tankard as he had done, "that are just right. And this is one of those cases. Fraser hands over all the money he has made from his crimes, including this latest counterfeiting caper. Mr Freame sees that the money is spent on worthy causes, with an eye to steering other young people away from danger. And he then makes a loan to Fraser and Kaufmann, to get them started in their new venture."

"In Vienna," finished Wilson.

I shook my head. "Actually, that was another condition of Mr Freame's involvement. He was of the view that Vienna would offer too much temptation – that previous unsavoury connections might prove irresistible, and that it is too hard to start again with a reputation around your neck. He has agreed to our plan, as long as the family goes to Canada instead – he has suggested Quebec."

"And he trusts Fraser to repay the loan, once he has set foot in Quebec and can disappear into that vast land?" asked Wilson.

I shook my head. "Mr Freame is no fool – you don't run a successful banking house for decades without developing a nose for this kind of thing. He doesn't trust Fraser, or at least not yet, but he does trust Kaufmann and even more so, he trusts Johanna. He went to Hunt Street and spoke to father and daughter, and he knows a strong woman when he meets one." I drained my tankard and cocked my ear to the sound of the church bells. "And talking of strong women, we had better be on our way, or it will be the dog-house for both of us."

Wilson put out a hand to stop me. "Aye," he said, "I can see all of that, but aren't you letting criminals escape justice? Fraser is a fraudsman and Kaufmann is a counterfeiter – if they get away unpunished, well, all the wild rogues in London will take heart."

"Freame has beaten you to it, my friend," I said. "As a Quaker he cannot countenance the thought of the scaffold, but he is very much in favour of criminals making amends to society. As a condition of the loan, Fraser has to put out the word that he has been snared by a scheme cleverer than his own, and that he and Kaufmann have lost everything and must flee the country in fear of their lives. He has also handed over the names of those involved in his frauds and the counterfeiting, so that we can visit them. If they seem amenable to mending their ways, we can steer them onto the right path – and if not, the magistrates can have them." I stood up. "And there's one final thing: Fraser knows of your move to the new police, and says to tell you that there's all sorts of rogues planning to join."

"Criminals joining the Metropolitan Police?" repeated Wilson.

"It's a clever idea, lad," I replied. "What better for a criminal than to be on the inside, getting information on how things are working, committing crimes with impunity, knowing you'll never have to face the magistrates."

♦

"That was kind of you, telling Wilson about Fraser's warning," said Martha, holding out her hand for my plate. I pretended to hesitate and then complied, so that she could serve me another ladle of stew.

"He can make better use of it than I can," I said, dipping my bread into the gravy. "Or at any rate, he will get more benefit from it. I'm long past the age when I need to prove myself."

Martha looked at me and tilted her head. "I hope that doesn't mean you're just going to sit around the place, getting in my way," she said. "You've plenty of fight left in you yet, Sam Plank. Old age comes soon enough –

there's no need to beckon it in." She sat back in her seat. "Have you thought about William's idea – about you helping to train the new police officers?"

"Not really," I lied. In truth, the closer came the launch of the new police, the more I realised how much I would miss my work. The magistrates would retain their constables, but our duties would be curtailed – and, I feared, our reputation would suffer in comparison with that of the new police. From what Wilson told me and from what I read in the newspapers, it seemed that the two Commissioners of the Metropolitan Police were setting up a professional, well-organised and efficient force, and I had no wish to end my working life playing second fiddle to them and begging for scraps from their table.

"If you say so," said Martha, standing to clear our plates and not believing me for one second. "Go and read the newspaper next door," she instructed. "I'll be through in a minute."

I was just dozing off when she came into the sitting room, wiping her hands on her apron before untying it and draping it over the back of her chair. She reached for her mending basket.

"Do you think Mr Freame and I are right about Fraser?" I asked.

"About letting him make a fresh start in Canada, you mean?" she asked. I nodded. "What's worrying you, Sam? It's not like you to have second thoughts."

I held up the newspaper. "There's a poor fellow in here," I said, "sentenced to hang for uttering. But when they went to his cell to collect him and take him to the scaffold, they found him dead in his bed, an empty vial of prussic acid on the floor. His friends said they knew he would do it – he'd told them he wouldn't 'dangle like a dog'."

"Acid is a painful way to go," said Martha, matching her thread to a piece of linen. "But uttering, Sam – it's a risk you take."

"Aye," I agreed, "but it says here," I opened the newspaper again, "it says here that he had a sweetheart. She was expecting, and he took the counterfeit note out of desperation. He was trying to buy things for the baby. He left a note for the prison surgeon, asking for his heart to be preserved in spirits and given to the young woman as a reminder of his love for her and their baby."

Martha put down the cloth and looked at me. "It's a sad tale, Sam, but why has it upset you?"

"The fellow didn't make the counterfeit note – he fell in with the wrong crowd and was tempted into crime," I explained. "It's the counterfeiter who is at fault – a counterfeiter like Fraser. And Kaufmann. Fraser may not have killed Madden, but who knows how many other fellows like this one," I tapped the newspaper, "have come to a dreadful end thanks to his work."

Martha leaned across and took the newspaper from me, then put her hand over mine. "Listen to me, Sam," she said. "After more than thirty years as a constable, surely you know that nothing is ever black and white – no-one is completely good and no-one is completely evil. People make bad decisions and foolish choices, and some of them never realise their errors. But Mr Fraser and Mr Kaufmann have chosen to turn their back on crime, and you and Mr Freame have chosen to help them. And Mr Conant thinks you are right to do so." She squeezed my hand. "Do you know how wonderful it is, Sam, that after three decades in your uniform you can still see the good in people who have done bad things? I pray you never change."

A thrilling ride

MONDAY 14TH SEPTEMBER 1829

We made an odd little group, standing in the yard of the Swan with Two Necks, waiting for the mail coach to Liverpool to board. It made more sense for them to leave London at night, to avoid being spotted by anyone who knew them, and I had secured two seats inside for Kaufmann and his daughter, while Fraser and the lad would sit on top. The promise of a thrilling ride had distracted Gregor – indeed, his eyes were like plates as he watched the bustle of the coaching inn – but the young bride Johanna was pale and quiet. From time to time her father looked at her and she gave him a tiny, brave smile. They had brought a basket of provisions made by Birgit and – Kaufmann told me – watered by her tears. The maid's

Smithfield porter had asked her to marry him and she was staying in London, but she was fond of the Kaufmann family and knew they were parting forever. To their supplies I added a walnut loaf and some apples from Martha, with a bag of barley twists for Gregor.

"Ah, there you are," called a voice, and I turned to see Edward Freame trotting into the yard. "I thought I would miss you – I'm not as fleet of foot as I used to be." He stopped alongside us and took a few deep breaths, then held out his hand. "Herr Kaufmann," he said, "Mr Fraser." He tipped his hat to Johanna. "And Mrs Fraser." He pulled an envelope from his coat pocket. "Constable Plank has already given you your tickets, I assume, for the coach?" Fraser patted the satchel that he wore across his body and nodded. "Excellent. You should arrive in Liverpool at about this time tomorrow evening, and you are to make your way to this address." He handed the envelope to Fraser. "It is our meeting house in Liverpool, and not far from the docks. There is a letter inside, addressed to Mr Thurston – he will make sure that you are given clean, safe lodgings for the night with one of our number." Fraser opened his mouth to speak, but Freame held up his hand. "We do not have long, Mr Fraser, and there is more to tell you." He pulled a second envelope from his pocket and handed it to Fraser. "In this one are the tickets for the boat. I have taken advice and chosen carefully: the *New Felix Souligny* is a modern vessel, and fast – you are expected to reach Quebec by the end of October. The captain, a fellow called Painchaud, is reliable and honest, and you need have no fears about him refusing your tickets. His consignment is salt, but he has berths for six passengers and is accustomed to taking settlers, so can help you with the formalities when you arrive."

"Mr Freame," said Kaufmann with emotion in his voice, "you do too much for us. We are in your debt."

"Nonsense, sir," said Freame brusquely, but I could tell he was pleased. "Everyone has a duty to do what he can for his fellow man. Now, there are not many Quakers in Canada, but in with your tickets I have put a note introducing you. I believe that the largest Congregation is based at a place called East Farnham, some one hundred and fifty miles from the port where you will arrive, but should you decide to ask for their help, it will be given. I have written the address on the paper."

"Liverpool!" shouted a man. "The Albion for Liverpool – leaving in ten minutes!"

Johanna grasped her father's arm and he patted her hand and said something quietly to her, I assume in their own language.

"A word, Mr Fraser, if I may," I said to him, stepping away from the group. He followed me. "Now you remember our arrangement," I said. "Mr Freame is a kind man and a hopeful one, always looking for the best in people, but he is no fool: the Quakers are not the only people he knows in Quebec, and word will soon reach us if you're up to your old tricks."

"It's not Mr Freame who'll keep me in line, Constable Plank," Fraser said, nodding towards Johanna. "When you first knew me, I had nothing to lose. But now, well, she's made it very clear that it's an honest life for all of us, or I'll be on my own. And I have lost the taste for the bachelor life."

"I'm glad to hear it," I said. "And you've been spreading the word here that you're on the run, only one step ahead of the hangman?"

"I have, yes," he said. "But won't it look bad for you, me slipping from your grip? After all, there's plenty that know you've been after me for a while."

"I'm past caring what strangers think of me," I said, "and those whose good opinion I value will know the truth. Anyway, I'm on my way out – it's the new police who'll have to worry about your successors."

"Come, Edward," called Johanna. "It's time." She gathered her bags as we walked back to them. "Constable Plank, please thank your wife for the loaf and the fruit. Gregor, what do you say to the constable, for your Süßigkeiten?"

Gregor tore his eyes from the spectacle long enough to say, "Thank you very much, sir." He was dancing from foot to foot, impatient to start his adventure.

Fraser helped Johanna and her father into the coach, handing in their bags which they tucked around them and under their feet. He checked that their trunks had been secured to the roof of the coach and then clambered up himself before leaning down and pulling Gregor up after him. At the boy's pleading, they had reserved the two seats behind the coachman, but I suspected that later in the journey Fraser would switch to ones further back, in the lee of the luggage, to give them some protection from the elements.

Freame and I walked up to the coach. I put my head inside and said farewell to the father and daughter, who had secured the two forward-facing seats and were talking quietly to each other. We then walked round to look up at Fraser.

"You have been afforded a second chance, Mr Fraser," I said.

"And you are wondering whether I deserve it," he said.

"It is not for me to say," I replied.

"Indeed," agreed Freame. "That is for God alone to decide. But for what it is worth, I would rather see you living an honest life in Quebec, bringing up a family of honest children, than rotting in a gaol in London, or swinging from a rope. You have assured me that you are capable of an honest life, Mr Fraser, and so I put my trust in you." He reached up and held out his hand to Fraser, who shook it. "I wish you Godspeed, sir," said the banker.

Fraser looked at me and held out his hand. I reached up and shook it. "May you fade into honest oblivion, Mr Fraser," I said, smiling. "You will understand if I say that I hope never to hear of you again."

As the coach pulled out of the yard, I turned to Freame. "Are we doing the right thing, my friend?" I asked.

The banker looked at me and shrugged slightly. "Only God knows the answer to that question, Sam," he said. "But I do know that sometimes punishment is not the best outcome."

I had to hope that he was right.

Parchment
and posterity

WEDNESDAY 16TH SEPTEMBER 1829

Martha indicated with a twirl of her hand that I should turn around. I sighed but did so.

"I'll not be meeting the King," I said.

"Who's to say?" she replied, plucking a piece of dust from my shoulder. "This is an important day for William, and you can't expect Alice to stand for hours waiting for him, not the size she is, so you'll have to do." She put her head to one side and looked more closely at my buttons. "Pass me the cloth," she said, taking it from me and giving each of the eight buttons a final rub. "With all those handsome young men on parade, you need to look your best."

"No-one is going to be looking at me," I said. "Everyone will want to see the new police, not an old campaigner like me."

♦

But I was wrong. When I arrived at Guilford Place and joined the small crowd waiting to be allowed into the grounds of the Foundling Hospital, two gentlemen approached me and asked whether I was a magistrates' constable, and then asked what I thought of the Metropolitan Police. One of them was making notes of my comments for a newspaper and I was careful to say how important it was for a growing city like London to have a modern police force. He asked whether I had heard about men leaving the force before they had even started their duties, but thankfully the gate was opened at that moment and we abandoned our conversation.

Of course, I knew from Wilson that there were some who, when they heard the regulations read aloud during one of their drill sessions, had decided that it was too much work for too little money and had resigned immediately. And the requirements were certainly considerable: a constable in the new force was expected to be available even when off duty, in case of emergency, and the pay was far from generous, particularly as the men had to buy their own uniform in instalments. Indeed, Wilson would be earning less as a Metropolitan Police constable than he had alongside me at Great Marlborough Street. But he would not be a constable for long, I was certain: his responsibilities and remuneration would increase, and a young man with a growing family must think to the future.

I took advantage of the funnelling of the crowd through the gateway to lose my two curious gentlemen and chose a position about a third of the way along the railings surrounding the parade ground. I knew that Wilson was in Division D, and guessed that his division would enter the ground fourth out of the six divisions. And with his surname being at the end of the alphabet, he would be at the rear of his division, which gave me some idea of where to look. With more than nine hundred men expected to drill, I wanted to be able to tell Martha and Alice that I had actually seen Wilson.

As the bell of the new church in Regent Square tolled nine, all eyes turned to watch the two Commissioners of the Metropolitan Police ride through the gateways. Charles Rowan, the former soldier, was about my age and sat comfortably on his horse, well accustomed to the parade ground. Richard Mayne, a barrister, was considerably younger than both of us, but looked much less at ease with his horse and his surroundings. The two men rode the length of the ground, finishing a long way from me, just in front of the porticoes of the main building of the hospital, and turned their horses to face back down the ground. Once the Commissioners were in position, the men of the Metropolitan Police began to march onto the ground. They filed two abreast through the twin gateways and then fanned out until they were marching eight men across. Sir Robert Peel's vision had been for a force that was disciplined and smart, yet did not remind Londoners of either an army or a secret police, but the influence of Rowan the soldier could be seen in the way the men marched. They were not yet in uniform – the contractors had been hard pushed to clothe so many in such a short time – but all wore sombre trousers and dark coats.

As luck would have it, Wilson was positioned on my side of the parade ground, only one man in from the side, and I had a good view of him. Martha had told me to whistle to attract his attention but of course I did no such thing. Nonetheless, I saw his eyes flick in my direction as he passed and I nodded in acknowledgement in case he had seen me.

♦

What passed between the Commissioners and the men was observed only by the assembled dignitaries, but Wilson told us about it later, as we gathered for a celebratory meal. I would have chosen a pie – Martha's pastry is a wonder to behold – but it was William's choice and so his first dinner as a constable with the Metropolitan Police was chops followed by plum crumble.

"I wish I could have seen you," said Alice, bouncing George on her knee and trying to distract him from reaching for everything on the table. He was at that age where everything he grabbed went straight to his mouth, and his chubby hands were surprisingly fast.

"You wouldn't have seen him anyway," I said. "With nigh on a thousand men marching past. Quite the sight, though."

William reached for the jug of custard and emptied it into his bowl. Martha smiled and wordlessly refilled the jug from the pan and passed it to me.

"What was it the Commissioner was reading out to you?" I asked. "I could hear the odd word here and there, but not all of it."

William swallowed a mouthful of pudding. "The General Instructions," he said. "We're each to get our own copy soon, when the printers are done. Telling us our duties and obligations. Nothing that we hadn't been told already, although some fellows seemed surprised and a few decided not to sign up."

"Ah," I said, "I wondered who they were, walking off the parade ground like that. What was their objection, do you know?"

"Some said that they didn't want to wear the uniform all the time, or that they didn't want to give up their other jobs," he replied, scraping his bowl with his spoon in search of drops of custard. "They thought that as we'll be working nights, they could carry on working during the day as well."

"And then what did you do?" asked Alice, catching George's hands in hers and playing ride a cock horse with him.

"Then we had to attest," said William. "We had to raise our right hand – like this – and swear to act as a constable for preserving the peace, preventing robberies and other felonies, and apprehending offenders against the peace."

Just then George let out a wail of frustration at being denied another swipe at the table, and we all laughed.

William held out his arms and Alice passed the child to him. "Let's see if I can preserve your peace, my little man," said William fondly. George continued to squall and William passed him quickly on to Martha, who handed George a wooden spoon, which he gnawed on happily and silently. "And then," continued William, "I had to sign my name on a roll of parchment to confirm that I accept the conditions of the job. The attestation register," he said grandly.

"Now you see why I made you practise writing your name, William," said Martha approvingly. "If it's on a parchment, stored for posterity, it needs to be neat."

Alice looked enquiringly at me. "What does posterity mean?" she asked quietly. I smiled at her; it had taken some doing, but we had finally persuaded Alice that asking questions was not a sign of ignorance but rather the most sensible way to learn.

"Forever," I said. "For all times. Wilson's name will be on a piece of parchment in a government department and centuries from now people will be able to read it and know what a good man he was." Martha looked at me with shining eyes and I cleared my throat. "Sadly, it will not record his gluttony when it comes to scoffing my custard."

CHAPTER TWENTY-FOUR

Officer 38
of D Division

MONDAY 21ST SEPTEMBER 1829

When I arrived home that evening, the kitchen was in turmoil. Martha and Alice were examining something on the table while Wilson sat to one side, bouncing George on his knee. I hung my coat on the peg and put my hand on Martha's shoulder. She half-turned to me, presenting her cheek for a kiss, but her attention stayed with what I could now see was a set of clothes. A uniform.

"Look, Uncle Sam," said Alice, turning to me. "It's William's new uniform."

It had taken Alice four years to reach the point where she could stop calling me Constable Plank. Although she called Martha by her Christian name alone, she was clearly uneasy doing the same for me, and when I suggested this compromise, she seized on it. Martha had later told me that as Alice had no blood family of her own, she liked people to think that she at least had an uncle.

"Aye, so I see," I said.

Alice held up a blue swallow-tailed coat, with eight gilt buttons down the front. Each button had the words "Police Force" written on it, surmounted by a crown. "Here's the pocket for his truncheon," she said, indicating a long pocket in the coat. "He's not been given that yet – not until he's properly on duty." She glanced at Martha, who smiled reassuringly.

"Don't you worry, my girl," said Martha. "William's a sensible fellow – he knows to walk away from trouble. The truncheon is for show really, isn't it, Sam?" She looked at me with wide eyes, signalling that I should support her in this claim.

I nodded. "A deterrent, Alice," I said. "That means something to put them off."

Alice smiled and turned her attention back to the coat. There was a leather stock for stiffening the collar – "In case some bluff fellow gets his hands round my throat," said Wilson, earning himself a hard look from my wife – and on the collar was a badge identifying Wilson as officer 38 of D Division.

"They wanted him at Holborn as well," said Alice, looking at her husband with pride, "but the two stations are the same distance from home and William likes Marylebone better."

Wilson shifted his son to the other knee. "We need to be able to get to the station within thirty minutes," he explained to Martha, "in case the fellows on duty don't turn up and we're called in. I've put in for a place in a station house, but for now, I'll have to gallop in from Brill Row." He reached across and picked up the black leather top hat, holding it over George's head to make the lad laugh.

Alice took it from him, stroking it carefully before putting it back on the table. "Careful with that, William – we can't afford another one."

"It's quite a list, Sam," said Martha, handing me a slip of paper. "Uniform: Constable – Metropolitan Police" it said.

"We've not been given the cape yet," said Wilson. "They're on order for the winter."

"What's this?" I said. "White trousers?"

"Aren't they smart?" said Alice, holding them up.

Martha laughed. "They certainly are – for about five minutes. Whoever chose those clearly knows nothing about laundry. You'll be washing them more often than wearing them, William."

"There's a blue pair for winter – the white ones are for summer," said Wilson.

"You'd think you were going to guard the King, not chase thieves down dark alleyways," I said. Martha shot me a warning look, and it's a brave man who ignores one of those. "And two pairs of boots," I said with more enthusiasm. "One pair on and one pair airing – very sensible."

"And there's this," said Alice, holding out a button brush and stick.

Martha took them and her face softened. "I remember when I first polished the buttons on Sam's coat," she said. "Now I'm a real constable's wife, I thought." She realised that we were all looking at her and put the brush and stick smartly back onto the table. "Perhaps one day men will stop fussing about shiny buttons and instead invent one that doesn't need polishing."

Mr Harmer's hospital

WEDNESDAY 30TH SEPTEMBER 1829

I had just walked down the steps of the police office when I heard a halloo. I turned to see James Harmer waving at me, a folded newspaper in his hand. I stopped and waited for him to make his way along the street, holding up my hand to show that there was no rush. I had noticed in recent months that the lawyer's expanding girth was starting to slow him down, although he still walked everywhere unless an urgent appointment demanded a coach. He reached me and paused to catch his breath, putting his free hand to his heart.

"How is it, Sam," he asked between breaths, "that I grower wider while you do not?"

"I daresay an alderman is invited to finer tables than a constable," I said, smiling.

"I resolve to eat and drink less," he said, shaking his head sadly, "but those who have known want in their early life never forget the feelings of hunger. And when a feast is set before me, I cannot resist." He was lost in thought for a moment and then remembered himself. "Have you seen this?" he asked, holding up the newspaper he had waved at me. "The new police have had a good review for their first night."

The window above our heads opened and John Conant leaned out. "Harmer," he called down, "I thought I heard your voice. Have you time for a drink? You too, Sam. Have you read this?" And he too waved a newspaper at me.

◆

Both men had a copy of the *Morning Post*.

"Not my usual reading," said Conant, "but Mr Neale pointed it out to me."

"Nor mine," agreed Harmer. "One of my clerks spotted it."

"May I?" I asked, holding out my hand. The magistrate passed me his paper.

"There," he said, pointing, "just a short piece, but positive. Read it out, Sam."

I started to read the couple of paragraphs, written, as the author admitted, after a "slight observation" of the new police on their first patrol. "Such as were stationed along the great thoroughfares of Holborn and the Strand moved backwards and forwards at a slow pace, without any indication of that offensive inquisitiveness and unnecessary meddling which too often marked the conduct of the watchmen."

"Ha!" interjected Harmer. "That should silence some of the criticism about the cost of the new police – do you remember the fuss they made in Marylebone about paying more in police rates than in watch rates? For a little more money, they're getting a professional body of men and no more unnecessary meddling."

I continued reading aloud. "Many of them have rather the appearance of respectable tradesmen than of persons taken from the more humble classes. Their dress is not so glaring as to attract notice, and their insignia of office are in a great measure concealed by a dark-coloured greatcoat."

"There," said Conant with satisfaction. "Rowan's choice of uniform for his men was right: respectable and understated."

The clock on his mantelpiece struck six. There was the sound of light running footsteps on the stairs and we all three turned to the door. It was flung open and in came Lily Conant, her hat slightly askew and her cheeks pink with exertion.

"Papa," she began, and then stopped when she caught sight of Harmer and me. "But you are busy, I see," and she smiled at us. "Constable Plank, Mr Harmer," she said, inclining her head at us in turn.

"Miss Conant," said Harmer, on his feet and bowing elegantly. "You will forgive an old man for saying how very charming you look this evening."

"I will forgive any man for saying that," said Lily, "even one who pretends to be old. It is a great pleasure to see you, Mr Harmer." She unpinned her hat and put it on the sideboard and then turned back to Harmer. "Actually, it is fortuitous that I find you here, Mr Harmer, as I have something to ask you." She indicated that Harmer should take his seat again and then carried over one of the dining chairs and put it alongside him.

"Lily," said her father, "are you sure that Mr Harmer has time for you this evening? And aren't we due somewhere else – you haven't run here for nothing, I assume."

"We are expected at the Nortons for supper," said Lily, "but it is a large gathering and we will not be missed. No, it is much more important that I speak to Mr Harmer."

"Forgive my daughter, James," said Conant, shaking his head.

"Nothing to forgive, sir," said the lawyer. "Now, Miss Conant, how can I help?"

"I have been reading about your hospital," said Lily.

"The General Institution, in Greville Street?" asked Harmer. Lily nodded. "Well, it is hardly my hospital, you know, Miss Conant," he continued. "Mr Marsden is the gentleman in charge – a surgeon. I simply gave him my support at various meetings, as I agree with his work."

Lily nodded vigorously. "As do I, Mr Harmer," she said.

"What do you mean, Lily?" asked her father. "What do you know of Mr Marsden's work?"

"I know that he believes everyone should be able to have treatment for serious conditions, even those who cannot pay," said Lily. "Imagine: he found a young girl dying of sickness and starvation, and he picked her up and carried her to two hospitals, which both turned him away because she had no-one to make her case to the governors or to pay her bill. He resolved there and then to start a free hospital, and Mr Harmer helped him." She looked at the lawyer with something approaching adoration. "And I too would like to help him."

Conant looked startled; he walked over to his daughter and put a hand on her shoulder. "Help this hospital?" he said. "By raising funds, you mean? Holding a gala of some sort?"

I could tell from the uncertainty in his voice that he rather feared that this was not what his daughter had in mind.

"Oh, that too, papa," said Lily, her eyes shining. "But what I would really like to do is train to be a nurse."

"A nurse?" barked Conant. "Good heavens, Lily…" Thankfully he caught sight of the warning on my face and stopped speaking.

"Yes, papa," said Lily, a stubborn note in her voice. "I have always known that I do not wish to be one of those silly women waiting at home for her husband, passing the days in shopping and idle chatter. I wish to do something useful – something worthwhile. Like you, papa."

"But Lily…" he began, and she interrupted him.

"Mrs Plank works in a school for unfortunate girls," she said, "and I know how much she enjoys it, and what good it does. Isn't that so, Constable Plank?"

Everyone turned to look at me. "Well, yes, Miss Lily," I said. "But a constable's wife becoming a teacher is not the same as a magistrate's daughter becoming a nurse."

"I am disappointed in both of you," she replied, straightening her back and setting her shoulders. "Papa, you have always encouraged me to use my mind, and to have compassion for those who are less fortunate. And you, Constable Plank, you permit some women to have purpose in life but not others."

"Lily," admonished her father. "Your depth of feeling is no excuse for rudeness."

His daughter bit her lip and nodded. "Forgive me, Constable Plank. That was unfair of me."

"It has certainly given me something to think about," I replied.

"But you, Mr Harmer," said Lily, turning her most appealing face to the lawyer and clasping her hands in beseech, "I know you will help me."

"In what way, Miss Conant?" asked Harmer, looking uneasy. "I hold no sway with the governors of the hospital – they run the place as they see fit, including the appointment of surgeons and nurses. I cannot interfere in the medical side of things."

"And no more would I ask you to," said Lily. "All I ask is that you introduce me to Mr Marsden, so that I can make my case directly to him. If he says that my plan is hopeless, well, then, I will think again. But if I have to spend the rest of my life going to suppers with people like the Nortons, then I shall go quite mad."

Harmer leaned over and put his hand over Lily's. "Miss Conant," he said, "I can see that you have grown into a young woman of ability and determination. I shall arrange this meeting for you on one condition: that your father agrees." Lily opened her mouth but the lawyer held up a hand to silence her. "As a lawyer, let me tell you that an agreement based on only one condition is a rare beast, so do not dismiss it out of hand. My dear girl, you are the age my beloved Clarinda would have been, had the Lord spared her, and I know only too well the responsibilities and hopes of a father." He paused, taking a handkerchief from his pocket and blowing his nose. "Your father wants the very best for you, Miss Conant – he wants to see you happy and settled and loved. Let me discuss this proposal with him and we shall see what we can work out."

Miss Lily looked over her shoulder at Conant, who nodded. And then she stood up, bent down and very gently kissed the lawyer on the cheek.

He put his hand to his face. "Good heavens," he said quietly. "What was that for, my dear?"

"That was from Clarinda," she replied.

♦

"Tell me again," said Martha, sitting opposite me at the table and looking me in the eye. "Exactly as you heard it. Tell me again."

"Miss Lily said that you work in a school for unfortunate girls," I said for the third time, "and that she knows how much you enjoy it and what good it does."

"Well," said Martha, leaning back in her seat. "Well. I had no idea she thought all that."

"Nor did Mr Conant," I commented. "I wonder what your father would have thought of what you do."

"My father?" said Martha, with a bark of laughter. "My father was too drunk most of the time to remember that he had a daughter, let alone give much thought to what I actually did. As long as I kept the place clean and put his meals on the table, I daresay he didn't think of me at all."

"No-one could accuse Mr Conant of that," I said. "The poor man doesn't know what to do for the best. Miss Lily is more worldly than most young women of her acquaintance, but nursing? All that disease and death and the physical side of things? No father would choose that for his daughter."

"I suspect there's more to it than that," said Martha. "Miss Lily has already rejected two or three proposals, I think." I nodded and she continued. "Mr Conant will be thinking to the future – wanting his daughter to be settled – and not many men are as broad-minded as he is, or you. If word gets around that Miss Lily is spending her days in a hospital, I can't see many mothers pushing their sons in her direction."

Miss Jenkins and Miss Deane

SUNDAY 4TH OCTOBER 1829

"At last," said Martha with a huff. "You'd think I'd asked for a ride along the Serpentine in a golden barge, instead of a simple walk in the park."

I pushed on the door to check that it was closed properly, turned up my collar – not because I was cold, but to make the point to my wife that I would rather be sitting indoors in the warm – and then offered her my arm.

"What you sometimes forget, Martha," I said as we turned northwards, "is that I spend all week walking. On a Sunday, I like sitting."

"And what you sometimes forget, Samuel," she replied, "is that I like to show off my handsome husband to the world, and I rarely get a chance to do it." She squeezed my arm and looked up at me with a smile. "It's a lovely day, Sam, and I want to see the autumn colours in the trees. After all that rain, I need some fresh air."

We were not the only ones to have had the idea of a Sunday afternoon stroll; the bright blue sky after almost a fortnight of heavy clouds and rain had brought out the families and the lovers, the fit and the infirm. We crossed York Terrace, thanking a jarvey who pulled up his coach to let us pass and flourished his whip in a cheery manner, and walked through York Gate into the Regent's Park.

"There," said Martha, sighing and sweeping her arm above her head. "Aren't they beautiful?" The avenue of trees was indeed lovely; their leaves were turning red, yellow, orange and gold, and the effect against the blue sky was like a painting. "I don't even mind the mud," she continued happily.

"You wouldn't say that if you were the one cleaning our boots on a Sunday evening," I replied.

We walked over the bridge that crossed the ornamental water and stopped to look down at the little island which split the stream. A group of ducks circled below us, having learned that people are a good source of food. Indeed, to my right a nursemaid had crouched down next to a little boy and was handing him scraps of bread, which he was hurling at the ducks while she kept a tight hold on his collar.

"Gently, now, Bertie," she said in a country burr. "You want to feed them, not brain them."

Martha smiled at them and said to me, "That will be our little George before too long."

"Aye," I said, "and woe betide those poor birds – he's quite the bruiser, our George."

"What a thing to say, Sam," said my wife, tugging at my arm. "Although he is sturdy, I'll give you that."

As the ground was so sodden we decided to stick to the path, and we had just passed the entrance to South Villa when Martha stopped.

"Look, Sam, there's one of the new policemen," she said, indicating with her head. "He looks very smart."

"He does," I agreed, "but he should not be standing and talking to those ladies."

"He may be off duty, Sam," said my wife, "and perhaps he is accompanying his sisters on a walk."

I raised an eyebrow. "Perhaps," I said. "Let's see, shall we? Wilson told me that discipline is still a concern among some of the young recruits."

We walked towards the little group; as we got closer, I could see that the two ladies he was talking to – girls, really – were certainly not his sisters. They were clutching each other's arms and looking alarmed, and the police officer's face showed no brotherly affection, only an unpleasant sneer.

"Good afternoon, constable," I called out. All three turned to look at us, and Martha gasped.

"Louisa Jenkins!" she said. "What on earth are you doing here? Is Miss Jenkins in difficulty, sir?" she asked the constable.

The constable blinked rapidly as he tried to work out what was happening. "These two ladies," he said eventually, clearing his throat, "that is to say, I was walking through the park, on my way to the station house, when these young ladies asked for my assistance." He looked at the girls – a hard look.

"Then you are in luck, constable," I said. "Miss Jenkins is a friend of my wife, and we can assist her and her companion with whatever they need. You would not want to be late, and your station house must be quite a step from here." I had looked at his collar: it identified him as officer F27 – and Division F was Covent Garden.

"It is very kind of you, sir," said the constable. If he was surprised that I should know so much about his occupation, he hid it. "I shall be happy to leave these ladies in your care. Miss Jenkins, Miss Deane." He bowed his head and walked off quickly in the direction of York Gate.

I turned to look at Martha, and she was standing with her arms folded across her chest, glaring at Louisa Jenkins. For a small woman, my wife can be remarkably fierce, and Miss Jenkins clutched even more tightly at her friend's arm. "Well?" said Martha. "Do I need to ask you again?"

"It's like he said, Mrs Plank," said Miss Jenkins, and her friend nodded vigorously. "Ellie – Miss Deane – and me, we came out for a walk, and we got lost. We saw his coat and knew he was a policeman and we asked him the way to the gate. Isn't that right, Ellie?" Miss Deane nodded again.

"Now Louisa," said Martha, uncrossing her arms and speaking much more gently. "What you may not know is that my husband is also a constable." Miss Jenkins' eyes darted to me and then back to Martha. "And one thing that constables can do very well is tell when someone is lying. Isn't that right, Sam?"

"Aye," I said. "People tell lies for all sorts of reasons – sometimes because they have done something wrong, but often because they are scared. And I think you're lying to us, Miss Jenkins." She opened her mouth but I held up a hand. "You see, when that policeman left, he said both your names. Now, when we first saw you we said your name, Miss Jenkins – but no-one said yours, Miss Deane. So how did this stranger of a policeman, a fellow you had met only moments before to ask for directions – how did he know your name?"

♦

By the time we reached home, the pair had given up all pretence of being worldly young ladies. On our walk from the Regent's Park they flanked Martha like ducklings, one holding onto each of her arms, and I brought up the rear – looking for all the world like a protective papa out with his family. From the conversation I overheard, I gathered that Miss Jenkins was one of the girls at Martha's school, while Miss Deane was her childhood friend. I remembered Martha telling me of a Louisa with a special facility for dramatic reading aloud and wondered whether this was the same girl. After the girls had both visited the privy and settled at our kitchen table, I cast a look of despair at Martha and she nodded; we both knew that the girls would talk more freely without me. I picked up the newspaper that I had brought home the day before and retreated to the sitting room.

I had finished the newspaper and just shut my eyes when Martha came in and asked me to return to the kitchen.

"Constable or papa?" I asked quickly.

"Constable, I think," she said gravely.

When I walked into the kitchen, I could see that both girls had been crying, which made them look even younger. I sat in my usual place and Martha sat down next to me.

"Now, girls," she said, "as I explained, my husband is a constable, but he is not part of the new police. He works directly for a magistrate – you have heard of them," they both nodded, "and he takes his instructions only from the magistrate."

It was a rather simplified explanation but it was near enough the truth.

Martha continued. "This means that you have nothing to fear from telling him what you told me. He does not work in the same force as the man in the park." She put a hand over mine. "He has been a constable since before you were born, and he is a good man." She smiled at me and then at them. "So you can tell him what you told me."

I leaned back in my seat and reached into my coat pocket for my notebook. "If you will permit, ladies," I said seriously, "I will write down what you say. You can then look over what I have written, so that we all agree that I have a true record of it. May I?"

Louisa and Ellie looked at each other. "Yes, sir," said Louisa.

I opened my notebook. "You are Miss Louisa Jenkins and Miss Ellie Dean," I said, writing. I turned the notebook so that they could read it. "Is this right?"

Ellie whispered to Louisa. "There is an e at the end of Deane," said Louisa.

I retrieved the notebook and corrected the spelling. "You see: our system is already working well," I said. "Now, may I ask how old you are?"

"I'm nearly sixteen," said Louisa, "and Ellie is fourteen."

"And you live with your parents?" I asked.

"My pa died last year," said Louisa, "so it's just me and ma and the little ones. Ellie lives with her gran – her parents died when she was a baby."

"And how long have you been going to the school where Mrs Plank teaches?" I asked.

"Nearly two years now, isn't it, missus?" asked Louisa. "Ellie wants to go to the school as well, but her gran needs her to do sewing and laundry, so I tell her what I learn. Better than nothing, isn't it, El?"

The silent Ellie nodded.

"Well, you can recognise your name, Miss Deane" I said, "and spot when it is written wrong. You're obviously a quick study." Ellie flushed at the attention and the compliment.

"Lou reads to me," she said in a whisper, "and I put my finger on the words as we go along."

"That's exactly how I taught Mrs Plank to read," I said, smiling. The two girls looked astonished.

Martha nodded. "Oh yes. When I first met Constable Plank I was just the same age as you are now, Louisa. I could read my name, like you, Ellie, and I knew the numbers, but that was all. I longed to read stories – to learn about people I didn't know and places I hadn't seen. And that's what we did: Constable Plank brought home books of stories, then he read them to me and I followed the words on the page – and one day I didn't need him to read them to me because I could read them by myself." She laughed at the faces of the two girls. "What – did you think some people are born knowing how to read? We all have to learn."

"The cleverest thing is knowing that you want to learn," I said. "It's a fool who thinks the world has nothing to teach him." I looked at the girls again. "Now, Mrs Plank has told me that something happened to you in the park today, something that frightened you both. I am assuming that it involved the policeman we saw."

The girls were sitting close together and I could tell from the movement of her arm that Ellie had taken hold of Louisa's hand under the table. Neither of them said anything.

I waited a few seconds and then spoke again. "Did you happen to notice the policeman's coat?" I asked. "His smart blue coat." They both nodded. "And did you see that he had something written in silver letters, here?" I indicated the left side of my own collar. They nodded again. "Well, that tells me exactly who the man is," I said. "Every policeman has his own number, and I have taken a note of it. It means that he cannot lie about who he is, or which police division he belongs to. And we do that because we expect policemen to be good and decent and honest, and to protect people. If he has done something wrong, we can find out who he is and stop him doing it again." I could see them listening intently. "There is a very good man in charge of the new police, called Sir Charles Rowan. He was a brave soldier who fought at

Waterloo. And he demands the best behaviour from his police – he even sacked the very first man he recruited, on the fellow's very first day as a constable, for being drunk!" As I had hoped, Louisa and Ellie both smiled. "So you see," I said, looking at them earnestly, "if a policeman has done something wrong, we must stop him. And you can help us."

Louisa looked at Ellie and then at me. "It's... it's not..." She looked pleadingly at Martha.

Martha leaned over and patted Louisa's hand. "Perhaps, Sam," she said, "you could look the other way. Turn your chair around – that's it – and then Louisa will feel more comfortable telling you this next bit. There, you see, girls: this way Constable Plank can hear it directly from you, and make a note of what you tell him, but he can't see you while you say it. Remember what I said: he is a good man. And he won't be shocked by anything you say: he's a married man, so he knows enough."

I heard Louisa take a deep breath and then she began. "It started the week before last. I came out of the school and he was standing on the corner and called me over."

"When you say he called you," I asked, "did he use your name?"

"I don't think so," replied Louisa. "He just called me miss. But I could see from his coat that he was police – you told us all about them, missus, you remember – and so I went. He said that a gentleman had told him I'd pinched a guinea from his pocket, but I never. I said it wasn't me, but he said the gentleman saw my face and would swear to the magistrate that it was me. So it was his word against mine. Then he said he would take me to the station house unless… unless I did things for him." I heard the sob in her voice. "I wanted to tell you, missus, I really did, but he said that if I told anyone no-one would believe me because he was a police constable and I was nobody."

"You are certainly not nobody, Miss Jenkins," I said. "And you have been very clear and helpful so far – I have it all noted. Now, what did he make you do?"

"Tell him, my dear," said Martha softly.

"I didn't want to," said Louisa.

"Oh, I don't doubt that for a moment," I said. "Miss Jenkins, if someone makes you do something you don't want to do, by frightening you or threatening you, it's their crime and not yours. And to make sure this man faces justice for his crime, I need to know what he did."

"He made me touch him," she said, "his privates. And he touched me – my…"

"Her privates, Sam," said Martha, who could see where the girl was indicating, "and her breasts."

"Did he force you to lie with him?" I asked, keeping my voice as emotionless as I could.

"He tried once," replied Louisa, "but someone disturbed us and he was worried they would see he was a police constable."

"So you met him more than once, Miss Jenkins?" I asked.

She was silent for a few moments.

"It's just for the notebook, Miss Jenkins," I said. "So that when this man is made to answer for what he has done, we can ask him about everything. We wouldn't want him to get away with anything."

"I met him three times, including today," she said. "The first time I told you about. The second time, it was two days later, and he was waiting again. He made me walk with him to the churchyard near the school, and that's when…"

"That's when he tried to lie with her, Sam," Martha explained, as she could see Louisa's face and gestures when I could not.

"And why were you meeting him today?" I asked.

"It wasn't her." Ellie had been silent until now. "He thought he was meeting me. But I was scared and told Lou, and she came with me."

"So when Louisa turned him down, he went looking for what he hoped would be easier pickings," said Martha bitterly. "He must have seen Ellie waiting outside the school."

"And did he spin you the same story, Miss Deane – about you stealing from a gentleman?" I asked.

"He said I'd been seen taking some lace from a shop and that the shopkeeper had recognised me from when I bought some buttons," she said. "I never bought buttons from a shop, but he said she remembered me."

"And when was this, Miss Deane?" I asked. "When did he tell you this?"

"Yesterday," she said. "He said that if I met him in the park today he'd probably not tell the magistrate. He said I wasn't to tell anyone, if I didn't want everyone to know that I was a thief. But I'm not, and I told Lou, and she said she'd come with me."

"I can look after myself," said Louisa, more to convince herself than anyone else, "but Ellie's, well, Ellie. I can't let him hurt her."

"You are lucky to have such a good friend, Miss Deane," I said. "And you, Miss Jenkins, are a brave young woman. I'll turn back now, if you'll permit me, ladies. It must be nearly four o'clock, and I believe that Mrs Plank has made some little queen cakes. They are far too dainty for an old fellow like me, but they will suit you ladies perfectly. For myself, I will just reach for this walnut loaf."

◆

Martha was silent as we readied ourselves for bed. I knew that her anger was not for me, but I also knew – as all husbands eventually learn – that it could be easily turned on me if I said the wrong thing. And so I chose to say nothing and simply waited. She climbed under the covers and pummelled her pillow into the right shape, throwing herself down onto it. Still I waited.

"He knew exactly what he was doing," she said grimly after a minute or two, "and he planned for any objections. He warned Louisa not to tell anyone and said that as a police officer his word would be worth more than hers." She thumped me lightly on the chest for emphasis. "Honestly, Sam, it makes me so angry: these girls have had years of being told that they're nothing and nobody, and just when we start making some progress with them at the school, giving them reason to believe that they're worth something…"

I caught hold of her hand and brought it to my lips, kissing it gently. "If that girl had thought she was nothing, she would have done what he demanded. But she said no, and what's more she gave her friend the courage to say no. And that courage came from what she has learned from her time at school – that if she works at her lessons there is more in store for her than drudgery and, well, the rest of it. You can't change the men who prey on these girls, Mar, but you can change Louisa, and she can change Ellie."

My wife was quiet, but I felt some of the stiffness go from her body as she lay against me. She looked up at me. "You're right, Sam. I can't change the men – but you can."

Snow in October

TUESDAY 13TH OCTOBER 1829 – MORNING

"There, you see," said Martha, standing looking out of the kitchen window, her hands on her hips. "I knew we were right to have that walk last weekend, even with all your complaining. Snow again this morning."

She turned and held her hands out to warm them over the pot of porridge that was bubbling lazily on the stove.

"Snow in October," I observed from my seat at the table. "Doesn't bode well for the winter, does it?"

We heard a stamping of feet outside the door, followed by a knock. Martha opened the door and there was Wilson, a dusting of snow on his new coat and hat.

She pulled him into the kitchen and pushed the door shut against the cold air.

"Take off your things, William," she said, "and you can join us for breakfast. You look tired, lad."

Wilson did as he was told and sat at the table, yawning widely. Luckily for him, Martha was tending to the porridge pan at the stove, otherwise she would have reminded him of his manners.

"I'm sorry, sir," said Wilson, shaking his head as though to clear it. "I'm on second night relief, which wouldn't be so bad if I could get my head down during the day, but George has other ideas. Alice tries to keep him amused but with the weather like this they can't be outside all day just so that I can sleep."

"It will be better once you're in the station house," said Martha, putting a bowl of porridge in front of each of us. "There will be other mothers around, and Alice and George can spend time in their rooms while you sleep in yours. In the meantime," she turned from spooning porridge into her own bowl, "you tell Alice to bring George here. I can look after him for a few hours while you and Alice have a rest. Tell her that I'm missing him, then she won't feel guilty about it."

"Thank you," said Wilson, scraping his spoon around his bowl. He must have been tired because he didn't ask for a second helping.

"On your way, now," I said, putting a hand on his slumped shoulder.

Wilson pushed himself up from the table. He reached for his coat and then turned to me. "I've remembered why I came over," he said. He put his hand into his coat pocket and took out a small black book and handed it to me. I glanced at the cover: *Metropolitan Police Instruction Book*, it said in plain lettering. "We were given these today – last night. And I thought you might like to see it. I'm supposed to keep it with me, so I'll collect it this afternoon on my way back to Marylebone Lane."

"I'll make sure to read it," I said. "And Wilson," he turned back from the door, "there's something I need to discuss with you before you go to work, so come a bit earlier if you can."

Wilson nodded and went out again into the cold.

CHAPTER TWENTY-EIGHT

The Covent Garden watch house

TUESDAY 13TH OCTOBER 1829 – EVENING

Wilson looked much brighter when he returned at four o'clock. Alice and Martha were in the kitchen making pies, while George was covering himself and all around him with flour. Wilson bent to give his wife a kiss on the cheek but – in his dark blue coat – kept a wise distance from his son.

"We'll be in the sitting room," I said. "A pot of tea would be most welcome – and maybe a slice of pie, if there's any flour left in London. We've some police business to discuss." Alice looked up with alarm.

"Nothing to worry about, Alice," said Martha soothingly. "Sam has some information for William, that's all."

Wilson looked at me with interest and followed me out of the kitchen. I had lit the fire earlier, so the sitting room was warm enough, and Wilson took off his coat and laid it carefully across the back of one of the armchairs before sitting down. I settled into the other armchair.

"At the end of August, you and I had a talk about Edward Fraser," I started.

"The man in the canary waistcoat?" asked Wilson. "Set sail for Quebec with his family, and the trust of Mr Freame?"

"Indeed," I said. "I know you had your doubts about our course of action, but there it is." Wilson raised an eyebrow but said nothing. "And do you also remember that before Fraser left, he said to warn you about criminals planning to join the new force?"

"I do, yes," said Wilson. "Why?"

"Well, I think Mrs Plank and I have met one of them," I said. And I told him what had happened in the Regent's Park. During my tale Martha came in with the tea and two slices of pie.

"You can tell William everything Louisa and Ellie told us, Sam," she said as she finished handing out our plates and turned to go. "He needs to know."

"And you're sure of the collar number?" asked Wilson once I had finished. He put his hand to his neck, where he proudly wore his own number.

"F27," I repeated. "Covent Garden."

Wilson reached back to retrieve his notebook from the pocket of his coat and turned to a table he had drawn at the back of it. "Division F," he read aloud. "Superintendent is Mr Joseph Thomas. Bow Street." He glanced at the clock. "If we set off now we can speak to the inspector before he sends the first night relief out on patrol."

He stood up but I did not. "I'm not sure that we should both go," I said.

"Of course," he said. "This is Metropolitan Police business. I should go alone. I shall say, what, that a member of the public made a complaint to me and remembered the collar number?" He was putting on his coat but stopped when he saw me shaking my head.

"I meant that I should go alone," I said. Wilson opened his mouth to object but I held up a hand. "Hear me out. You're a constable in the new police, and you want to progress, don't you – sergeant, then inspector and so on?" He nodded. "If you march into another division, a mere fortnight after their first patrol, and complain about one of their men, well, you'll be seen as a trouble-maker at best, and a snitch at worst."

Wilson's shoulders slumped: I knew he could see the sense in what I said. "But they'll think the same of you," he observed.

"Aye," I said, "but I'm not hoping to work with them for years to come." I stood up myself. "I'll go to Bow Street now, and you come here tomorrow, before you go on duty, and we'll see what's to be done."

◆

As I turned into Bow Street, the feeble sun was setting and the evening air was frigid. I walked through the large arched doorway into the premises at number 4 and explained to the office keeper at the counter that I wished to speak to the inspector on duty.

"We've no inspectors here, constable," he said. "You'll be wanting the new police." He raised his eyebrows in question and I nodded. "They're not in this building. They're in the watch house in the churchyard – you can't miss it." He sniffed mightily. "Best place for 'em if you ask me."

I made my way down the side of the Theatre Royal and across the market. The stallholders were long gone, back to their gardens and smallholdings, and the area was now the province of the Covent Garden nuns. One or two of them called over to me until their friends pointed out my coat.

"Watch out, Lil," one cackled, "he's a constable, that one – have you up before the beak!"

"Constables is men," replied Lil. "He's got the same under his coat as any man, ain't you, handsome?" She swished her filthy skirts. "And he can have me up anywhere, long as he pays for it!"

I was saved from their further attentions by the arrival of three smart hackneys, spilling a crowd of young men on their way to the theatre. The women sensed easy pickings and loose wallets and turned away from me.

The office keeper was right: it would be hard to miss the watch house. To the left of the elegant church and the fine stone gateway to the churchyard stood a plain white building with a simple red roof. Two narrow arched windows with wooden shutters flanked the doorway, which – unexpectedly – had a row of flowerpots across its portico, while the upper storey had one small window only, again with flowerpots in front of it. Were it not for the words "WATCH HOUSE" painted in large letters at the top of the wall, I would have taken it for the home of an eccentric old woman from one of those stories by the Grimm brothers. Leaning on the high black railings in front of the building were three police constables, dapper in their blue winter uniforms and with their collar numbers clearly visible – none was F27. They followed me with their gaze as I walked up the three steps into the watch house.

There was no counter, but a man of about forty, judging from the slight greying to his whiskers, sat behind a small desk with a ledger open before him.

"Excuse me," I said to him. He looked up at me but did not stand. "I would like to speak to one of the inspectors, please."

"On police business?" he asked, none too friendly.

"Plainly," I said, "otherwise I would not be in this, well, what would you call it? A temporary station house, perhaps. While you new police find your feet."

"I am Inspector Cameron," he said, very much on his dignity. "And what is this business?"

"I rather think, Inspector Cameron, that you might prefer to discuss this in private," I said, as another four constables clattered up the steps, eyeing me curiously as they passed. "I am Constable Samuel Plank, of Great Marlborough Street, and I wish to speak to you about one of your men. He has been abusing his authority to importune young ladies. And one of them has reported the matter to me." The last of the four turned to stare and then quickly scurried after his fellows.

"Wait here," said Cameron brusquely. He followed the constables into a back room and I could hear him giving instructions – presumably to the second inspector on duty. He returned, retrieved the ledger from the desk, and beckoned to me. "Follow me," he said, and went up the narrow staircase. Upstairs was a room set up as a small apartment, with a small table and two chairs, a washstand, an armchair and a single bed – I guessed that the inspectors would take turns to rest up here during their long shift. Cameron pulled out one of the chairs from the table, indicating that I should do the same, and we sat opposite each other. He opened the ledger in front of him, turning to a fresh page, and pulled an inkstand towards him.

"Which man?" he said without preamble.

"F27," I said.

"Can you describe him?" he asked.

"I can, yes," I said.

He waited and then looked up at me.

"Do I need to describe him?" I asked. "Do you not know who wears that number?"

"Your informant – the young lady – may have been mistaken," he said.

"The young lady certainly informed me of the incident," I said, "or, to be exact, incidents, but I identified the man myself. And I know the number that I saw: F27."

"So the young lady informed you that they spoke and claims that he – what was your word – importuned her. But perhaps she approached him," suggested Cameron. "We both know, you and I, the effect a smart uniform has on the female eye." He smiled roguishly, but I kept my face neutral.

"Inspector Cameron, this was not a harmless flirtation." I leaned forward in my chair. "Your officer threatened the young woman. He said that he would see that she was prosecuted for theft if she did not do as he said. He tried to violate her. And when she resisted, he turned his attentions to her younger friend – a girl of fourteen. He is abusing his authority, inspector, and must be stopped."

The inspector closed his ledger without writing a word. He put down his pen with exaggerated care and sat back in his chair, folding his arms.

"Shall I tell you what I think, Constable Plank?" he said, managing to put a world of distaste into my name.

"I think you are a bitter man, looking your own demise in the face. I think you resent the new police for displacing you with something more modern and efficient. I think you have seen one of my men reject the advances of a foolish young woman and have decided to make trouble for him. But now you think about this, constable." He leaned forward again and jabbed at the table with his finger. "Who would a magistrate believe: the chatter of a girl who chases after fine uniforms, or the word of a Metropolitan Police officer chosen personally by Commissioner Rowan?"

I stood and pushed my chair back under the table.

"Thank you for your time, Inspector Cameron," I said. "It has been most illuminating to see the new police in action."

I walked down the stairs, across the small hall and out of the building. Behind me, the inspector called after me. "You magistrates' constables have always been second-rate, and you've always known it," he said. "I saw it when I was a Runner and I'm seeing it still."

CHAPTER TWENTY-NINE

Contravention one

WEDNESDAY 14TH OCTOBER 1829

B y the time Wilson arrived at four o'clock, I had worked out a plan. Martha made us a pot of tea and then left us at the kitchen table while she went to pay a call on a neighbour.

"And I have counted those biscuits," she said as she pulled the door closed behind her.

As promised, Edward Freame's wife had supplied her recipe for spiced biscuits and they had become such a favourite that – like the banker before me – I could not be trusted to limit myself. Martha would serve out a certain number on a plate – four, this afternoon – and would keep the rest in her cupboard, with a careful inventory.

Wilson drank noisily from his tea and reached for a biscuit. "These look a bit dainty," he observed, putting it whole into his mouth. "But good." He chewed and then smiled and reached for another. "Very good."

"Two each," I said quickly.

"One of the hardest things about working at night," he said, withdrawing his hand, "is knowing what to eat when. I should be having my breakfast now, but all I want is, well, tea and biscuits. And when I get home and want my dinner, Alice and George are having their porridge."

"Alice will have to make up your dinner plate and keep it warm for you," I said. "Going to an eating house now and then is all very well, but it's greasy food and you're never sure where the meat's from. There's nothing to beat a meal at home."

"You're right. Alice is coming on leaps and bounds since Mrs Plank started helping her in the kitchen," said Wilson, reaching for his second biscuit. "Maybe they can make these together. Bigger ones."

"Now," I said, putting my tea carefully to one side and pulling towards me the book Wilson had left with me the previous day and the notes I had made. "To work."

Wilson swallowed quickly and ran the back of his hand across his mouth, then took his own notebook from his coat pocket.

"Yesterday afternoon I paid a visit to the inspector of Division F," I said. "An Inspector Cameron. A former Runner." I raised an eyebrow at Wilson. "And he has taken his attitude with him to his new post."

"Unhelpful, then," suggested Wilson.

"Unhelpful, and arrogant and dismissive," I confirmed. "To my mind, we have tried the official route as recommended in your book." I tapped the *Metropolitan Police Instruction Book* with my forefinger and then pushed it towards Wilson. "Page 26." Although he read well enough, he always needed practice.

Wilson looked at his hands and then wiped them on the cloth Martha had left drying over the back of a chair before he took hold of the book and turned to the right page.

"Read it aloud for me," I said.

He did so. "If upon complaint made against a man, the Inspector shall think his conduct blameable, or deserving of punishment, he will, as soon as possible, communicate the whole matter to the Superintendent for his decision, in the meantime suspending him from duty, if the case requires it." He looked up at me.

I leaned forward. "When I told this Cameron about F27, he wrote nothing down. He dismissed my complaint as sour grapes, and obviously had no intention of making any enquiries or passing on the concern to his superior, let alone suspending the fellow." I smiled at Wilson. "Let's call that contravention one."

"Contravention?" repeated Wilson.

"Going against the rules," I explained. I sat back in my seat. "You see, the beauty of having a clear set of rules – which the new police force now has – is that no-one can claim that they didn't know what they should be doing. Now," I pointed again to the book. "Page 41 – the last sentence."

Wilson leafed through the book. "This is about constables," he said, looking up at me and I nodded. "He will be civil and attentive to all persons, of every rank and class; insolence or inci... inciv..."

"Incivility," I prompted. "Rudeness."

"Incivility will not be passed over," he completed.

"Now that's contravention two," I said. "I have an agreed statement from Miss Jenkins and Miss Deane that officer F27 was both insolent and uncivil to them."

"I see what you are doing, sir," said Wilson, looking up at me. "But this will not make me popular – pulling out my instructions and pointing to people's shortcomings."

"Indeed not," I said. "I did this by way of illustration – to show you how it could work. No: you need to be cleverer than that. What you need to do," I leaned forward once more and spoke earnestly to him, "is think of a way to make sure that this behaviour by F27 – and there may be others – is witnessed by those who will take action. You need to identify the good men in your division and have them on the look-out for contraventions. And this is not just to catch this one rogue, Wilson: the new police has many enemies, and they will seize on any excuse to run you down. So learn your rules," I pointed at his book, "keep to them at all times, and take pride in them. They are a structure for good men and a trap for bad ones."

Wilson nodded solemnly.

"Now, don't tell Mrs Plank," I said, getting to my feet. I reached into the cupboard and pulled out the biscuit tin. "One more each, I think." And I put four more biscuits on the plate.

CHAPTER THIRTY

A smart young bachelor

MONDAY 19TH OCTOBER 1829

I had just raised my hand to the knocker of Mr Harmer's premises in Hatton Garden when the door opened and there stood the man himself.

"Splendid timing, Sam," he said, flapping his hand to indicate that I should go back down the steps. He pulled the door shut behind him. "If we stay here we won't get a moment's peace." He indicated the bulging satchel under his arm. "If I'm at my desk, Mr Welby brings me more and more work." Welby had been Harmer's clerk for as long as anyone could remember. "But if I'm out of sight..." He smiled impishly. "Now, Sam, what do you say to the Saracen's Head?"

Five minutes later, we were sitting by the long window of the tavern, watching the bustle in the coaching yard.

"I can't imagine why anyone would want to leave London," said Harmer, almost to himself. He turned to look at me. "My wife has family in Kent and talks of moving, but a man could suffocate out there – all that fresh air. Ah – here we are."

The pot boy leaned across me and put two tankards on the table, and then two pork pies, still steaming from the oven. Harmer picked up a knife and, holding them still with the tips of his fingers, cut our pies into quarters. "In case you think this pie the product of pure generosity," he said, indicating my pie with the knife, "I should confess that I wish to pick your brains. About John Conant and his daughter." He picked up a wedge of pie and blew on it before biting into it. I could see him considering his words as he chewed. "As you may recall, I find myself caught between them."

"With her talk of hospitals and nursing, you mean," I said.

The lawyer nodded, sending a shower of pie crumbs down his front and brushing them away with an impatient hand. "She's a clever one, catching me like that – taking advantage of my own foolish vanity about the hospital. And now, if I help her pursue this idea of being a nurse, John will be angry, and if I don't, she'll be vexed." He shook his head sadly. "Trapped, Sam. A man of my education and experience, too," he winked at me, "but then I'm not the first to be charmed by a young lady." He leaned forward. "And then I remembered that you know Miss Lily much better than I do – she's been to your house, I understand."

"Well, yes, once," I said, "but that was..."

Harmer held up a hand. "No matter – compared to me, you're an expert on Lily Conant. So tell me, Sam: what should I do?"

I was struggling to answer when a welcome distraction arrived in the form of a trim young man with a pleasant, open face making his way determinedly through the crowd to our table.

"Mr Harmer," he said as he reached us.

"Mr Barnes," said the lawyer, with exaggerated politeness and a bow of his head.

"Mr Harmer," repeated the young man, "Mr Welby suggested that I might find you here."

"Josiah Welby is a tattletale," said Harmer almost petulantly. "Sam, this is Richard Barnes, my junior. Mr Barnes, this is Constable Samuel Plank of Great Marlborough Street."

314 | SUSAN GROSSEY

I reached up and we shook hands.

"I have heard tell of you, constable," said Barnes, smiling genuinely. "It's a pleasure to meet you."

"Have you come to drag me to court?" asked Harmer. "I checked my book and was not aware..."

"I have not, sir, no," said Barnes. "I am on my way there myself, however, and Mr Welby asked me to deliver some papers to you, for a matter tomorrow." He reached into the satchel he carried over his shoulder and started to unload papers onto the table. "Forgive me," he said distractedly as the pile of papers grew. "My sister has written a pamphlet and I promised to distribute it for her."

I angled my head to read aloud the title of the top pamphlet on the pile. "A Brief View of the Nature and Effects of Negro Slavery as It Exists in the Colonies of Great Britain." I raised an eyebrow. "Your sister wrote this, Mr Barnes?"

"Elizabeth is a woman of opinions," he said. "Our father was a great believer in common humanity." He paused the rummaging in his satchel. "He taught us that all human beings are equal: white, negro, man, woman, rich, poor. For my part, I can support and promote our beliefs through my work – alongside Mr Harmer. But the options are more limited for Elizabeth, even though she has the better intellect." He flashed a smile like a schoolboy. "But I will never admit that to her face, of course." He held a bundle of papers aloft with triumph. "Aha – here we go." He passed the bundle to Harmer and then proceeded to stuff his sister's pamphlets back into his satchel. I took one.

"May I?" I asked.

"Of course," said Barnes. "Elizabeth will be delighted to hear that a constable is interested in her writings." The clock of St Andrew's on Shoe Lane started to toll the hour and the young lawyer cocked his head to listen. "And now I am late and must run. Mr Harmer, Constable Plank." He bowed to each of us and was gone.

"Just like his father," observed Harmer, signalling to the pot boy. "Idealistic. But at least he had the good sense to take up a profession. The father was a clergyman – a good speaker and an excellent brain, but poor as a church mouse. You'll have another?" He indicated the tankard and I nodded. "The boy, on the other hand – he has more of a commercial head on his shoulders."

"Has he a wife?" I asked.

Harmer dabbed at the pie crumbs on the plate with his finger and shook his head. "Lives with that sister of his – Elizabeth. He'd be a fine husband for someone, but with those progressive views of his about women and the rest... He'll want a clever wife and an understanding father-in-law." He sighed. "Ah, here we go." The pot boy put down two more tankards and cleared the dead men.

I waited as Harmer took a drink and I looked at him levelly. He put his tankard down and looked back at me. "What? You have your own drink."

"For one of London's leading lawyers," I said, "you are slow off the mark today. Here we have a smart young bachelor, looking for a clever wife to share his passion for social justice. If only we knew of such a creature and could push them together." I raised my eyebrows at him.

Harmer frowned for a moment and then his face cleared. "Lily Conant!" he bellowed. A few faces turned towards us and I held up my hands in apology. "If we introduce them and she likes the look of him, she'll forget all about nursing and start thinking about weddings."

"I'm not sure she'll be diverted quite that easily," I said, "but a man with a good brain and a sense of justice might catch her eye and offer another way for her to live the worthwhile life she craves." I drained my tankard and stood. "But then you'd have another problem." Harmer looked up at me. "Finding a way to explain to John Conant exactly why you introduced her to the man who would take her away from her father. Rather you than me."

CHAPTER THIRTY-ONE

Two shillings honestly earned

THURSDAY 29TH OCTOBER 1829

"**A**lice wants to have things shipshape in their rooms at the station house by the time the baby arrives," said Martha, bumping me aside with her hip as she reached into a cupboard. "But with William working all the hours that God sends, she needs a hand. She's a determined little thing, but with that belly on her, she can hardly be on her hands and knees scrubbing the floor, can she?"

"I suppose not," I said, sitting at the table to get out of her way.

Martha paused and looked at me. "I know you miss him, Sam. But we all agreed – you agreed – that this was best for him. With everything you've taught him, he'll be streets ahead of the others in the new force."

"Sergeant by Christmas, inspector by Whitsun," I said, trying to smile.

Martha put a hand on my shoulder and I put mine on hers. She kissed the top of my head. "Something will come along, you'll see," she said. "It always does."

And then, as if by magic, there was a knock at the back door.

"There you are," she said triumphantly. "If the lad looks hungry, there's an apple in the basket he can have." And she left the kitchen, no doubt in search of more things to help the young ones on their way, as she had it, thinking I wouldn't notice the contents of my home shifting gradually to the station house in Hadlow Street where Wilson and his little family had been assigned quarters.

I opened the back door and looked down at the message lad. He was bending over, hands on his knees, puffing, but when he saw my feet appear he stood upright, almost to attention, and smartly handed me a note. I nodded seriously.

"From Mr Young," he said. "At the Horse Bazaar."

"Help yourself to a drink from the tap," I said, indicating the one in the yard. He went over and put his mouth to the tap and drank noisily.

"Any reply?" he asked, wiping his mouth with the back of his hand.

"No," I said.

He looked crestfallen. I reached into the pocket of my coat, hanging in the kitchen, and felt for a coin, and then picked up the apple that Martha had mentioned. I handed them both to him and he grinned.

"The coin is for your speed," I said, "and the apple is for your breakfast." I remembered being his age and never feeling full. "And have another drink before you go – it's good clean water."

♦

When I reached the Horse Bazaar I stood quietly for a couple of minutes in the yard, watching a lad trying to brush down a handsome grey horse that was dancing around him. Then I went into the building and up the stairs to George Young's office on the first floor. He must have spotted me from his windows, as he was waiting at the open door and held out his hand to welcome me.

"Thank you for coming so promptly, Constable Plank," he said. "I have some information that I know you will want to hear. But first: some refreshment. Take a seat." He waved towards the armchair and then leaned out into the corridor again. "Vaughn!" he called. "Vaughn!" I heard footsteps running up the stairs. "A pitcher of fruit cordial – quick as you can. We're parched up here."

Young came back into the office and picked up one of the chairs, placing it closer to the armchair where I was sitting.

"That's a fine animal in the yard," I observed.

"You've a good eye," said Young, raising an eyebrow. "One of our best hunters – excellent sire and dam. He'll go for a decent price on Saturday."

We heard steps on the stairs and both turned to the door. In came a young man carrying a tray on which was balanced a pitcher of pale red liquid and two short, wide glasses. He put the tray on the desk and left silently.

Young stood and poured our two drinks, handing one to me. "Cherry, if I am not mistaken," he said. "Very popular with the ladies. My wife tells me that they like the taste, and the colour it gives their lips." He raised an eyebrow and smiled and then refilled both our glasses before taking his seat again.

"Now, constable, to business," he said. "This morning Tom Dawson came to see me. You remember Dawson? Big lad, but, well, a ninny."

I nodded. "Aye. I spoke to him here, in the late summer."

"That's right," said Young. "And you told him to look out for the fellow who offered him five pounds to attack the poor Madden boy. Dawson does well when you give him a clear instruction, and he says he's seen the man again."

"He's seen the man who wanted him to assault Charles Madden?" I asked.

Young nodded. "I thought you'd be pleased. And he'll only tell you." He smiled wryly. "Says it's official business for Constable Plank only."

He stood and went out onto the landing again and called down the stairs. "Vaughn! Send Tom Dawson up here." After a few minutes there was a slow tread on the stairs and then a timid knock on the open door. "Come in, come in," said Young, beckoning Dawson into the office. "Constable Plank is here to see you."

I stood and spoke to him. "Mr Dawson," I said. "I understand from Mr Young that you have seen him again – the man who tried to tempt you to hurt Charles Madden."

Dawson nodded. "But I didn't do it," he said. "And I remembered what you told me. To tell you if I saw him again. I remembered your name. You're Constable Plank – like the wood."

"That's right," I said. "You've a good memory. Now, tell me when you saw this man."

"Yesterday afternoon," he said. "Just before it struck four. Mr Young wasn't here but as soon as I saw him today, I told him."

"You did right, Mr Dawson," I said. He smiled broadly. "And where did you see the man?" I asked.

Dawson looked questioningly at Young, who nodded. The big lad bent down and carefully untied his laces and stepped out of his boots. He then walked across the office, almost on tiptoes, hardly daring to touch the rugs, and reached the window overlooking the yard. He pointed. "Down there," he said. "On a coach. A black coach."

"In a coach?" I repeated.

He shook his head. "On a coach – at the back. Standing."

"A footman, you mean?" I asked.

He shrugged. "He was standing at the back and when the coach stopped he jumped down and opened the door for the man."

"And you're certain it was the same man?" I asked. "If he was a footman, they all wear a similar sort of uniform – dark breeches and coat, pale stockings, black shoes with buckles." I took out my notebook and turned back a few pages. "That's how you described him to me last time. Perhaps you have confused him with another footman."

Dawson turned to me and frowned. "No," he said, shaking his head emphatically. "It was him. After his master had gone inside, I walked past the coach and he looked at me and then spoke to the driver. They both looked at me and laughed. I remember his laugh. People always laugh at me, so I'm good at remembering what they sound like."

"More fool them, Mr Dawson," I said. "You have given me some very useful and important information. And there is a reward for that."

Dawson's eyes widened. I reached into my pocket and took out two shillings. Dawson looked at Young, who nodded, and then Dawson walked over to me and held out his hand. I put one coin into it. "This one is for you to take home to your sister, as I am sure that keeping a big lad like you well fed costs a pretty penny," I said. "Tell her that it was given with thanks by a constable for your good work. I am sure she will believe you, but she can always check with Mr Young." And then I put the second coin onto his palm. "And this one is for you to spend as you wish. Perhaps you have a young lady who would like a new ribbon for her bonnet." From the flush that spread on Dawson's face I could tell I had hit the mark, and Young turned away quickly before Dawson could be offended by his smile. "It's not five pounds," I said, "but two shillings honestly earned is better than a hundred pounds from crime."

Dawson beamed at me and the smile stayed on his face as he bent to put on his boots, and as he bowed when he left the room – and I daresay all the way down the stairs and out into the yard.

"A black coach with one footman and a driver, yesterday afternoon at four," I said to Young.

"I'll ask around the yard and let you know," he replied.

A magistrate's warrant

SUNDAY 31ST OCTOBER 1829

John Conant and I looked at each other. Although nothing was said, I am certain that we each knew what the other was thinking. For my part, I was wondering whether it was wise to go alone to confront the subject of the warrant that the magistrate had just signed. And he was deciding whether he should risk offending me by suggesting that I take a younger constable with me. In the end, we both kept our counsel.

Conant looked down at the warrant again and then picked it up to shake the powder from it into the fireplace. He folded it carefully into three and handed it to me.

"A sad situation," he observed. "When will you call?" he asked.

"I sent a lad to make enquiries," I said, "and the maid told him everyone will be at home this morning but heading to the country this afternoon."

"This morning it is, then," said the magistrate.

♦

The rain was falling in a fine autumn drizzle by the time I arrived. In the end I had taken another constable with me, in case we needed to restrain our man on the way back to Great Marlborough Street, but I told him to wait in the coach. I knocked on the door and it was opened by the same footman as on my last visit. He looked at me but said nothing.

"I would like to speak to Mr Forster," I said. "It is a matter of some urgency. Constable Plank, of Great Marlborough Street, with a magistrate's warrant."

A flicker of alarm crossed the man's face but he quickly mastered it and stepped to one side to allow me into the hall. As before, he showed me into the drawing room.

"Wait here, please, sir," he said. He pulled the door shut behind him but I could hear his footsteps hurrying across the tiles, presumably to Forster's study. I glanced around the room; the black crêpe had been removed from the mirrors and pictures and the curtains were opened as wide as possible, but the heavy furnishings and the rain-filled skies meant that it was still a joyless room. Not for the first time I thought how strange it is that the people with the most money often have the least welcoming houses, while our own little place on Norton Street has only a few treasured, threadbare pieces and yet is a true home.

The door opened and in came Roger Forster. No silk banyan this time; he was dressed for an excursion to the country, with rough trousers and a thick coat, and serviceable boots rather than fashionable slippers.

"Constable Plank," he said. "As you see, you catch me leaving town. If it is something that could wait…" He made to turn from me, hoping to dismiss me with his impatience.

"It is not, sir, no," I said. "I have a warrant signed by a magistrate, requiring you to appear before him at a hearing this afternoon. It is my duty to escort you to that hearing." I reached into my pocket, took out the warrant and held it out to him. He looked at it but did not reach out for it.

"A hearing?" he said. "What business could a magistrate possibly have with me? Pass the matter to my lawyer or my banker, as you see fit. And now, constable, I must ask you to leave."

He yanked open the door and I saw the footman rear away – he had obviously had his ear pressed to the wood.

"Mr Forster," I said calmly, "it makes no difference to the legal process whether you take the warrant or not – it is still my duty to enforce it. I can, if you wish, share its contents with your lawyer and your banker, but the obligation to appear at the hearing is yours." I held out the warrant again. "My advice, sir, if you will forgive me, would be to take this, read it, send a note to your lawyer, and then come with me. I have a coach."

Forster snatched the warrant from me and tore it into pieces, throwing them angrily into the fireplace.

"You and your advice, constable, will leave my property immediately," he said. He looked around for the footman and then strode ahead of me to the front door. He opened it wide but I stayed in the hallway.

"Mr Forster," I said, "I have no choice in the matter. I cannot leave unless you accompany me."

Forster looked out in the street. Waiting just outside the house was a coach, the horses shaking their heads in the drizzle.

"If you think this is a mistake," I said, "you will be able to explain that to the magistrate at the hearing. I cannot leave unless you accompany me, and I imagine you would prefer to walk to the coach unescorted."

Forster all but snarled at me but said nothing. He snatched his hat from the table in the hall and walked briskly out into the street. The constable inside the coach threw the door open for him, and he stepped in. I looked around for the footman but he was nowhere in sight, so I pulled the door of the house closed behind me and climbed into the coach. The driver lifted his whip and we set off, turning into Brook Street.

Only a few yards later we pulled to a halt. I looked out of the window to check what was holding us up and saw a huddle of three men in the middle of the street, lurching around in an inelegant dance, as two of them struggled to hold onto a third, who was kicking and struggling.

"Hey, you there," I called out. "Clear the way!"

One of the men looked across at me, and I saw that it was Wilson.

"You head back to Great Marlborough Street," I said to the other constable, "and see to the paperwork for Mr Forster. Four o'clock hearing before Mr Conant. I'll see you there."

I climbed down from the coach, shut the door and signalled to the driver to carry on. The horses looked warily at the three men but stepped past them and the coach bowled away.

"Constable Wilson," I said. "I had no idea that this area was part of your new responsibilities."

"Ah, Constable Plank," said Wilson, dodging to avoid a fist flung carelessly in his direction. "You are quite right – I am well outside my allotted beat. But I am not yet on duty today. My friend Mr Dawson and I were out for a stroll and we spied this gentleman running down the passage behind these houses. My friend recognised him and said he thought you might want to speak to him, and how lucky that you should be nearby." He ducked again and this time grabbed the man's fist in his own hand and bent his arm up behind his back. "Now then," he said to his captive, "you can either stop that and quieten down, or we can quieten you down. Either way, I've had enough of it."

The footman tried to free himself again but realised that it was hopeless. He made a sound rather like a growl and cursed under his breath.

"I wondered where you had gone," I said to him. "Mr Forster is to appear before the magistrate, and the question really is whether he will admit his guilt, or let you swing for his crime."

The footman looked at me, narrowing his eyes.

"Oh yes," I continued. "The only fact we know for certain is that you asked Mr Dawson here whether he would attack young Charles Madden in exchange for five pounds."

"But I said no," said Dawson, looking at me.

I nodded. "But Mr Dawson said no. Now, Mr Forster could well say that it is nothing to do with him. Indeed, thinking about it, I'm sure that's what he will say. He will say that you and Charles Madden had a falling out – about a debt, perhaps, or a woman. And that you wanted your revenge." I looked at the footman, who was still scowling but nonetheless listening intently. "Now, personally, I think that's unlikely. I doubt you'd choose to waste five pounds on Charles Madden. But it's not what I think that matters: it's what the judge and jury think that matters. And Mr Forster has friends, I'm sure.

No-one likes to see a gentleman go to the scaffold. Do they, Constable Wilson?"

Wilson shook his head. "Much better to blame it on a servant, I should say."

"Less tawdry," I said. "Not so much scandal."

The footman's eyes darted from me to Wilson and back again.

"Unless," I said, as though the idea were just occurring to me, "unless someone could give us evidence about Mr Forster – about why he might want to have his stepson killed. If we had a motive, well, it might start to make sense."

♦

"I shall look forward to seeing Mr Forster at four o'clock," said Conant when I called into his rooms to tell him what had happened.

"He's none too pleased at being detained," I said, "and said some very unkind things to Mr Neale."

The magistrate smiled wryly. "I find it a mistake to insult those who have your comfort – or otherwise – in their gift."

"On a similar theme," I observed, "we have also brought in Mr Forster's footman. The one who offered five pounds to have Charles Madden attacked. He might well tell us who told him to make that offer, and why."

Conant raised an eyebrow at me. "The who is no mystery at all, Sam. The interesting thing – as ever – is why he did it."

"Another interesting thing," I said, "is how Constable Wilson came to be at just the right spot this morning. It's as though someone sent him a message to let him know what was going on. As though someone knew I would be attending that address with a warrant, this very morning, and might need assistance."

"Indeed," replied the magistrate, putting on his spectacles and reaching for a pile of papers. "As you say, interesting."

♦

The footman – whose full name, I now knew, was Robert Leedham – was brought into the back office by Tom Neale. The right side of Leedham's face was colouring into a bruise. I indicated it.

"Is that the work of Constable Wilson or of Mr Dawson?" I asked.

Leedham felt his cheek and winced. "An elbow, I think," he said. "Hard to say whose."

"Sit down, Mr Leedham," I said.

Leedham hesitated and then lowered himself into the chair opposite me.

"Were you in the same cell as Mr Forster?" I asked conversationally.

Leedham stared at me. "He's here?" he asked. "In this building?"

"Oh yes," I replied. "He's appearing before Mr Conant, the magistrate, at four o'clock. I understand from Mr Neale that he has requested a visit from his lawyer, so no doubt the two of them will be deciding just what picture to paint for Mr Conant. The heart-broken father – stepfather in name only, so fond was he of the lad – horrified to hear that the murderer is someone in his very own household. Yes, that would be my guess."

"I'm no murderer!" exclaimed Leedham, leaning forward. "I only offered the money."

"More than once," I reminded him. "Tom Dawson turned you down, but someone else didn't, did they? Someone else took the money and killed Charles Madden."

"Someone else, yes – someone else killed him, not me," said Leedham quickly.

"Ah, but that's where the law is a bit tricky," I said, shaking my head sadly. "Now, if the death had been accidental – a fight that got out of hand, let's say – then a charge of manslaughter might be possible. But murder now, that's premeditated, deliberate killing. And I'm sure Mr Forster's expensive lawyer will be able to argue that you, by paying someone five pounds, had in mind a killing – premeditated, because you planned it, and deliberate because you knew what would happen. The fact that you didn't want to get your own hands dirty will not change the argument that you incited a murder." Leedham opened his mouth but I held up my hand. "I'm simply thinking like a lawyer, Mr Leedham – and like the judges in the Old Bailey. The question will be why you did it. And with Charles Madden dead, there'll be no-one except you to dispute what the lawyer suggests. They could go with envy on your part, or a disagreement over a woman, but given Charles Madden's history of gambling, I think they'll say that he borrowed – perhaps stole – money from you and refused to pay it back."

Leedham slumped back in his chair, his face pale under the bruising.

"I'll swing for murder, won't I?" he said quietly.

"This time last year," I said genially, "it would have been worse. A servant killing a master was tried as petty treason, and then you'd have been hanged, drawn and quartered. But they've changed the law and now it's murder, plain and simple. So yes, you'd hang – with your body sent to the surgeons to be dissected and anatomised."

I might have gone too far, as Leedham looked as though he might faint. He gripped the table and swallowed hard. I took pity on him.

"But there is an alternative," I said. "If – as I believe, but then I am not the magistrate or the judge – the person who planned the murder and paid the five pounds is Roger Forster, then all eyes will turn to him. You would not be completely blameless, but as a servant obeying the orders of his master, well, your actions would be more acceptable."

"And that is what happened," said Leedham hotly. "That is exactly what happened."

"The difficulty will be explaining why Mr Forster would do such a thing," I said. "He's a stepfather, yes, but a stepfather who tried to share his interests with his stepson." I turned back several pages in my notebook. "Mrs Forster told me that they went to horse sales together, and to Crockford's. In fact," I glanced up at Leedham, "she suggested that Roger was fonder of Charles than the other way round but could not find any reason for the young man's dislike of his stepfather – beyond the usual dislike of seeing his father replaced in the household. And with Charles not able to speak for himself, the court will hear only from Roger Forster and his wife." I closed my notebook deliberately. "Unless you can shed any light on things – unless you know what would drive Roger Forster to murder his stepson."

"I'm caught, aren't I?" said the footman, almost to himself. "Either way, I'm involved – but one way I'll hang and the other way I have a chance."

"Mr Leedham," I said, "you certainly are involved: you handed over five pounds to someone so that they would attack Charles Madden, and that attack resulted in his death. It is right that you should answer for that. But if you were acting on behalf of someone else, and you know their motive, you must tell me."

"Money," said Leedham, and then again, louder, "money."

I opened my notebook again. "Gambling debts?" I asked.

He shook his head. "That's what I thought at first, but no. It's more complicated than that."

An incomplete scheme

MONDAY 2ND NOVEMBER 1829

"So we are losing Constable Wilson to the new police, but not you, Sam," said James Harmer with a smile, putting down his satchel next to an armchair. "Although I can't help thinking that they would be wise to recruit you – it's never a good idea to have an entirely new service without some experienced fellows on board. I know you're a loyal old dog and you'd miss everyone here, but still, it's worth considering, you know." He looked at me for a long moment. "Worth considering, yes." He walked over to the sideboard where Conant's footman had put a pot of fresh coffee, poured himself a cup, sipped it and grimaced. "Too strong for me – plays havoc with my digestion." He walked to the door, opened it and yelled down the stairs. "Billy – tea, if you please!" He then sat down, indicating that I should do the same, and glanced at the clock.

"I've sent word to Mr Conant that you are here," I confirmed.

We heard footsteps on the stairs and, as if I had conjured him up, the magistrate appeared. We all stood, and Harmer and Conant shook hands. I carried over a chair from the dining table, leaving the two armchairs for the magistrate and the lawyer. Conant poured himself a cup of coffee, glancing at the discarded one on the sideboard. "Tea, James?" he asked.

"Your man is seeing to it," said the lawyer, just as the door opened and Thin Billy appeared with a pot of tea. Drinks distributed, we sat down.

"It is good of you to come so quickly, James," said Conant. "We have need of your legal expertise to pick the bones out of a tale we have been told."

"A tale?" echoed Harmer. "You don't believe it?"

"I don't know yet," admitted the magistrate. "It hinges on an understanding of inheritance law, and mine is rather cursory."

"Well, inheritance can be a slippery beast," said Harmer. "Let's hear it."

Conant turned to me and nodded.

"We have a case of murder," I started. "The victim is a young man who was attacked so viciously that he died. The attacker was paid – we think five pounds – for his work. The victim's stepfather says that the footman is responsible, and the footman accuses the stepfather."

"As you mentioned inheritance, I assume that we need to explore the position of the stepfather," said Harmer, reaching into his satchel and pulling out a notebook and pencil, rather like my own.

"Mrs Forster, the victim's mother," I continued, "was widowed ten years ago, when her son was twelve. When he was nineteen, she remarried, to Roger Forster."

"Did the first husband die intestate?" asked Harmer, making notes.

I nodded. "Yes: Mrs Forster herself told me that."

"And so a third went to the widow and two-thirds to the children," said Harmer.

"Just the one child," I said. "Charles Madden."

Harmer shook his head. "I am always uneasy when a child inherits," he said. "Did he run wild?"

I looked back through my notebook to my record of my meeting with Mrs Forster. "His mother said that he was 'headstrong and rudderless', and 'set about spending it'," I read aloud.

"As might we all, gentlemen, had we been left a pot of money at an age with no responsibilities and no eye to the future," said Harmer with a chuckle. "But so far I can see nothing that needs my legal expertise, as you so flatteringly call it, John."

"Indeed," agreed Conant. "But the footman claims that the stepfather wanted to kill his stepson in order to inherit his fortune, and Constable Plank and I are not certain whether such a plan would be feasible."

"Ah," said the lawyer, sitting forward with interest. "So we have a young man of, what, twenty-two?" I nodded. "Unmarried?" I nodded again. "And in possession of a sizeable fortune. He has a living mother – any siblings from the second marriage?" I shook my head.

"And I should imagine he has no will," I added.

"Which of us does, at that age?" said Conant. "I certainly thought I was immortal. Age makes us more cautious – and less certain."

"Indeed," said Harmer. "If I understand it, your question is: what happens to this young man's property in the case of his death?" This time, both the magistrate and I nodded.

"The short answer is that it goes to his next of kin," said the lawyer. "Interestingly, that term is not defined specifically in statute, but the principle is that it turns on bloodline. Ordinarily, of course, a father comes before a mother in that reckoning, but a stepfather does not – the blood is what matters. And so, for your young man, the sole beneficiary would be his mother – Mrs Forster."

Conant looked at me. "Well, then, surely the footman is lying," he said. "Roger Forster does not benefit financially from his stepson's death."

"Not yet, no," I agreed, "but Mr Leedham – that's the footman – claims that the scheme is only part-completed. Mr Harmer, you say that Mrs Forster will inherit her son's estate – in other words, she has now inherited everything from her late husband, apart from the portion already spent by her son."

"That's right, yes," said the lawyer.

"And what would happen if Mrs Forster were to die?" I asked.

"Do we know if her husband has permitted her to make a will?" asked Harmer.

"I don't know," I replied, "but it would seem unlikely, given what I have seen of the man. I doubt he is one to give up control."

"Let us assume not, then," agreed the lawyer. "In that case, her estate would pass to her widower – to Roger Forster."

"And is that the scheme, then, Sam?" asked Conant.

"According to Leedham," I confirmed, "Roger Forster's intention was to wait a suitable period and then arrange the death of his wife, thereby inheriting the entire estate."

"A fortune hunter," said Harmer.

"It could work, then, the scheme that Leedham described?" I asked. "Kill the son, then the mother, and inherit the lot?"

"Yes, indeed," said Harmer, putting away his notebook. "Some men make quite the career of it."

♦

"And yet the newspapers are full of stories about women marrying wealthy men," said Martha, as we sat at our fireside that evening. "Mind you, to my way of thinking some of them earn their money, when you see the dull, fat old men they choose."

"You sound rather world-weary, Mar," I commented.

"Do I?" she asked. "I hope I'm not. But the more I hear about people, the more I realise that very few things are simple. When I was a little girl and saw the fine ladies in their carriages, with their handsome footmen and their rich clothes, I envied them: I thought that if I had those things, I'd be happier. But money doesn't solve your problems: it just gives you different ones. If Mrs Forster had married a poor man – or even just an ordinary one, perhaps a constable," she smiled at me, "then her son might still be alive and her husband wouldn't have been plotting to kill her."

"We're not certain that he was," I reminded her. "The judge and jury will decide that. He says he's innocent."

Martha shrugged. "Of course he does: he's facing the scaffold. But the footman couldn't have invented that story – they're hired for their looks, not their brains. And Mr Conant thinks there's something in it, or he wouldn't have sent him to Coldbath." She shook her head. "Poor Mrs Forster – I wouldn't be in her place for all the fine clothes in London." She gazed into the flames.

"Talking of fine clothes," I said.

"Hmm?" asked Martha, her eyes still fixed on the fire.

"I said, talking of fine clothes," I repeated, "you might have to buy some new trimmings for that blue dress of yours."

Martha turned to look at me. "My blue dress? What has my blue dress to do with anything, Sam?"

"You remember me talking about Mr Harmer's junior lawyer, Richard Barnes, and how he might suit Miss Lily?" I asked.

My wife raised an eyebrow. "I remember thinking that you are rather stout to be playing Cupid," she said tartly.

I put on an injured face. "That's not kind, Mar," I protested. "You women think you know everything about marriage and romance, but we men – we're really the soft-hearted ones."

Martha smiled and held out her hand, and I took it. "I'm sorry, Sam," she said. "That was unkind of me. Tell me about Mr Barnes."

"On the advice of Samuel Cupid here," I said, "at the end of our meeting this morning Mr Harmer sent for Mr Barnes to bring him some papers. Because someone," I pointed to my own chest, "someone knew that Miss Lily would be calling in to accompany her father home. And if the two young people were to meet and engage in conversation…"

"Pah!" said Martha, releasing my hand and sitting back in her seat. "Blue dress, indeed! Do you really think that there will be a wedding on the strength of a short conversation in front of the girl's father? Miss Lily is far more choosy than that."

"Indeed she is," I agreed. "But tell me this, Martha Plank: how many times, to your knowledge, has Miss Lily missed dinner with her father in order to accompany a young man to a concert?"

Martha looked at me with narrowed eyes. "Not once," she replied.

"Precisely," I said. "And yet, can you imagine who is, at this very moment, sitting in a City of London amateur concert alongside a young lawyer of pleasing appearance, considerable intellect and upstanding morals, while her poor father dines alone at home?"

Repercussions

TUESDAY 3RD NOVEMBER 1829

I t was a damp, bone-chilling morning as I turned into Dorrington Street and headed for the entrance to the Coldbath Fields house of correction. When I was a young constable it had had a brutal reputation as a crowded, filthy, pitiless place, and although the first was still true, its keeper John Vickery had done everything within his power to address the other two concerns. He was a former Runner and had every reason to view his inmates with disgust, but – like John Wontner at Newgate – his compassionate nature triumphed over any despair he felt at the endless supply of rogues sent into his care. I glanced up at the stone fetters strung in warning above the gateway and shivered, before knocking on the heavy wooden door. The bolt was scraped back and the door opened just enough to allow a turnkey to peer around at me.

"Constable Samuel Plank," I said. "Here to fetch Roger Forster for his hearing." I passed the warrant through the gap and the turnkey took it and pushed the door closed again. After a moment, he opened it fully.

"'E's in the sixteen, o' course," said the turnkey through his few remaining teeth. "Although there's no danger o' that one topping hisself, I can promise you. Paid good money for his bed and board." He cleared his throat and spat onto the ground. "Straight in, or see the guvnor first?"

"I'll see Mr Vickery, if he's here," I said.

"Know your own way, d'ye?" asked the turnkey.

"I do," I replied.

The turnkey nodded, returned the warrant to me, and disappeared back into his guardhouse – I caught sight of a little pot-bellied stove in the corner, with a kettle steaming on the top of it.

The keeper's house – where he lived and worked when he was not patrolling the prison – was a strange building: it formed part of the wall surrounding Coldbath, with its front door on the inside and two large windows looking to the outside. It was six months or more since I had called on John Vickery, and the change

in his domestic circumstances was plain to see: the front
step was swept but not polished, while the door knocker
was dull. Nonetheless it served its purpose, and a young
maid opened the door to me. She took one look at me
and called over her shoulder "Constable 'ere to see ya!"
before retreating once again to the back of the house and
leaving me to find my own way. I reached the door of
Vickery's study just as he opened it and we shook hands.

"Another one of your good causes?" I asked.

"It's this or back on the streets," he said, smiling.
"Since Phoebe – you remember my girl – since she married and went up to Edinburgh, I've had to shift for myself. Her new husband's coaching inn, meanwhile, is the
most efficient it has ever been." The smile faded a little;
a widower, he had been very fond of his daughter, and I
knew it pained him to see her move so far away. "She's
the third one I've tried," he said, nodding in the direction
of the kitchen, "and, if you can believe it, she's the best of
the three."

"You've never thought to marry again?" I asked.

"Who'd have me?" replied Vickery, pointing to himself. "My back aches, my hair's going grey – and I live
with a thousand prisoners on my doorstep. But not for
much longer, Constable Plank."

"You're moving on?" I asked.

"Retiring," said Vickery. "At the end of this year I'll have done my seven years, and then I receive my pension."

"You'll be sorely missed," I said, meaning it. "Do you have any say in the selection of your successor?"

The keeper shook his head. "I did ask but was told in no uncertain terms that it is a matter for the prison commissioners. Anyway, I've done my years, and my son-in-law has kindly asked me to move in with them and help with the inn. With new routes being set up all the time, and their prime location on Princes Street, they have more custom than they can manage. Or at least that's what he tells me. I suspect they just feel sorry for this old carthorse, being put out to pasture."

"You forget that I have met your daughter, and I know she's not one to hide her true feelings," I said. "If she says she wants you to live with them, then she wants you to live with them. And I'm sure they'll get the better of the deal; you've always been a hard-working fellow, and I can't see that changing just because some prison commissioners say it's time for you to go."

Vickery clapped me on the shoulder, which I took to mean that he was pleased. To save him further embarrassment, I held up the warrant. "Now, how have you fared with Mr Forster?"

"I try to remember my Bible," said the keeper. "Love your enemies, bless them that curse you, do good to them that hate you, and pray for them which despitefully use you, and persecute you. And I've been praying a great deal since Mr Forster's arrival."

As we walked into the prison, I found myself distracted – as I always was – by the sound of Coldbath's dozen treadwheels being turned by prisoners. I hated the sound: it seemed to me the most pointless of punishments, requiring men – thirty at a time – to climb steps that constantly rotated towards them, in an utterly exhausting and entirely unproductive exercise. At least the women prisoners, put to work picking oakum, had something to show for their labours at the end of the day.

"Did you know that the fellow who invented the treadwheel meant it to be used for the grinding of corn?" asked Vickery.

I shook my head. "I hope he regrets his work," I said.

"You know we're headed to the sixteen?" asked the keeper.

"Your turnkey told me," I replied. "He also suggested that it wasn't for the usual reason."

"Ha!" said Vickery, holding yet another door open for me as we gradually made our way towards the very centre of Coldbath. Here were the sixteen private cells; they were completely internal, without much light, and originally intended as places of punishment and sole confinement or to keep a close eye on anyone considered at danger of self-murder, but the alternative was a berth in a crowded, noisy and perhaps dangerous room with a dozen others. "It's impossible to fool the turnkeys. They've seen it all. When Forster was brought in on Saturday, he put on quite a show. Insisted I was summoned from my dinner to deal with him personally, wept on my shoulder, asked me to send for the chaplain – wrung my hand piteously when I took my leave, saying that we might not meet again in this life. A couple of the sixteen cells were empty, so we put him in there for the first night – and he's paid handsome garnish to the turnkeys to stay put." He held open one final door, revealing a turnkey dozing on a chair against the wall.

"Mr Longden," said Vickery, and the turnkey woke with a start and stumbled to his feet.

"Sorry, sir," he said, rubbing his face with his hands. "Nothing to report – all quiet."

"We'd like to see Mr Forster," said the keeper.

The turnkey lifted the bunch of keys that hung from his belt and sorted through them. He walked to one of the thick oak doors leading to the cells and unlocked it, then stood to one side to let us open it and enter the cell. Roger Forster was sitting on one of the two chairs by the table and stood as we walked in. With three of us in the cell, which was only seven feet wide by ten feet deep and contained a stump bedstead, a washbasin on a stool and the table and chairs, it felt very crowded.

"Mr Forster," said Vickery. "Constable Plank is here with your warrant, to accompany you to Great Marlborough Street for your hearing."

"And not before time," said Forster, reaching for the coat hanging over the back of his chair. "Once the magistrate hears how I have been treated, you can both expect repercussions. Anyone with a modicum of wit will soon see that your suspicions are ludicrous."

"Indeed, sir," said Vickery mildly.

Forster snatched up a small leather bag from the bed and stuffed into it his few possessions. He spoke over his shoulder. "You, constable," he said. "You've spoken to Leedham. You should be careful about believing what he says. He's a liar – he'll say anything to save his own skin. I know for a fact that he and my stepson argued about money – Charles borrowed from him and he turned nasty. He knows people, does Leedham – dangerous people. I said as much to my wife: Charles brought it on himself, but Leedham's behind his death, you can be sure."

"That must have been a great comfort to her," observed Vickery.

Forster rounded on him, jabbing a finger into his chest. "And I shall certainly be making a complaint about you, Vickery," he spat.

"About me, sir?" asked the keeper.

"I gave your man a message to deliver to my wife, and he took my money but the message was not delivered," said Forster. "I have had no reply."

"Ah, well, sir," said Vickery, "those are two different matters. I can assure you that your message was delivered to your wife. And my man, as you call our senior turnkey, waited more than an hour for a reply. And was told very clearly that there would be no reply, no matter how long he waited. It seems that your wife no longer wishes to hear from you."

"You're lying," said Forster, narrowing his eyes. "My lawyer will see to it that your foul lies are exposed."

"It's interesting that you should mention lawyers," I said. "Mr Conant had a word with a lawyer only yesterday, discussing your situation."

"My situation?" repeated Forster.

"Very interesting," I said conversationally. "Family structure and lines of inheritance. And Mrs Forster kindly confirmed what we thought: that she had inherited her son's estate, and that if she died before you, you would be her sole beneficiary."

Forster paled a little but maintained his bluster. "And why should my wife die before me? She's a strong and healthy woman – we both look forward to a long and happy life together."

"Once upon a time, maybe," I said, "but if she is not replying to your message, perhaps she is having second thoughts about that."

"It's a marvellous thing, the maternal instinct," commented Vickery. "No matter how much a woman may love her husband, her love for her children is always greater. I've seen a bitch turn on a dog twice her size when he threatened her pups. Tore a lump out of his throat, and he bled to death." He indicated his own neck and shook his head sadly.

"I've had enough of this nonsense about dogs," snarled Forster. "I'm no schoolboy, to be frightened by your simple allegories. If you think you'll scare me into confessing anything, you're sadly mistaken."

I looked at Vickery and raised an eyebrow. "Mr Forster talks of confessing, Mr Vickery," I said. "An interesting choice of word. Not one that would spring readily to the mind of an innocent man, wouldn't you say?"

I sensed rather than saw the movement of Forster's arm as he raised it to strike me, but Vickery – his reactions honed by years of exposure to men far more dangerous than the one before us now – grabbed Forster by the wrist and twisted his arm behind his back.

"Come now, Mr Forster," he said calmly, "that's not going to help your cause, is it? The magistrates don't look kindly on anyone who attacks their constables."

"Your mistake, Mr Forster," I said, "was to ask Leedham for help twice. All your eggs in one basket, as it were. As you say, there was no love lost between him and your stepson, but when you asked him to look for someone willing to murder your wife, he wasn't keen. A step too far for Mr Leedham."

"He certainly increased his price," snarled Forster. "Fifty pounds, he wanted. He could have set himself up with that, but instead he goes snivelling to you."

"I wouldn't be too harsh on him," I said, standing to one side so that Vickery could push Forster out of the cell ahead of me. "He didn't say a word to us about your wife. But now we have your confession, he won't need to."

♦

"And once he realised that the game was up," I said to Martha as I dried the dishes, "he told us everything."

"A bit late for that," said Martha tartly.

"Indeed," I said, "but it made the hearing more straightforward. It seems that he was a member of Crockford's and ended up with some of their counterfeit banknotes, which gave him the idea. He passed them on to his stepson, encouraging him to spend them at the Horse Bazaar, as he knew that Mr Young was on the lookout for them. From there it was simple for him to suggest that Young had set his thugs on Charles Madden in revenge – all the while paying someone, through his footman, to make it look like the beating from the thugs had gone too far."

"And all this," said Martha, standing back from the sink and drying her hands on her apron, "all this – the murder of a young man, the breaking of a mother's heart – just for money."

"We're lucky, you and I, Mar," I said, pulling her to me and kissing the top of her head. "We know there's more to life than just money – for us, it's always that: just money. But there's plenty who are made different, and to them, money is everything."

CHAPTER THIRTY-FIVE

Thrown to the wolves

WEDNESDAY 4TH NOVEMBER 1829

I was standing in front of the counter at Great Marlborough Street, stamping my feet to bring some warmth back to them after a chilly morning spent outside.

"Snow, do you think, Sam?" asked Tom Neale, looking up from his ledger.

"It wouldn't surprise me," I replied. "The sky looks yellow enough for it. Any chance of a pot of tea in the back office, to thaw me out?"

"I can go one better than that," replied the office keeper. "Mr Conant has sent word that he wants to see you, and no doubt Thin Billy has been brewing his delicious coffee in anticipation of your arrival." He winked at me.

Thankfully there was also a pot of tea, a tureen of vegetable broth and a covered dish of grilled meats ranged on the sideboard in the magistrate's room. The footman was setting the table.

"Good afternoon, constable," he said, indicting one of the dining chairs. "Mr Conant sent word that you're to start and he'll be up as soon as he can. There's the newspaper if you want it," he pointed to the magistrate's armchair, "and I'll just see to the fire before I leave you."

I was starting on a second helping of broth when the door opened and Conant came in. "Good to see you, Sam," he said. "No, no, don't get up – I'll join you." He walked over to the fire and held out his hands to warm them before turning to do the same for his posterior. "Is the broth any good?" he asked.

"Excellent," I said. "Vegetable and barley, I think."

The magistrate lifted the lid on the covered plate and sniffed at the meat before helping himself to a bowl of broth. He sat next to me at the table and we ate in companionable silence for a while, sharing bread and working our way through the meat that I had carried to the table once we had both had our fill of broth. At last, Conant pushed his plate from him, wiped his mouth and sat back in his chair.

"I thought you'd want to know about the Forster hearing yesterday," he said. "Mr Forster was not very complimentary about you – apparently you twisted his words while Mr Vickery twisted his arm. I assured him I would take the matter up with you." He smiled at me. "Which I have done."

"Mr Vickery and I may have encouraged him to think carefully about his situation," I conceded, "by pointing out some of the inconsistencies in his account."

"Mr Forster's situation is entirely of his own making," said the magistrate. "And whether it was his conversation with you and Mr Vickery, or his few nights' stay in Coldbath and our cell here, or indeed a sudden attack of conscience, he has finally told me the full story. Or at least, the version of it that he seeks to present at his trial. He claims that although he did consider seeing off first his stepson and then his wife, in order to inherit the estate, once the first killing was done he changed his mind." I raised an eyebrow but said nothing. Conant continued. "When he saw how distressed his wife was at the death of her child and realising belatedly that he too was fond of the lad, he decided not to go any further. He had already asked Leedham to find a second assassin, but was planning to rescind his instruction, on the very day that he was arrested."

"Convenient," I observed.

Conant shrugged. "That is not for you – or me – to decide. The judge and jury will have that pleasure. But this will amuse you, Sam: Forster asked me whether I thought he should claim insanity, or perhaps admit to manslaughter, saying that he had never intended the attacker to kill his stepson, only frighten him."

"I trust you declined to express an opinion," I said.

"I did," confirmed the magistrate, standing and walking over to the sideboard. "Coffee, Sam? Or tea?"

I chose the latter and we moved over to the armchairs to take advantage of the fire.

"And what of the footman – Needham, was it?" asked Conant.

"Leedham," I replied. "Robert Leedham. After a little persuading by Constable Wilson, he has come around to our way of thinking. As you know, he admitted that he paid five pounds to the man who attacked and killed Charles Madden, and told us that Roger Forster then asked him to arrange the murder of his wife. Luckily for her, Leedham was quite fond of her and didn't want any part of it despite the generous inducement."

"Indeed," said the magistrate.

"When Mr Leedham finally understood that his master might well throw him to the wolves, we convinced him that offering up the name of the killer would be to his benefit. He was uneasy – and who can blame him? A paid assassin would have no compunction about killing again. But just this morning he has sent me word of the man's name. I have been dropping questions in the right ears and hope to hear soon."

CHAPTER THIRTY-SIX

The highest standards of public service

FRIDAY 6TH NOVEMBER 1829

The message lad bent over, hands on knees, catching his breath. "Mr Atkins says you're to come quick," he puffed. "Says there's an officer of the new police, drunk as…" He caught sight of Martha's face and corrected himself. "Very drunk, missus."

Martha nodded at him and finished cutting the slice of fruit loaf. She handed it to the lad. "You eat that while Constable Plank puts his coat on," she said, "and if you're lucky he'll take you with him in the hackney back to the

Blue Boar. Unless you'd rather stay round here for your next job."

The lad shook his head vigorously, swallowing quickly. "Oh no, missus, thanks all the same."

I smiled to myself as I buttoned my coat; no lad of that age would turn down the chance of a ride in a coach.

"It'll be a long journey, mind," I said. "We've to go to the station house on Hadlow Street first, to collect another constable."

The lad beamed widely: with coins from his errand, a belly full of fruit loaf and now a long ride in a coach, he was most satisfied with his morning.

♦

Wilson yawned as we barrelled along Woburn Place. "Sorry," he said, shaking his head to clear it. "George woke me early – he can't understand why I'm at home but not playing with him. And Alice is restless these days."

"Aye," I said. "Less than a month to go, Martha reckons."

The message lad, sitting opposite us, nodded solemnly. "My sister was the same, with her youngest. Couldn't settle to anything. Drove my ma to distraction."

Wilson and I took care not to catch each other's eye, for fear of laughing at his weary wisdom, and looked instead out of the coach windows. I had told the jarvey not to go right up to the Blue Boar but to stop some way back, just in case our quarry took fright. And he did as requested, pulling the horses to a halt on the corner of King's Gate Street. The lad jumped out, put a hand to his forehead in salute, and disappeared into the crowd on High Holborn. Wilson and I climbed down more slowly, keeping close to the buildings, and walked towards the inn. We stood to one side to allow a dusty coach and its steaming horses to turn into the courtyard, and then crossed the yard ourselves and went into the kitchen, as instructed in the message. The cook spotted us, called across to the pot boy and he raced off to find George Atkins. Instead, his wife appeared; she was as tall and spare as her husband, and with a welcoming manner and ready laugh to match his.

"Constable Plank, Constable Wilson," she said, above the din of the kitchen. "You are just in time." She beckoned us to follow her and led us out of the kitchen and into the corridor that ran towards the main public rooms of the inn. "He's in the drawing room," she said in a low tone. "He was making to leave, so I sent Florrie in to do a bit of tidying and catch his eye. She's a good girl, Florrie, but handy for distracting a gentleman." She winked and then indicated that we should peer into the drawing room through the next doorway, while she herself returned to the kitchen. Wilson looked first and then turned to nod at me, before I had a quick look myself.

Sitting at a table in the corner of the room, two tankards in front of him, was a Metropolitan Police officer. He had that loose, slumped posture of the drunkard, and his collar was undone. His hat lay on the floor under his table. Florrie – who I had to admit was a pretty girl, with tempting curves – was keeping her distance from him but taking her time about dusting the ornaments on the mantelpiece. I looked again at the officer's drink-reddened face and turned to Wilson.

"You're in luck, lad," I said quietly. "That's Inspector Cameron."

"The one you saw at the watch house in Covent Garden?" he asked.

I nodded. "And that means you'll have to deal with him on your own – we can't have him running to the Commissioners with accusations of conspiracy or persecution, if he thinks I'm after him."

"But he's an inspector," whispered Wilson. "I'm only a constable."

"A constable who is sober, wearing his uniform correctly and upholding the good name and reputation of the Metropolitan Police," I said. "None of which applies to him." I jerked my thumb in the direction of the inspector. "You have your notebook?" I asked. Wilson nodded and patted his coat pocket. "And your *Instruction Book*?" He nodded again and patted the other pocket. "Then you're ready," I said, and gently pushed him into the room.

From my hidden position behind the door, I saw the inspector look across at Wilson, and then sit more upright when he spotted the uniform. Sensing trouble brewing, Florrie bobbed a quick curtsy to Wilson and left the room. Her eyes widened when she saw me hiding behind the door but I put my finger to my lips and she nodded and scurried off down the corridor.

"Constable," I heard Cameron say. The drink had made his voice thick, but he said the word with as much authority as he could muster.

"Constable William Wilson, D38, Marylebone," said Wilson.

"Inspector Cameron," said the fellow. "I am waiting for the coach..."

"Inspector Cameron, if I may," said Wilson. Cameron looked startled. Wilson took out his notebook and made a show of reading aloud from it. "I believe that you are Inspector Cameron, F Division. Based at the watch house in Covent Garden." He looked at the inspector, who gazed at him but said nothing. Wilson continued. "Under your command at F Division is a constable, name unknown, bearing collar number F27. Complaints have been made about the conduct of this constable, but you have declined to take action, on the basis that…" he enunciated carefully, "we all know the effect a smart uniform has on the female eye".

I could see on the inspector's face the struggle his ale-soaked brain was engaged in, to make sense of what he was hearing and work out where he had heard it before.

Wilson closed his notebook, put it away and then took out his *Instruction Book*. "As a constable myself, I have been issued with one of these," he said, holding the little book aloft. "I have read it carefully and assume you have too."

Cameron nodded dumbly.

"And so you will be well aware of the restrictions placed on us as officers of the Metropolitan Police, of the need for us to be seen as a new force, serving our fellow citizens and upholding the highest standards of public service," continued Wilson, warming to his theme.

"Such as this: He shall at all times appear in his complete police dress."

Cameron looked self-conscious and put his hands to his neck to fasten his collar, while looking around for his hat.

"And then this," said Wilson, turning a few more pages of the book. "On no pretence shall he enter any public house except in the immediate execution of his duty." He looked up at Cameron, his face a picture of innocence. "You mentioned that you were waiting for a coach, inspector – which coach is that? Are you waiting to apprehend someone? In the immediate execution of your duty?"

Cameron sat forward as though to look out of the window but then slumped back in his seat.

"What do you want, Constable Wilson?" he asked. "Something to do with F27, it seems."

Wilson closed his Instruction Book. "Constable F27 is abusing his authority to make approaches to young women – to girls. He is forcing them to lie with him, by threatening them with accusations of theft. He is a shameful Metropolitan Police officer, and a shameful man. I do not know or care why you chose to protect him, but it will stop. You will include a full account of his actions in your next report to your superintendent, and you will make sure that constable F27 is dismissed and that his fellow constables in F Division are told why." Wilson stopped to draw breath. "That is what I want, sir."

Cameron thought for a long moment. "And if I do as you suggest," he said, "this… meeting will be forgotten."

"Completely forgotten," agreed Wilson, nodding. "I have friends in F Division," he lied, "and they will let me know once constable F27 has gone. If I do not hear from them…" He left the sentence unfinished.

The inspector held up a hand and then struggled to his feet. He cast around and Wilson pointed to the floor beneath the table; Cameron bent down with some difficulty and retrieved his hat, jamming it onto his head. He then smoothed down the front of his coat and with exaggerated dignity walked to the door. I ducked back into the shadows and watched as he made his way along the corridor, one hand on the wall to steady himself. In the drawing room, Wilson collapsed into a seat.

"Thank God that's over," I heard him say.

♦

"I'm not sure I approve of blackmail," said Martha when I had finished telling her what had happened. She bit off the thread and shook out the nightdress she had been mending.

"Blackmail?" I echoed. "Hardly that. Blackmail is more when you force someone to do something they shouldn't, whereas we were simply encouraging Inspector Cameron to do something he should. Whitemail, perhaps."

"Whitemail?" said Martha. "There's no such thing, Sam." She yawned and stretched. "How did you know that the inspector would go to the Blue Boar?"

"I didn't," I said, standing and checking the fire. "I sent a note to George Atkins, asking him to keep an eye out for any Metropolitan Police officers from F Division drinking on duty, and to ask other innkeepers to do the same. After Atkinson and Alcock, I knew it was a weakness of the new force."

"Atkinson and Alcock?" asked Martha.

"The first two Metropolitan Police constables who were attested, on the same day as Wilson," I explained as I put the guard in front of the fireplace. "They were given collar numbers one and two – and were dismissed the very same day for drunkenness."

"That's shameful, Sam," said Martha. As the daughter of a toper, she had little sympathy for those who overindulged.

"I reasoned that it was only a matter of time and patience before someone spotted an officer from F Division in a public house," I said, "and then we would be able to use that to put pressure on Inspector Cameron to do the right thing about the officer who threatened Louisa and Ellie. Not for one moment did I think we'd catch Cameron himself."

"No wonder he was so tolerant of his constable's bad behaviour," said Martha as she walked into the kitchen, "with his own standards being so low."

"Aye," I said, checking the bolt on the back door. "When you recruit so many men so quickly, you're bound to get some bad apples in the barrel. And if a man is inclined to abuse his position, no *Instruction Book* is going to stop him."

"No," said Martha, "not in his own hands. But in the hands of a good man, well, that's different."

We were just at the foot of the stairs when there was a knock at the back door. Martha looked over her shoulder at me and rolled her eyes.

"You go on up, Mar," I said, patting her rump, "and I'll be along soon."

I went to the back door and pulled open the bolt. Standing there, his breath clouding in the cool night air, was one of the message lads.

"Good evening, Jake," I said. "You're out late."

"Last job, sir," he said. "Just on my way home and Mr Neale asked me to bring you this. Said you'd want to know." He reached down his front and took out a note, handing it to me. He looked past me into the kitchen. "Mrs Plank gone to bed already, sir?" he asked.

"So that's your game, is it, lad?" I said, teasingly. "Wait there and I'll see what I can find."

I went to the corner cupboard, and as I opened its door I heard Martha's voice – she was obviously sitting on the stairs, waiting for me. "There's a slice of pigeon pie on the blue plate, Sam," she said. "And a pear from the bowl."

I wrapped the pie in a sheet of paper and handed the two items to Jake.

"Ta, Mrs Plank," he called.

"Good night, Jacob," came the reply. "Get off home now – your sister will be worrying about you."

Jake disappeared into the dark and I closed and bolted the door again.

Martha reappeared in the kitchen. "What does Mr Neale want?" she asked.

I unfolded the note. "He says he's had word about Jed Hawkins – the man Leedham paid to attack Charles Madden." I looked up at my wife. "Hawkins has been

380 | SUSAN GROSSEY

found – pulled from the river earlier this evening. A knife wound to the chest."

Martha put her hand on my arm. "I'm sorry for his mother, or his wife," she said, "but it saves the hangman a job."

Eighteen pounds

THURSDAY 19TH NOVEMBER 1829

"I can't imagine what Mr Freame would want with me," said Wilson as we walked towards the banking house.

"Nor can I," I admitted, "and yet his note was quite clear." I pulled the paper from my pocket and read it aloud once more. "'If Constable Plank and Metropolitan Police Constable Wilson would care to attend the banking house of Freame and Company at eleven o'clock today, they will receive news of great interest to them both.' He's a sensible fellow – he won't be dragging you across town on a fool's errand."

"Still," said Wilson, pulling his coat collar tighter around his neck, "it's a cold morning and I could have stayed home in the warm."

"You can hardly hold the man responsible for the weather," I said. "Anyway, you're here now."

We pushed open the door of the banking house and the heads of the three clerks behind the bench looked up in unison. A blast of cold air followed us into the hall. The senior clerk, Mr Harris, hopped down off his stool and came across to greet us.

"Constable Plank, Constable Wilson," he said, bowing his head. "Mr Freame is in the parlour – he will be very pleased to see you."

"Mr Harris," I said as I handed him my hat, "do you have any idea what this is about?"

"I do, sir, yes," he replied.

"But you are not going to tell us?" I asked.

"No, sir, I am not," confirmed Harris, walking ahead of us to the door leading to the back rooms of the banking house. He knocked on the door of the parlour and looked into the room.

"Are they here?" I heard Edward Freame ask. "You didn't say anything, did you, Harris?"

"Yes, sir, and no, sir," said the senior clerk, and stood aside. "Constables," he said, and left us.

Freame jumped to his feet. "Come, come, come," he said, holding out his hand to shake first mine and then Wilson's. "Please, sit." He was smiling like a man with a secret. And for all his earlier complaints, I could see that Wilson was charmed by the banker's enthusiasm.

"Constable Wilson," began Freame, "I understand that you were uneasy about our decision to allow Edward Fraser and his family to evade justice and go to Canada."

Wilson shifted in his seat. "Well, that's not quite…"

Freame held up his hand and smiled. "I sometimes forget that you are a much younger man than either of us," he indicated himself and me, "and that for you the world is a much simpler place – right is right and wrong is wrong. I remember it well." He sighed. "But the years have taught me – us – that it is often much more… muddied. And I hope that what I have to show you today, Constable Wilson, will go a little way to showing you that sometimes bad people can turn out to be surprisingly good."

Wilson looked at me and I shrugged. Freame reached under his chair and brought out a slim packet. He looked at me and smiled broadly, and then handed the packet to Wilson.

"Go on," said the banker. "Open it."

Wilson turned the packet over in his hands and then unfolded the paper. Inside were banknotes. He counted them.

"Eighteen pounds," he said.

"And now look at the paper I wrapped them in," instructed Freame, on the edge of his seat.

Wilson turned over the paper and flattened it. "It is an advertisement," he said, "for an auction. Two days ago, held by Messrs Robins, in Covent Garden." He looked at the banker. "You have sold something and made eighteen pounds?" he asked.

"Precisely," said Freame. "A painting. A very accomplished painting, as the sale price suggests. By a renowned Austrian artist."

"Austrian?" I repeated.

Freame nodded. "Ernst Kaufmann of Vienna. He painted it here in London, and when they left for Canada he told his maid to have it sent to me. I knew nothing of this until the painting arrived here at the end of September, with very clear instructions. I was told to sell it for the best possible price, and as Mr Robins is a friend of mine and a man of great charitable generosity, I knew he would do his utmost to help – he even waived his auctioneer's commission. And so, eighteen pounds."

"But for what?" Wilson looked from Freame to me and back again, the banknotes in his lap.

"Why, for the family of Mr Robertson," said Freame, suddenly serious. "The poor fellow transported for uttering. In his letter, Mr Kaufmann said that he was sorry he could not do more for Robertson himself, but that this might be of some help to those he had been forced to leave behind." He held out his hand and Wilson passed the banknotes to him, and Freame handed them on to me. "Sam, you can make sure that this money is given to Mrs Robertson."

"I shall," I said, putting it into my pocket. "What type of painting was it, Edward? A portrait? Landscape?"

Freame smiled broadly. "This will amuse you, gentlemen," he said. "It was a fine London scene: the Picquet marching past the Bank of England."

Downstairs

WEDNESDAY 2ND DECEMBER 1829

"We can't leave her downstairs, like a dog," I said quietly to Martha as she readied herself for bed.

"When a woman is about to have a baby," she said, unpinning her hair and putting the pins one by one into the little dish on the dresser, "you must just do as she asks. Alice had her first baby in our sitting room, in front of the fire, and that is what she wants again."

I wondered – but didn't ask – why a woman would want to remember giving birth to a baby who was no longer with us. From time to time one or other of us would say, do you remember when little Martha did this or that, and we would all smile bravely.

Martha turned to look at me. "And if you are thinking of little Martha – and I know you are, from that look
on your face – then stop worrying. We had her for two
wonderful years, and none of us would wish that away.
Alice will think about her daughter every day for the rest
of her life, regardless of if and where she has more babies. And if being here, nesting among the cushions in
our sitting room, gives her peace, then that's what she
can do, for as long as she wants." She stood and
shrugged on her nightdress. "Anyway, we can't leave her
on her own at the station house while William is on duty.
William's mother has George, and we have Alice and
whatever baby God chooses to send her. Now shift
over." I did as I was told. Martha wriggled down and
curved her body against mine. She put her arm across
me and spoke into my chest. "And you mustn't be afraid,
Sam. Don't be afraid to love this baby. We must take it
into our hearts and love it for as long as we're given."

♦

When I woke in the night to use the pot, Martha had
gone. I put on my dressing gown and went downstairs.
I knew better than to go into the sitting room, from
where I could hear a low, animal moaning, but I knocked

gently on the door. Martha's head appeared; she looked worried.

"Anything I can do, Mar?" I asked.

There was a sharp yelp and Martha ducked back into the room. I waited.

Martha reappeared. "Put a pan of water on the stove, Sam – you'll need to stoke it up. The big pan. There's a pile of cloths on the chair in the kitchen – put them near the stove to warm." There was another yelp. "And then put your coat on, Sam, and fetch old Sadie. Tell her to bring her birthing bag. Quick as you can."

♦

I had fallen asleep in the kitchen, my head on the table, when I was woken by the shrill sound of a baby crying. Groggily, I knew that was good news and I stretched my arms above my head and bent my head this way and that to relieve the stiffness in my neck. I was just putting the kettle on the stove when I heard the sitting room door open.

"Tea, Mar?" I asked without looking round.

"Oh, Sam," she said, a sob in her voice, and as I turned around she collapsed into a chair. I went to her and crouched down beside her, my knees cracking.

"What is it, Mar?" I asked, although I dreaded the answer. "I heard the baby – but Alice?"

My wife leaned her head against mine. "She's not dead, Sam, but only by God's mercy. She's so small, so slight, and the baby is a big lad."

"A boy!" I said.

"She's been... damaged, Sam." Martha sat upright and looked at me. "Not just from this, but from, well, you know: before."

When Alice first came to us, she had been running away from a life that she could never tell us about. But she was fourteen, and with child, and wearing fine clothes that only a man of wealth could have bought for her. We knew only too well how she had earned those clothes.

"Is she in pain?" I asked.

Martha took my hand. "At the moment, yes – most women are after having a baby. But that will heal; Sadie has prepared a poultice and has bound her belly. But there will be no more children, Sadie thinks."

I stood. "Then this little fellow," I said, "is all the more precious. We must get word to Wilson that he has another son."

"A son called Samuel," said Martha, and burst into tears.

The absence of floggings

THURSDAY 17TH DECEMBER 1829

"Is that coat of yours warm?" were the first words out of the mouth of Commissioner Charles Rowan, who was himself wrapped in a heavy greatcoat, its collar turned up.

I looked down at myself. "Aye," I said.

"In that case," he replied, "I propose we have our discussion outside. I always think better outside than when cooped up in an office." And with that, he strode off ahead of me, out of the door into Whitehall Place. I caught up with him as he was crossing Whitehall, and together we walked through a narrow alleyway alongside Horse Guards and out onto the parade ground.

392 | SUSAN GROSSEY

"Ah," he said, breathing deeply. "That's better. I don't know how those fellows stick being inside so much." He turned to me with a ready smile. "Forgive me, constable." He held out his hand. "Charles Rowan."

I shook it. "Sam Plank," I said.

"A pleasure to meet you, Sam," he said. "Shall we?" With that, he headed off across the parade ground towards the Birdcage Walk. "We're of an age, you and I," he said, looking across at me. "Plenty still to offer the world, but with whippersnappers at our heels." As if to prove his point, a group of five smart young soldiers walked past, laughing and shoving each other and barely even acknowledging our existence.

"I've served my time, sir," I said, "as have you."

Rowan stopped and turned to me, an earnest look on his open face. "You speak as though it's all in the past," he admonished.

"If I may be frank, sir," I said, and the Commissioner nodded. "I received a note saying that you wanted to see me. I was intrigued and curious, and so here I am, but I don't see what a Commissioner of the Metropolitan Police wants with a worn-out magistrates' constable."

"You do yourself a disservice, Constable Plank," said Rowan. "I find myself in need of certain skills, and having asked several men for their suggestions, a name that came up again and again was yours. Allow me to explain. But let's walk on – my mind works better with movement, after all those years on the battlefield. The waiting, the standing still – that's what does for a man, not the action." We set off again. "As you know, we have recruited nearly two thousand men to the Metropolitan Police in the past three months. What you may not know is that half of them have had to be dismissed – for not turning up for duty, for drunkenness, for taking bribes, for frequenting taverns and prostitutes and so on. Half of them. Although my first instinct was to recruit from the navy and the army – I know how to work with a military man – the general opinion was that this would be unwise as it might give the impression of an army on the streets of London. And so we have taken men from all walks of life – with the all but inevitable result that discipline is sadly lacking."

"Aye," I said. "I have read about it in the newspaper."

"I could resort to punitive measures," continued Rowan. "But when I was in the army I found I achieved better results when my men wanted to do the right thing, rather than when they were forced to do it. Discipline in my regiment was measured not by the number of floggings given, but by the absence of floggings."

"An admirable approach," I said, meaning it.

"From everything I have heard about you, I thought you might hold similar views," said Rowan approvingly. "But a lack of discipline is not just a waste of time and resources – although it is certainly that. For instance, we've already had complaints from the clothing contractor about the expense of altering and re-issuing so many uniforms. It also risks losing us what little public confidence we have gained. We urgently need to instil in our new recruits not only discipline, but pride in their work and determination to do it well. In short, Constable Plank," the Commissioner stopped again and turned to face me, "we need experienced men who can tell them – and show them – how to work effectively and professionally as a police force."

CHAPTER FORTY

A constable to the core

SATURDAY 19TH DECEMBER 1829

"Sam," said John Conant as he walked into his rooms. "Is all well? It is not like you to lurk up here waiting for me."

I stood. "I asked Thin Billy and he said that you are dining alone before your afternoon hearings, and I wanted to talk to you. About the future."

"Indeed," said the magistrate, lifting the cover of the dish on the sideboard. "I see that we have enough for two, so shall we discuss it over a plate of food?" He leaned forward and sniffed. "Kidneys, if I am not mistaken." He helped himself to a serving and indicated that I should do the same, and then we both sat at the table.

Conant poured himself a glass of wine and offered me one; I took a small glass and diluted it with water from the jug. He tore off a piece of bread and dipped it into the gravy on his plate. "So, Sam – the future."

I cleared my throat. "As I understand it, sir," I started, "despite the arrival of the new police, there are no plans for them to take over the duties of magistrates."

"Absolutely not," said Conant. "It is essential for public trust in the new force that there is strict division between those who arrest people for alleged crimes, and those who decide whether or not they are guilty."

"I can see that," I said. "Which means that your work here at Great Marlborough Street will continue as before."

"Busier, if anything," agreed Conant. He offered the bread to me.

"But if the new police are arresting people and bringing them to the magistrates for hearings," I said, "what is to become of the magistrates' constable? Will we become a second-class force, treated like the watchmen, as old fellows who should have been put out to pasture?"

"Ah," said Conant, leaning back in his chair. "Well, this has been a topic of some discussion, as you can imagine. When Mr Peel first suggested the new force, people wondered what would happen to the old force. Just as they did when we introduced magistrates' constables and wondered what would happen to the Runners."

"But the Runners are still active," I said.

"Precisely," said Conant. "You cannot switch from one system to another overnight. And we shall not do that this time either. Eventually, yes, I imagine that magistrates' constables will be replaced by the new police, but it is accepted that this will take a decade or more – certainly more than enough time to see us both out, Sam. In short, your job is safe for as long as you want it." He looked at me more seriously. "And more selfishly, I very much hope that you will continue working as a constable here, with me." He sighed. "It seems that my daughter has at last met a man who meets her very exacting standards, and from the way they look at each other, I live in daily dread of his requesting a meeting with me."

"Richard Barnes?" I asked.

The magistrate nodded. "If he weren't about to steal my daughter from me, I would like him very much," he said. "Intelligent, compassionate, modest, good at debating – which he will need, if he takes Lily as a wife. Not much money, but then I have more than enough for all three of us." He sighed again. "I didn't expect – or want – her to stay with me forever, but it will be a wrench."

"At least, with Barnes being a lawyer, they won't be moving to the country," I said. "His work – and his causes – are here in London, and likely to remain so."

Conant smiled weakly and then seemed to gather himself. "And with you staying on, Sam," he said, "I shall not want for sensible company."

"Actually…" I started. Conant looked at me enquiringly. "I have been approached by one of the Commissioners. Of the Metropolitan Police," I continued.

Conant smiled and held up his hand. "I thought it might happen eventually," he said. He stood and went across to his desk, sifting through a couple of piles of papers until he found what he wanted. He brought it over and handed it to me. "There," he said, "second column, halfway down the page."

It was a newspaper – the *Morning Chronicle*, from the 14th of August.

"Look at the paragraph that begins 'All the parishes',," instructed Conant.

I read it. It explained that although the Metropolitan Police required that recruits should be under thirty-five years of age and at least five feet seven inches tall, regard should be given to taking on men who might not meet that standard but who had "knowledge of police matters". I read the last sentence to myself and then aloud.

"By this arrangement many persons will continue to be employed, and give the new system the benefit of their experience, who would, by too rigid adherence to the regulations, be excluded."

Conant touched the side of his nose and smiled. "There's no need to ask who made that suggestion to the Commissioners, about recruiting men with knowledge of police matters – but I was certainly not the only magistrate to support the idea, Sam. It would be of little use to any of us to have a new force of novices, who might be young and tall but lacking, how do they put it, the benefit of your experience. Tell me: what precisely have they asked you to do?"

♦

Martha cleared the plates, wiped down the table, folded up her cloth and then turned to look at me. "Now," she said, "just when are you planning to tell me about you joining the new police?" She laughed at the look on my face. "Heavens, Sam – surely you don't think you could hide that from me? Two days ago you get dressed to the nines for an important meeting that you don't want to talk about, and today you say you'll be home late because you have to see Mr Conant about something to do with our future."

"But after everything I've said," I started. "About being too old, and leaving it to the youngsters like Wilson."

"Too old to be a constable on the beat, yes," she agreed. "And I'm long past the age where I would consider living in a station house surrounded by constables and their wives."

"So am I," I said. "I like my home comforts."

"But that's not to say that there isn't plenty you could do," continued Martha. "I've been reading in the papers you bring home about the lack of discipline among the new men. Most of them started out as soldiers, didn't they?"

I nodded. "Commissioner Rowan is a former soldier himself, so he recruits what he knows. And Commissioner Mayne is a barrister, so he knows about the law but not much about enforcing it."

"Well then," said my wife, as though the matter were settled, "if they have a soldier and a barrister, what they're lacking is an experienced constable. Soldiering's one thing, and knowing the law is useful, but running a force of men on the streets of London, well, that's something special. Something you know more about than almost anyone, I should think."

"I wouldn't go that far, Mar," I said. "But it's pretty close to what Commissioner Rowan said when I met him – dressed to the nines."

"You're blushing, Sam," said Martha, poking me in the side. "You've never been any good at accepting praise. But we all knew they needed you in the new police – Mr Harmer, Mr Conant, me. And William too – he said you should join."

"Aye, he did," I admitted. "But for all that, I can't imagine he'd be best pleased to have me looking over his shoulder, so I think I'll leave him to it at Hadlow Street – let him make his own mark in D Division. It's been suggested that I join C Division – St James's."

"Well, that makes sense," said Martha. "It's a familiar area for you."

"Very familiar," I agreed. "I'm told there will be four bases for Division C – and one of them is going to be at Great Marlborough Street."

"Close to the court, then," said Martha.

"More than close," I replied. "We'll be sharing the same building. It's until the new police get their own premises – perhaps build a new station house – and to my mind it's a good idea. It means we'll be able to help them find their feet in their new jobs. I'm being taken on as an honorary sergeant, charged with educating the new officers – sharing what I know about our local rogues, teaching the new recruits how to question people and so on. And making sure they do their work with pride and honesty. Here: this explains it."

I reached over and took a small black book from my coat pocket. I patted the seat beside me and Martha sat down.

"*Metropolitan Police Instruction Book,*" she read aloud from the cover of the book I was holding.

"The Home Secretary has given one of these to every man in the new police," I explained, opening the book. "Commission Rowan gave this one to me."

Martha continued reading aloud, shifting closer to me and angling her head to get a clearer view. "The principal object to be obtained is the prevention of crime…" I turned the page for her, "better effected than by the detection and punishment of the offender after he has succeeded in committing the crime," she finished. "Well, that makes sense, Sam: prevention is always better than cure."

I turned over a few more pages – there were sections on the divisions and the ranks within them, the conditions of admission into the new force, and the general duties of the new officers. I stopped at the page dealing with the rank of sergeant.

Martha read on. "You're to show alacrity and skill in the discharge of your duty." She turned to look at me. "Alacrity?" she asked.

"Eagerness," I said. "Speed, haste." I glanced at her. "Are you smiling?"

She shook her head, biting her lip. I prodded her in the ribs and she squealed. "Does this mean you'll stop being a magistrates' constable?" she asked.

"I spoke to Mr Conant about that today," I said, "and he says he thinks the magistrates' constables will go on for another ten years or more. He has suggested that I divide my time between the two: three days a week as a magistrates' constable, and three with the new police. He said he can agree it with Commissioner Rowan."

"And would you like that, Sam?" asked my wife, leaning back so that she could look me full in the face.

I looked steadily at her. "I think I would," I answered. "One foot in the past and the other in the future. But what about you, Mar? Would you be happy about it?"

"You're a constable to your core, Sam," she said, "and I can't imagine you doing anything else. Seeing what a difference you have made to William – how you've pushed and pulled him into shape – well, it would be a waste if you didn't do that for more young constables."

She stood up and put her hands to the small of her back to stretch. "But I do have one condition."

"Oh yes?" I said.

"You find a laundress for those fancy white trousers you're going to be wearing. I don't mind polishing the extra buttons on your new coat, but I'm not going to spend my time washing the soot and grime of London from a ridiculous pair of white trousers."

Glossary

Almack's – an assembly rooms in King Street in St James's known as the "marriage mart", where people of social standing went to find a husband or wife – exclusivity was assured by the patronesses, who issued signed tickets to the dances (known as "vouchers") and kept track of who was socially "in" and "out"

Banyan – an informal, knee-length dressing gown worn by a gentleman at home, over his shirt and trousers (especially at breakfast, and while playing cards, writing letters or reading)

Barouche – a large, open, four-wheeled carriage, heavy and luxurious, with a collapsible hood over the rear half, and drawn by two horses

Beau monde – literally "fine world", used to signify the world of fashion and high society, what we might call the upper crust

Bluff – fierce, surly

Bow Street Runners – London's first professional police force, originally consisting of six men and operating out of Bow Street magistrates' office. Their role was gradually taken over by magistrates' constables – like Sam – and by 1828 they were spending most of their time using their city-honed skills to investigate offences outside London. The runners were formally disbanded in 1839.

Bravo – a mercenary murderer, who will kill anyone for a price

Bridge – to bridge someone, or throw him over the bridge, is to deceive him by betraying the confidence he has placed in you and, instead of serving him faithfully, to involve him in ruin or disgrace

Brooks's – a gentlemen's club, founded in Pall Mall in 1762 and moving to St James's Street in 1778, favoured by members of the Whig political party – notable members have included prime minister William Pitt the Younger, artist Joshua Reynolds and anti-slavery campaigner William Wilberforce

Clipper – someone who clips metal off coins, creating coins that contained less precious metal and keeping the clippings

Coiner – a maker of fake coins, usually by making a sand mould from a genuine coin and then manufacturing counterfeit coins with sub-standard metal, colouring them to look right

Cork-brained – light-headed, foolish

Covent Garden nun – a prostitute

Dead men – empty bottles, glasses or tankards

Drover – a fraudster whose role is to find further victims, so-called because he drives them to slaughter as a drover does his animals

Fetters – a device used to restrain a prisoner, consisting of two manacles (for the wrists or, more usually, the ankles) joined by a chain

Gammon – flattery, deceit, pretence (to gammon a person is to give him false assurances to achieve a particular end)

Gaolbird – one used to being shut up in gaol, like a bird in a cage

Garnish – in Newgate and other prisons, the payment of garnish to the warder will mean that the prisoner is not shackled in chains but is allowed free movement of his limbs, and further payments will secure other comforts such as better food, or the services of a cleaning woman or prostitute

Georgie Mac – a criminal from Sam's past, featuring in the plot of the second Sam Plank mystery, "The Man in the Canary Waistcoat"

Gold sovereign – a coin worth about £68 in today's money

Gulling – the practice of finding gullible people (known as 'gulls') to exploit

Hackney coach – a vehicle for hire, with four wheels, two horses and six seats

Hazard – a game played with two dice and often seen in gambling houses – craps is a modern simplification of hazard

Jarvey – the driver of a hackney coach, see also *Hackney coach*

Macaroni – a foppish man, fond of excessive fashion, luxurious fabrics, tall wigs and the like

Minuscule – lower-case (as the concept of upper- and lower-case letters did not take hold until printing was commonplace, referring to the upper and lower trays in which the letters were kept by the typesetters – in Sam's day, when almost exclusively handwritten, they were known as minuscule and majuscule letters)

Oakum – see *Picking oakum*

Out at heels – in declining circumstances

Pelisse – in women's fashion, a long, fitted coat with set-in sleeves and an Empire waistline, often with military-style fastenings or braid to refer to its derivation from the short, trimmed jacket worn by Hussars, slung over their shoulder

Picking oakum – picking oakum was used as a punishment in prison, and as a way of earning board and lodging in a workhouse. A prisoner serving hard labour would cut an old ship's rope into a two-foot length and hit it with a mallet to remove the hardened tar coating it. It would then be passed to a woman or child to uncoil, unpick and shred the rope (and the fingers...) into fibres – known as oakum. Oakum could then be mixed with tar or grease and used as caulking to fill in the gaps between the wooden planks of ships to make them watertight.

Picquet – the nightly guard on duty at the Bank of England

Pigeon – a weak, silly man, easily imposed upon or cheated

Queen cake – a traditional fairy cake made with currants (and, in wealthier households, rose-water and almonds)

Queer screen – counterfeit banknote

Rum cull – a rich, silly fellow, easily cheated and exploited

Rum diver – a dexterous pickpocket

Runners – see Bow Street Runners

Serle's – a coffee-house in Lincoln's Inn, popular with barristers

Shaver – a cunning fellow, one who trims close to the limit, an acute cheat

Smasher – someone who utters (i.e. presents) counterfeit banknotes

Spencer – a short jacket extending only to the waistline, with long sleeves but no tail; worn by both men and women, the jacket is named after George, 2nd Earl Spencer, who started the fashion for them in the 1790s

Square toes – an old man, as they are fond of wearing comfortable shoes with room around the toes

Süßigkeiten – the German word for sweets or candies

Swell mob – a group of criminals who dress fashionably and act with seeming respectability

Toper – a drunkard

Utter – to utter a forged document is to knowingly pass it on or use it, and uttering is considered as serious a crime as the forgery itself

Wild rogue – a rogue trained from the cradle, i.e. what we would call a career criminal

Thank you for reading this book. If you liked what you read, please would you leave a short review on the site where you purchased it, or recommend it to others? Reviews and recommendations are not only the highest compliment you can pay to an author; they also help other readers to make more informed choices about purchasing books.

ABOUT THE AUTHOR

Susan Grossey graduated from Cambridge University in 1987 and since then has made her living from crime. She spent twenty-five years advising financial institutions and others on money laundering – how to spot criminal money, and what to do about it – and has written many non-fiction books on the subject.

Her first work of fiction was the inaugural book in the Sam Plank series, "Fatal Forgery". "The Man in the Canary Waistcoat" was her second novel, "Worm in the Blossom" her third, "Portraits of Pretence" her fourth, "Faith, Hope and Trickery" her fifth, and "Heir Apparent" her sixth. "Notes of Change" is the seventh and final book in the Sam plank series.

Susan is now plotting a new series of five novels, again set in the 1820s, but this time with a university constable in Cambridge at the heart of them. He might well be called Gregory.